ASCENSION

FACETS OF FEYRIE BOOK TWO

ZOE PARKER

CONTENTS

For my children, as always. Also, my ever faithful, tolerant other-half. And my Savage Squad you got me here. Also for Kyle, I didn't know you, but I know the woman who made you and she is one of the most courageous, caring people I know. So I imagine that you were too.

ASCENSION

CHAPTER ONE

za

ROAD TRIPS ARE kind of fun when you're traveling with three awesome snots. I'll never tell them that, though. The fun bits anyhow— I'll call them snots all I want.

My eyes alight on each of them briefly.

Knox, with his mossy green eyes and baby-soft hair. He's acting more like a kid every day, though I'm not sure he'll ever shake those shadows from his eyes completely. These days his laughter comes easier and more often.

Ruthie's hair is growing out to a velvety brown, which goes well with those brown eyes of hers. A week ago, she decided pink is too 'high maintenance.' She's blossoming, not that I'm surprised. She's smart for a kid her age and pretty, too.

Although at seventeen years old, she's still considered a baby in human years. Quite possibly, if we were human, her life would be much different.

Only we're not human.

1

These kids have no idea that I'm only four years older than Ruthie, and I feel like that number should have a zero behind it. Some days I just feel so damn old. I'm glad they have a chance to be kids, since I didn't.

My eyes move on to Michael, with those baby blues. He's still quiet, reserved. The timid is starting to fade away, showing peeks of the true strength underneath. He's still quite shy with people, which is mostly okay; there's a difference between shy and timid. Something I'm slowly finding out about him and life in general.

I don't miss the way his eyes follow Ruthie either. That's going to be an interesting thing to see one day. She watches him the same way.

When they both realize it, there's going to be entertainment to be had.

"Iza, why are you looking at me so funny?" The stupid smile on my face fades as Michael's voice penetrates my happy little reverie.

Little shit caught me staring.

"You have mustard all over your chin," I taunt, then sigh when he checks. Really? He hasn't eaten anything with mustard on it.

"How many miles left before we're... *there?*" I ask. Maybe if I don't say its name out loud, I can play the denial game a little longer?

"Just under 200 miles. Do you want to push through tonight or stop somewhere?" What Ruthie means by that is, *please stop somewhere and give me a steak or shoes.*

She's got a bit of a shoe fetish. There's a bag in the back full of nothing but shoes, her shoes. And the steak well, we all like steak.

"We can stop at the next place that has a Wally-World store." I answer, giving her a yes to her unanswered question.

Ruthie nods and pushes her dark glasses back up her nose, a satisfied grin on her face. I'm right. It's shoes this time. Which is fine; the kid has gone through hell. She can have all the shoes in the world if she wants.

"Iza, can we get a place with a pool?" Knox asks, tugging a little on my arm.

Smiling over at him in the seat beside me, I answer, "Sure, but you still have to wear your vest." And I can't go in any deeper than my waist.

A week before, I discovered in a panicked moment that Knox can't swim, and unluckily for us both, neither can I. Of course, I found out the hard way. He started flailing, and I jumped in to save him, and we both sank like rocks. Fortunately, Ruthie and Michael both know how to swim.

It was careless of me because I didn't think about jumping in. I saw Knox struggling and in I went. I'm not sure if it's a good or a bad thing yet.

When the car suddenly stops I hit the back of the front seat with my shoulder.

"You should wear your seat belt, Iza. They give you tickets here. click it or ticket," Knox whispers, unfastening his own seatbelt. I ruffle his hair and climb out of the back seat.

Ruthie, my dear shoe hoarder, finds a Wally-World within a few minutes. She wants those shoes! Once inside, Michael takes Knox's hand, and they head off to look at whatever boys look at here. Ruthie heads straight for the clothes and such.

Which leaves me standing there twiddling my thumbs.

We can't have that, can we?

Setting off through the store, unsupervised, I browse and touch anything appealing, adding all sorts of goodies to the empty cart I snag from an aisle. Eventually, my wandering brings me to the ones with the real goodies.

The pharmacy area.

The shampoo section is a quick tour. My senses can only briefly handle smelling so many fruits and flowers. Each consecutive aisle snags a piece of my attention. I scamper out of one before I'm seen—I left a bit of a mess.

My curiosity has a cost sometimes.

Coming around the corner of the last aisle, I find myself standing next to the maxi-pads. Using my shirt sleeve to wipe the taste of the foulness of my minutes past adventure off my tongue, I stare at the rows of neatly lined up, brightly colored packages. Because of TV, I know what these are. Maxi-pads have a useful purpose, the whole menses thing.

A blue box with a strange looking item on it catches my attention. Curious, I open the box and then the crinkly plastic package.

What in holy hell is this cotton ball-stringed thing?

I swing it around by the string experimentally. Is it a toy? Boring one if it is. No noise. No flashy lights. Hmm. I sniff it, ignoring the grumbles of the old lady standing in the diaper department.

They have diapers for adults here too, which look rather comfortable. I bet she's wearing one right now. Maybe full of poo, the way she's staring so hostile-like at me.

Ignoring her, I sniff it again. This thing smells kind of like paper. Huh? Picking the discarded blue box up off the floor, I read the instructions.

Wait, you put it where?

"Iza, what are you doing?" Michael's voice pulls me out of the hell this box says to go through to insert these things into—ahem, places.

Why in the world would you do that to yourself on purpose?

I hit him in the cheek with the tam-poon, totally accidentally on purpose, and he snags it as it falls with a red face.

Ha, Michael knows what they are!

Giggling, I go to the "mess" aisle and grab a random pack of condoms off the shelf and toss them to him as well. This useful item's purpose I already understand, after I tasted one. Bleh. It looked like candy and it said strawberry flavored on the box. It didn't smell like candy. But humans are weird, so I thought... why not?

I need to be more careful about what I put in my mouth.

4

CHAPTER TWO

 za

WE ENDED up getting a hotel with a pool for the night. Not that I'm complaining. I don't tell them no often. These kids deserve more than they've been given in life, and I'll make sure they get as much as I can give them.

Staring out the window into the night, I tighten my grip on the cup of caffeinated goodness in my hands. Normally, I'd be content and occupied by my favorite beverage. But the butterflies of anxiety in my stomach are a bit troubling.

Tomorrow, I'll be at the Sidhe.

There's no more room for denial. No more avoidance of it. We're too close to take it any slower than we already have. Not to mention, the Magiks inside of me are screaming and pushing at me to get there already.

Bossy shit.

I know that it's childish for me to be so reluctant, but who wants to take on the responsibility for so many *other* people? Not anyone with any sense, that's for certain.

Good thing for this Magiks crap, I don't have much sense.

"Iza, why does it scare you so much?" Michael's soft question causes me to jump and drop the cup in my hand.

Soda splashes all over my socked feet.

Frowning, I question internally, *Who, me? Scared? Ha.* Nothing scares me. Something as stupid as some prophesied shepherd isn't scary, right? I'm an immovable wall of badassery. Snorting, I move to clean up the mess.

Maybe if I think it hard enough, it'll be true.

Grabbing a towel off the towel rack, I hastily work cleaning the soda stain up. Deciding to look busy and to not answer Michael's question. Denial does work in some ways.

"We got your back. You don't need to worry," Michael says again, more gently this time.

For a second, I pause in my task. Letting myself absorb the importance of his words. Feeling my cheeks heat with emotion, I finish cleaning up the soda.

I'm not embarrassed, but damn if I don't feel like crying.

"What kind of car was it you said you wanted?" I mumble, knowing he'll hear me.

His whoop of joy is enough to make me cringe, which gives me an excuse to hide the smile on my face.

"Hey, what about me?"

I flat out laugh at Ruthie's tone. Deciding to mess with her, I look up at her.

"Car or Choo shoes?"

Her mouth opens and then closes. The little minx is debating. Laughing, I shake my head. Until recently these three kids were afraid to ask for *anything*. Apparently not anymore.

I'm okay with that.

"You don't think I'll buy one for him and not you, right?"

I hit the floor hard enough to knock the breath out of me. Squashing the instinctual urge to lash out, I relax. A laughing teenage girl is hugging me for all she's worth. Two seconds later the two boys join her.

Mentally sighing, I want to say I don't like the puppy pile. But I'd be a liar. With a growl, I toss all three of them, giggling, on the bed and pounce.

CHAPTER THREE

Iza

Fate is a dillhole. A massive, flipping dillhole.

Those words repeat in my head, several times, as I stand here, staring at the decrepit old house in front of me. Absolute dread is like a rock weighing heavily in my stomach.

The once white paint is now peeling and stained from age. At least, I hope it's from age. The discoloration in some places makes me wonder about that. The shutters, what's left of them, are crooked and broken.

Don't get me started on the windows. I'm fairly certain that the entire upstairs doesn't have a single intact window. Or frames. The wooden porch, sagging and ancient, is even falling in. I'm reasonably sure there's a hole right next to the front door, as well.

This house is the Sidhe? This is where I've sent people?

Well, shit. Have any of them stayed?

"Iza, look," Michael says from beside me, pointing towards the front of the house.

So, I look. The front door is now open and in it stands a familiar woman. A dragon to be more accurate. I know that face.

"Nika?" I question, taking a step towards the house. Maybe she can clear up what's going on here.

As I take another step closer, my Magiks blast awake inside of me, freezing me in place. Arcing out of me in a wave of blacks and purples, it hits the house with a boom.

For a heartbeat, nothing happens, and then the house begins to glow, to change right in front of my eyes. The peeling paint turns whole; the shutters, hanging so haphazardly, lift and reattach themselves to windows that are no longer broken.

As the minutes tick by I'm stuck there, gaping like an idiot, watching the miracle happening before me. The entire house is changing, turning into the house of my dreams—one I dreamt of as a bloody, miserable kid curled into a ball in a damp cell crying for a life I would never have.

A hush falls over us, broken only by the sounds of the Magiks gathering in a storm cloud above the house. Uh-oh. That can't mean anything good.

The impact of the first wave slings me back into the truck knocking the wind out of me. Wheezing, I fight to catch my breath, only to lose when the rest of it kicks in. Images bombard my mind as the Magiks flood into me.

It pulls me within myself where, for the very first time, I see a full-on view of the web attaching me to every Feyrie. The web is a tangible representation of the Magiks that have been my forceful, annoying boss... up until now.

I've got a feeling that things are going to change.

Guided by something greater than myself, I climb to my feet, a puppet to the Magiks. Those strings walk me through the, newly renovated, front door and into a space too large to belong to the house on the outside.

The Sidhe and the Magiks inside of it are welcoming me home.

The room is empty except for an old wooden chair that beckons my gaze, pulling my body against my will. Sitting in that chair will put me on the path I can never leave. Briefly, I struggle against the force pushing me forward. In my head, I even picture turning around and running.

It doesn't happen, of course. I lost this battle the minute I got out of the car.

Accepting—no, momentarily defeated, I force myself to relax, letting my steps continue unhindered. Not that fighting made any lick of difference. But I'm a contrary creature.

The second my butt touches the seat, a change comes over the chair. The wood morphs into black bones, moving and growing beneath me, and in my heart, I know they belong to my mother. The Magiks entwined with them whisper the knowledge to me.

Eyes burning, I exhale a shaky breath.

The Sidhe, my prophesized birthright, is waiting. It's waiting for me to say one simple word... yes. I'm surprised by its hesitance but not the least bit surprised by its impatience. Fate or not—it's at least giving me a choice. I can't say I'm happy about any of this fate shit, but for this... I admire it a little too.

There's no turning back now. I let out one more long breath. Well, here we go. Seeing as I'm not one to drag things out, I rip down all the mental walls protecting me from that deep dark, inside... and out.

Oddly, it continues to wait.

Maybe there isn't anything to let inside? Rather anticlimactic really. I was expecting a few more fireworks and sparkles. Maybe a fairy godmother or—with a rush that tears a cry through my clenched teeth, it floods into me.

I grunt at the strength of it. *Jerk Magiks.*

It builds inside me like a growing fire. Blazing into an inferno that overtakes everything. This time there's so much more... stretching my psyche, my body.

I feel like I'm going to pop like a too full balloon if this keeps up.

My inner self reaches out to that Web that scares me so much—finding those directly connected to me. These creatures of the dark.

There is no stopping it this time, no denial to hide behind, no more walls. I close my eyes as the final wave of power washes through me. My back bows, and I rise into the air. I can do nothing but be amazed at the feeling of the Magiks crawling over my skin, digging down deep inside of me.

Changing me on a physical and a Magikal level into something else.

The skin of my forearms turns black all the way to my clawed fingertips. Underneath the blackened skin, there's movement. The monster I am beneath, the one I've been hiding from the world, is hinting at its existence.

For now.

In my mouth, my teeth lengthen, the sharp points of them dig into my tongue, flooding my mouth with the taste of copper. My eyes burn and a brief searing pain makes them water. Just as suddenly the pain ends, and a new lid moves sideways when I blink.

Again, the Magiks question me.

"I accept," I say in barely a whisper, but it's all the Magiks and the Sidhe need.

It's like I have a backseat to my own body. All I can do is watch as someone else drives the car. At least they don't drive grandma-style like Ruthie. This ride will be over fast.

The fiends gather closer, circling me in a vortex of darkness that grows tighter and tighter every second, as I feel myself rise even higher into the air.

Whispers fill my mind. Whispers from the past, from the present, of the future to come. I imagine touching a finger to the glowing center of the web where I'm connected to all the Feyrie. Including my father and my mother's spirit. All the ones I've found along the way, their strands glowing along the lines of the web.

Fascinated, I watch the center flare and send a flash of light down all the strands of the web—which is so much larger than I imagined it to be. Line after line lights up. Each one connected to a being some-where out in one of the worlds. Over and over it does this, until there are so many I lose count.

Among so many, one draws my gaze. One strand is isolated from the others interweaving only through the center. It's dark, lit differently than any other, and feels different.

Phobe.

The strand that's Phobe, the essence of him, is completely interwoven with mine in the center.

That's interesting and unexpected.

Distantly, I hear wood creaking from the strengthening power, feel the room around me slightly give and bow outwards. There's so much now. Too much, maybe. It's quite mesmerizing, really. But it would be cooler if it wasn't happening to me.

If none of this were.

I focus on the massive webbing of Feyrie, so many yet so few. I can feel so many of them. Feel them watching, feel them waiting. Feel their awareness of me being aware of *them*.

Wow. Just wow.

Lightning flashes across the strands of the web inside of me and I become aware of those that have come before. I hear their voices of sadness, their fears for their people, their power all combining into my own.

Lastly, I feel their rage at what has become of their people... *my* people.

My eyes jerk open, and they follow the darkness crawling along my body to converge into the solid form of the fiend armor, a purple-black that shines ethereally in the dark. Wicked and sharp, it covers me from head to toe in pure dark power.

The legion of fiends are giving me their strength, their protection. Some of them sacrificed themselves to become this armor, the daggers. A hot tear rolls down my cheek and is ripped away by the Magikal winds.

The Magiks don't give me time to grieve for them.

My mind is opening, casting away the shadows of doubts. There are no more illusions, no more fears. There's only the power, it's awake, and it's *me*.

A scream leaves my throat raw as the web ripples, lighting each strand even brighter.

I call you to me.

Dormant dark marks flare to life. I can feel them all. Feel them raise their faces to the sky, hearing my call, every single dark creature in existence.

Melting through the ceiling into the unnaturally colored sky I rise higher on Magikal winds. A bubble of solid dark power surrounds me, black lightning bolts rippling across its surface. With a final exhale I stop fighting at all because there's always a little fight in me and, let the dark reign.

A sensation of feathers tickling me on the inside turns into pain as the Magiks seep into every pore, every part of me. Something inside stirs that has long slumbered.

My Ascension is here.

"We awake," I whisper, my voice the voice of thousands. My power pulses like a light blinking. "No longer shall we slumber."

With each word my voice grows stronger, more powerful. The Magiks pulse again and the bubble surrounding me grows.

'Let go, Iza.' My father's voice drifts through my mind.

My scream turns into a roar, echoing with the anger of all who came before me. The bubble shrinks with a thunderous sound, like a Magikal back draft drawing more Magiks to it, compressing and then exploding outwards. A shockwave of pure dark power races in every direction at the speed of sound.

My eyes close as the darkness envelops me. Shit, this is going to hurt. Falling is the last thing I feel before oblivion takes me.

CHAPTER FOUR

 hobe

"IT's STARTED," Sergean says softly, appearing beside me.

His eyes are on his daughter floating in the Magikal storm above us. It is a rather entrancing sight; Iza accepting the power she will need for the future.

She is fully becoming the creature she is meant to be.

Underneath the layers of Magiks I can see the physical changes beginning. Her dragon half is letting some of itself out. I can see it in the black creeping along her skin and the movement underneath it.

Iza is embracing her fate. The Shepherd is born.

Her scream pulls at me; her roar of rage even more so. Although there are other's voices in that roar hers is the loudest. Her voice is the strongest, and hers is the one they will fear.

Beautiful.

Abruptly, like a star, she flares brightly and winks out, falling from the sky. I jump to catch her. Landing in the center of the roof, her limp body in my arms, I stare down at her. I almost forgot what it feels like to hold her.

My arms tighten around her pulling her closer. The smell of ozone from the Magiks is strong on her. The scent of cinnamon is stronger. The fact that something as simple as her smell must be the strongest amuses me.

Sergean studies me intently. I can feel it but, it is not he that holds my gaze. I cannot look away from her.

"She is struggling to adjust to this. As you can see by her delay in getting here."

At his statement I give a slight nod. I know what he means. He means that she needed me and, I was not here for her. My intention was not to remain gone so long but, once on the path, my task required completion. I also needed time to think.

"For God's sake, don't tell her I told you either. She has a bit of a temper." There is amusement and affection in his tone.

Iza bonded with her father.

Pulling my eyes away from her I turn to look at him in his sudden silence. He tucks both his hands in his pockets. "You have changed, darkness," he comments with a smile hovering about his mouth.

I say nothing. I do not disagree. Nor do I fully agree. The ways he believes I have changed are not going to be correct. Either way it is not his concern.

"Did you find what you sought?" he asks more seriously.

Tucking Iza's head to my shoulder I hug her closer to my chest and nod. There will be no more slave stones in our future but, that is not all.

"I know you tried to free me more than once." At my words he exhales.

He tried and failed several times. He is the only one ever to try. That is until his daughter came along and succeeded.

"No matter what I did it didn't work," he says, the frustration coming out in that statement.

Clenching my jaw, I stare at the man who helped force me into slavery. I do not like him. I never will.

I do not hate him either.

"Did you know about her?" I ask.

"He told me that you would save the most precious thing in the world to me one day," he answers.

I shake my head at those words.

"I did not save her. She saved me." I reply.

Leaning down, my glamour swirling around me, I kiss the cheek of the woman who haunts me no matter how far away I go or how long I am gone. Placing her gently in her father's arms I step off the roof into a pool of darkness.

Hiding is cowardly but, I am not ready for her to see me. Yet I am not ready to leave her presence either. I am annoyed with myself for it but, I cannot deny the want to keep her in my sight.

Hidden, I follow on silent feet and watch them from the shadows, using every skill I possess to cloak my presence.

To be utterly honest, if I were a conscience-ridden being, I would have stayed gone. Iza can be vicious, she can be cold and loves violence but, that is not what makes up the majority who she is. She is also kind,… soft-hearted. I am neither of those things.

Since I am being honest with myself the time away from her was the most uncomfortable experience of my life. Extremely close to being intolerable.

This creature who fathered her will never know these things.

Sergean carries her to an underground chamber guided by the Sidhe. Initially, I am 'kept' from following them into the room. Being what I am and as determined I am to get in, eventually I do.

Having to fight my way in does not bother me. The Sidhe is simply protecting her which is what it is supposed to do. With her being as vulnerable as she is right now nothing else besides me will have the strength to get through.

Which gets a small bit appreciation from me.

The fiends also contest my entry initially. I manage to persuade them without hurting them. They would die to the last one to protect her; their devotion knows no bounds. Her happiness is their happiness. Her will is their will. She is all and everything.

I am sure Iza does not comprehend that level of loyalty.

I do.

My eyes eat up the sight of her lying so still and pale on the pillows. Her physical transformation is complete. She no longer has the minutest look of humanity. No one with any sense can look at her and mistake her for one ever again.

Unless she wants them to. Her glamour is quite good.

The black claws on her hands are now long and razor-sharp. Her skin is so pale there is a slightly blue cast to it, much like my own. Her hair is long and so bright now that it can easily be mistaken for a pool of blood across the pillow. The black medusa strands are alive, writhing around her head even in her slumber, and separating her even further from a mortal.

She may not have the build of a Feyrie, being rather short in comparison to them, but her real beauty comes from the look of feralness about her. That she has in spades.

Her mouth is now wider to accommodate her bigger, sharper teeth. The ones I can see through her slightly parted lips. Her opalescent eyes are a little larger and, I know beneath her lids rest nictitating membranes. Her nose is still tiny but flatter.

Iza has come into her Otherness. She is now more monster than a woman.

God, she is beautiful.

So much so that she draws my gaze over and over and holds it there with invisible strings. I fight the pull to go to her side instead of remaining here, in the shadows, watching.

A 'creeper' she calls me. Considering how I have stalked her, since I returned to this world, that word is accurate. I have indeed been creeping on her.

Sergean walks back into view holding a robe to cover her nudity. Her transformation burned her clothes off. I refuse to turn my back as he dresses her and pulls multicolored socks on her small clawed feet.

Only a father thinks of socks.

Many times, I questioned why I became aware of existence. Why was I arrogant enough to take on flesh and overthrow the very balance of things? Why, of all punishments to suffer, was I bound to that stone and left at the control of the very creatures I will once again spill the blood of?

I get it now. Iza needed me to be in that dungeon.

I was enslaved and imprisoned to wait for the woman whose heart I can feel every beat of and through her feel everyone connected to her. Ours is an incredibly strong connection, stronger than any other I know of. Strong enough to survive my absence and the distance.

Not once did I stop feeling her within me.

Now it is significantly stronger.

Iza, who does not have an arrogant bone in her body, is deep within me, unintentionally holds me anchored to her, in a place that did not exist before her. A place created that first time I laid eyes on her.

Something I will never again deny the existence of.

I step out of the shadows just enough for Sergean to become aware of my presence. Even as powerful as he is I still have a few eons on him.

"I wondered where you got off to," he says quietly from his position at the foot of her bed.

"How is she?" I ask, careful not to awaken her with my voice.

He does not need to know I was unseen.

"Changing," he pauses and, I wait for the words to come. "Your absence had a good and bad effect. It gave her time to find herself. It also gave me time to get to know her without your overpowering presence." His dark eyes turn to me.

"Now that she can feel them all even at a distance she is going to be in a whole new world of pissed off," he finishes.

I briefly meet his eyes then look back at Iza.

Instead of continuing the conversation I watch the way the strands move around her face. I cannot say I like talking especially with her father. My silence is my answer—or lack of one.

"She will also have to deal with the rest of the Alpha and Lord bull-shit of the half-breeds. She's done well so far, but, those were just fringes." My silence does not stop him; he continues to speak.

I look over as he crosses his arms and watches her too.

"The two of you are a surprise," he muses.

To some those words would be cryptic, but I understand them. He is still undecided about my presence in her life. But this is not a discussion I am willing to have with him. Nor will I allow him to impact any of it.

I am *not* undecided about my place in her life.

"Have you heard anything about the schoth?" I ask him. Since he wants to converse I decide to at least get the answers to questions I have. Sergean is not someone whose mind I can touch.

The schoth I have found following her so far won't be coming after Iza again. Ever.

"Not so far but, they will try soon enough. My main concern is the near future and the creatures in this realm—Kael and his lackey Romiel among them. They will be at her soon like a rash, irritating and consistent." He sounds annoyed with the thought of it.

Not if I have anything to do with it.

"I'm surprised you have not killed Kael," I say, aware of whom he speaks.

More aware than Sergean knows. Kael is a dragon, Iza's uncle and the self-proclaimed dragon king. When Iza's mother was murdered Kael took the throne for himself instead of letting the throne choose another ruler.

Not that it hasn't chosen. The dragon throne rests in the Sidhe.

"The rules always apply," is his response.

Rules that I am not bound by.

"Do you think he will wait long to come here?" I ask.

Why has he not found a way around his precious rules? A loophole to allow him to rid himself of a menace? I will never understand why the Eldest follow the rules so carefully.

"No. Those two have their half-brains together trying to figure out how to replace her," he answers after a pause.

That job will be much harder than they realize. Iza is not a pushover. Once she truly accepts this task she will not give it up. Not without a fight.

Kael is well-known for his greed not for his intelligence. He is conniving, and that makes him an obstacle.

"Kael is the only threat out of the two. I don't consider Romiel one. I think she has a few friends that can deal with him adequately," he muses.

Sergean has a point with that. She does indeed.

"Do you know what he is planning?"

He shakes his head at my question. "They have layers of Magiks protecting them from my gaze. I've been trying for years to get inside the head of that bastard." He picks at an invisible piece of lint on his shirt sleeve. "He will not come at her straight on. He will try to come out of this with his hands as clean as possible."

"I could just kill him."

"He is mine!" he whispers fiercely.

His eyes glow like opals and then go black, like his daughter's. I can understand vengeance but not the risk towards Iza from him waiting for it.

"Do not let him get in my way," I caution.

This will be my only warning.

Iza stirs in her sleep, her thoughts coming to the surface. My mind automatically seeks hers out connecting with her unprotected one. It has been so long since I felt her actual thoughts. It causes me to pause in place.

"I will return shortly," I whisper.

I do not wait for his response before disappearing into the shadows. He casts one puzzled glance before turning to his daughter.

With one last look at her face I enshroud myself deeper in the darkness and head outside. Leaving is something I must do before I give in and do what I want to do.

Bloody fucking emotions.

Months passed for her since I left. For me it has been years and, I still have no idea how to deal with the emotions entangled with her. In this case I am at a bit of a loss of the correct procedure of reintroducing myself.

Even delving into the massive bank of memories from the ones I have consumed does not help. No one understands emotions.

But I *can* do some recon... or kill something. Yes, I will go kill something. That is so much easier than trying to figure out the mess inside of me.

With a goal now in mind I pass through the realms to a place I know is always good for hunting something.

CHAPTER FIVE

za

"IZA, THIS PLACE IS SO COOL!" Ruthie exclaims, running through the dining room, with its tables stretching as far as the eye can see. She grabs my arm and yanks on it like it's not attached or anything. Gently I remove her hands and turn her to face me amused, but very much wanting to keep my arm.

"Did you find a room? The boys too?"

She nods, smiling from ear to ear, at my questions.

"The Sidhe made rooms for each of us. I have a shoe closet!" She jumps up and down in place.

Good god, who knew closets were so exciting?

Then again I was a bit tickled when I saw my room which the kids shared with me last night. There's a large round bed, covered in a multitude of cushions, and it was so freaking comfortable I didn't want to get out of it this morning.

Not that I slept much.

Instead I lay there and stared at the gorgeous purple walls with three-dimensional dragons flying around on it. At the ceiling with stars and even a moon shining down on me.

The bathroom is even tailored to me specifically.

The Sidhe is trying to comfort me. I get that now. The feeling it's trying to saturate me in is... love. It's not an emotion I'm familiar with so, it took me a bit to figure it out.

Still, I'm not sure what to do with it. I have a connection with this place. It sings to me, soul-deep. So much so that late last night I could feel the leaves on the trees outside and the water lapping against the shore in the lake.

The dirt, I could feel the dirt. Still can.

It gets worse. Now I can feel every single Feyrie in existence. The Magiks will make sure I know what I need to know about each one of them. There is a reason I'm the one chosen for this. The reason it's not some goody two shoes with a silver tongue. The Magiks only want the loyal ones.

The ones who aren't shall be judged and brought to justice. Feyrie Justice. Not a slap on the wrist either, unless it's detached, then maybe.

That's something I can do better than anyone... almost anyone. Phobe is much better at it, but he isn't here. He's not connected to the Sidhe.

He's something else entirely. And did I mention... not here? The jerk.

"Iza, you okay?" Ruthie's concerned voice breaks into my reverie.

Shaking my head a little, I smile at her and say, "I'm good. Where're the boys?"

They're probably playing the gaming system again. The Sidhe provided a TV as big as a wall in the living room—every boy's dream.

"Playing video games. Michael is trying to beat Knox's high score in something. Have you met some of the folks here? Iza, there are dragons here. Real dragons! They have wings and everything." Ruthie flaps her arms but, she barely takes a breath before she continues to talk at twenty miles a second. "Did you see the Goblins? Or some of the other critters walking around here?"

She grabs my arm again and starts pulling me to people's tables. She's going to yank the damn thing off if she keeps pulling on it.

"What's here?" she asks, stopping us at a table.

God help me. The girl has no couth.

"Two imps and a shifter," I say automatically.

The three men at the table smile indulgently at Ruthie. Four tables later Ruthie gets distracted when Michael walks into the dining room with a chattering Knox.

The blush on her face is hilarious. I giggle. She deserves a little payback for dragging me around to play 'guess the creature.'

Leaning close to her I whisper, "When are you going to put him out of both your miseries?"

She swats at my arm. "Iza!"

"What? It's the truth. He makes puppy-dog eyes at you just as often," I whisper. Or at least try to. I don't have the best whisper voice — it carries.

Her face turns more red. This is awesome; she's going to pop like a little cute balloon.

Michael and Knox head right for us. When he gets to me my little alpha shifter wraps his arms around my waist and squeezes. I pat his head. I'm still learning this whole affection thing.

I'm a work in progress.

"Iza, he can't beat my high score so, he threatened to eat me," Knox tattles on Michael.

I look up at Michael, who blushes.

"He bit me," Michael says, showing the imprint of little teeth on his arm. The wound is already healing.

"He won't eat you, Knox. Right, Michael?"

Michael cuts a mock dirty look at Knox then nods.

"And of course, you won't bite him again over a stupid video game, right Knox?"

Knox looks up at me guiltily and then nods.

I take a deep breath and say, "Now, let's go meet some dragons."

Specifically those I remember from before, when I was a child. The very ones I've been avoiding all morning. Wow, I'm not awkward or anything.

"Who's that big bearded guy?" Knox asks, pointing as kids do.

No subtlety—a kid after my own heart.

"That's Alagard. He was the weapons master for the dragon royalty."

"What's a weapons master?" Knox asks, linking his hand with mine.

"Well, he trained soldiers for the dragon kingdom." At least I think that's what he did. I'm a little fuzzy about what it is too.

"It means that I was responsible for turning boys into soldiers. And am willing to do it again," Alagard says, winking at me.

I ignore the wink.

"Ask him, Knox. He can give you all the details."

Excited but shy Knox sits across from him at the table and stares at him expectantly.

I grab a seat beside him. I need to know these things too.

"So you're like a general?" Knox asks him.

Alagard shakes his head. "I teach them the skills. Someone else points them in the right direction."

Knox studies Alagard with that super serious look he gets and asks, "Why?"

I lean forward, resting my chin on my hand. It's a good question!

"Dragons are born with particular talents. It's part of our Magiks. Mine is with metals. Because of that I was chosen to train by the previous master and, now it is my duty to train. But my mind isn't analytical enough for directing soldiers in battles." As he answers Knox I watch his face and allow my Magiks to brush him.

He's telling part of the story. Alagard doesn't like sending people off to die. That's why he repeatedly failed at leading. Guilt.

It's all there in the song the Sidhe sings to me. My brain is just slow at figuring out what it all means. Certain notes make me feel certain emotions. The Sidhe doesn't have an actual voice just its beautiful songs.

I'm okay with that.

Right now it's singing about Alagard's misplaced guilt. His mind is wide open to the Sidhe. His loyalty to the dark, full and complete.

"Yeah, you're full of shit. But we'll talk about that another time, Alagard," I say when there is a pause in the conversation.

"Beg pardon, my lady?"

"You can't hide behind fear or guilt anymore. You don't deserve to feel either. Soon you and I will have a talk about things and your place in them."

Stunned, Alagard sits there and stares at me. Luckily for him I'm used to having that effect on people.

"Ha ha, you're gonna be a general now." Knox says, laughing.

CHAPTER SIX

 hobe

I CANNOT GO BACK INSIDE of the Sidhe. Not yet. But I can sense her in there even though our bond is sleeping. Because I had to make it do so to keep her from feeling me so close by.

Currently she is too aware of everything inside of the Sidhe. She might very well discover my presence before I am ready for that to come to pass.

For now I can see her on the days when she is outside. The kids are around her most of the time and, she watches them like a hawk. The dragons work around her too but, I can see their alertness.

They think she has no idea they are guarding her. The reality is that she is guarding them. Protecting her flock of sheep like the good shepherd that she is.

There are also moments where I think she is going to catch me watching her. She will pause and look right in my direction with a frown on her face. Then she shrugs it off and moves on in whatever task she is completing.

She looks a little lost at times too. Often there is a faraway look on her face; her forehead wrinkled in thought. The urge to reach out and touch her with my shadows, to search for what has her thinking so hard, is hard to resist.

It is during these moments I am the most thankful—yes, thankful —that Iza is not human and frail. No human mind could survive her life.

But even her mind did not survive it completely unscathed.

The difference is, she always moves forward.

Today, they are out picking up refuse that is strewn all over the Sidhe land. Iza is in the lead with the children close at hand, all the children. She is turning into a bit of a mother bear when it comes to her people.

Caring for these creatures will make things more difficult for her in the future. Not that difficult ever stops her. Iza does not realize how hard things are going to get yet. She will. Iza is smart. She will figure it out then adapt.

Unfortunately, her job as the Shepherd is to bring the people together. To get them ready to be lead, to hold them together and protect them. In essence, her duty is harder than any lost king's.

Her destiny.

She hates the word destiny. Says, and I quote, "It is a bullshit way to convince people to do stupid shit based on someone else's bullshit."

I think I am starting to understand what she means by that.

Today, she is not smiling much. A frown keeps appearing between her eyes. Something heavy is weighing on her thoughts. The impulse to reach out for her mind is strong and, I stomp on it.

Soon. Very soon. As soon as my gut stops clenching every time I think about standing face to face with Iza again.

CHAPTER SEVEN

za

JAMESON IS TOO nerdy for his own good sometimes. This time, however, it's working out for me. He is documenting everyone that enters the Sidhe. He's also working with the dragons in arranging identification for the residents.

This human world requires legal documents for everything.

Smart imp, Jameson. And he's also working non-stop at making up for the shit he did. Honestly, I'm kind of proud of him. The Sidhe likes him. I see him now for what he truly is.

Which helps me trust him more.

Not counting the house goblins, we have almost three-hundred people here. Which is a lot but not when you compare it to how many will be here soon. Thousands.

All the shifter children Ryan arrived with have been adopted out to other members of the Sidhe. Children are a rarity and, there are lots of folks who will love them. Jameson also sends a team led by Ryan out to get more stragglers daily. Mostly the old and children who need help getting here.

Apparently, Ryan has turned over a new leaf. Jameson said he always helps with whatever is needed. Ryan has a lot to make up for and this is a good start.

"My Lady, are you paying attention?" Jameson asks, snapping his fingers in front of my face.

He goes to do it again and, I grab his hand.

I'm only half joking when I say, "If you snap your fingers in my face again, Jameson, I'll break them."

Clearing his throat nervously, he pulls his hand out of my grasp and flips through his notebook again. "I'm making a list of council member families as well. I have a feeling this might be useful in the future."

"Find out anything you can on the government structure of this country. I read on the Google God, but I'm sure there are things it doesn't know. Or that I simply don't understand," I request.

He scribbles notes on his paper.

"Anything else, my lady?"

I think about it a moment and say, "Look for a property we can use for a potential business."

If you give people something to work on that they can call their own it helps morale. So says the Google God.

"Of course. That's fantastic and a way to make a legitimate income to keep the humans from being suspicious." He's nodding as he writes.

I roll my eyes. "Also, find out about the human holidays and customs. I would like to make sure we recognize them." As I speak, he keeps nodding and writing.

Yes, he's very useful. This is why I didn't break his fingers.

Staring at him I use the Magiks to really look at him. There is no doubt that Jameson did a selfish, dirty thing to Phobe and I but, I can see the goodness in him.

The untapped potential.

The Sidhe sings to me of his regret. Reaching out I pat his shoulder.

"Good job. Your help is invaluable." At my words he blushes, and I take that as my cue to walk off.

Jameson has done a lot here since he got his head out of his ass. He's still Jameson but, being here is good for him.

Perhaps it's good for all of us.

"Oh, by the way," I call over my shoulder to Jameson, "I found your... what do they call them? Blog. Yes, that's it. Your blog. How's that orgasm leaf fanning bit going?"

His gasp of outrage echoes and, I throw my head back and laugh. Jameson fanned a woman with a leaf and thought it would give her an orgasm. Leaf fanning. I laugh harder.

CHAPTER EIGHT

 za

A LONG NOTE of comfort from the constant song the Side sings to me means that my dad is— "What's got you so thoughtful, Dove?"

He climbs onto the bed beside me no longer hesitant to be affectionate with me. Since I'm not hesitant anymore either I lean against him and watch Knox who is staring out of the window a frown on his little face.

"He's been through a lot, Dove. He's trying to adjust just like you are," Dad says, giving voice to my thoughts.

I raise an eyebrow at him. Look at him being all wise and shit.

"Kids go through phases. I've seen it many times."

I settle in more comfortably and ask, "So tell me about the death thing?"

Dad chuckles and answers, "The movies are mostly wrong. I don't wear a long black shroud and go personally to collect the souls of the dead. They're escorted to the various afterlives by creatures similar to your fiends."

"So, there's more than one kind?"

"Essentially, yes. The One-God likes to give comfort to his human creations."

"Do you know everyone that dies?"

"No, not at all. I must be looking for them or know that they're dead. Souls do not get 'checked-in' to enter the realms of the dead."

Well, there went that theory; no ticket lines in the afterlife.

"All right, Dove. Think of the beginning of life like a big soup pot of soul energy cooking on the fire of creation. When someone is born their energy floats out from the soup and merges with a physical body. A lot like they're scooped into a bowl. When they die their soul returns from whence it came."

It sounds way more simplified than it probably is. My dad has gotten to know me well enough to realize that the simpler the better.

"What about heaven and all that?" I ask.

"Their experiences while in the soup pot are what they believe in while alive."

"You're saying that if someone believes they are going to hell when they die they'll imagine hell while in the pot?"

"Basically, yes."

Smiling, I pat his hand. "So what exactly do you do besides look pretty?" And if he isn't escorting the dead all over why does he disappear all the time?

"It's amazing how often creatures try to tamper with death. Not unlike your dark friend Phobe. They just have a lot less chance of success. There are also things that try to... escape at times. Since my existence is tied to the realm of the dead, I must protect it from those threats."

That makes a weird sort of sense.

"Why can't you interfere with things out in the living world?"

"If I break the rules, I lose my post and, I will be banished to the realm of my birth as long as I live," he says solemnly.

Well, then. That makes me feel a little like an asshole for resenting him leaving all the time.

"You were entitled to it. I could've always taken you and your Mother to my realm. We would've had a good life."

Freaking mind-readers.

"Would Mom have been okay with leaving her people behind?" I ask, trying not to sound like a little kid. My mother was incredibly loyal to her people. She fought for them, bled for them. She loved them.

"Yes, for you, Dove. Nothing mattered more than you to her." His answer gives me that weird warm feeling inside.

And that's enough of that.

"Dad are you ever going to find someone else?"

I'm not sure where the question came from but, it's out there and valid. There's no reason for him to stay alone. Mom has been gone a long time and, I really don't think she wants him alone.

When he shifts around, obviously uncomfortable, I giggle a little.

"I will never find another like your Mother." He clears his throat nervously after answering.

"Yeah, she was unique but, that doesn't mean you won't find another person to love, Dad." I'm not sure why this is so important to me but it is.

Dad doesn't need to be alone anymore.

"Besides, 'bout time you got laid, isn't it?" I look over my shoulder to meet his eyes and his smile.

"Are you saying I need a girlfriend?" He smiles as he asks.

"Or a hooker. It's up to you." Prostitutes need money too.

His laughter warms the room.

CHAPTER NINE

za

TWO AWKWARD WEEKS have now passed since I stepped into the Sidhe for the first time. Since I woke up... different. At least it's been awkward for me. Everyone else seems to be doing fine.

Which is a fact that I'm only a little pissy about.

To keep my head about me I've spent a lot of time tidying up the grounds and finding odds and ends to fix or do. At first I was told no a lot and treated like a fragile little flower. Annoyed, I stopped asking to help and just started doing things.

I'm not good at asking permission. They just give in and help now.

Currently, I'm out of things to do. The urge to get away makes me hurry through the dining hall at damn near a run. My plate is full of mashed potatoes and steak that the wonderful house goblins provided for lunch.

Running doesn't mean I can't have lunch.

Instinctively, my eyes search for the faces of my kids. I find them at a table full of other kids laughing and smiling. Well, hell. I'm not about to interrupt that. Turning on my heel I head towards the exit. I'll eat in my room.

Every few seconds someone says, "Good day, my lady", or "Hello, my lady." It's starting to get to me because, I don't know how to deal with this shit. It's more than enough motivation to make me never want to come out of my room again. Or quite possibly throw up on their shoes.

"Iza, what are you doing?" Alagard's words stop me dead in my tracks.

I look up guiltily holding my plate full of food in front of me like a shield. I take a few seconds to study the old dragon's scarred face as I debate how honest I want to be. His brown hair is long, almost as long as his beard. The scars on his face make him look menacing although he's a big softie.

And really, he doesn't scare me at all.

Alagard was, or is, my Godfather. He was like a loving uncle to my mother and, a weapons master to the dragon royalty for hundreds of years. He was kind to me as a child but, other than that I have no *real* memories of him.

He is extremely loyal to the traditions of his people. This I know because of the Magiks. He also defected from the dragon court to come to the Sidhe with Nika. That says a lot for someone who so faithfully served the dragon royalty for so long.

He came because the throne is here because this is where my mother's bones rest.

Decision made, I admit, "Running."

His golden-brown eyes lighten in amusement.

"From what, lass? No one here is going to hurt you." He motions for me to walk by patting my shoulder and nudging me forward. He falls into step with me. "Feeling a little overwhelmed?"

My cheeks heat and I answer, "A bit."

He pats me again and steers me into an alcove.

For some stupid reason I let him. It's totally because I don't want to drop my plate, right?

"Sit and eat. We'll talk and see if we can't help you with that."

So, like the little kid I once was in his presence, I sit. He sits across from me regarding me with kindness in his eyes.

"Now, what seems to be the issue?" he asks, that kindness now in his voice.

Nervously, I move the mashed potatoes around with a fork. Part of me wants to shove the plate at him and run. The rest realizes that's stupid. Mostly.

This time I opt to answer his question instead. "I'm no better than any of them. They are calling me 'Lady' and that's not a title I feel I deserve." Or understand, really.

"They do it out of respect, Iza. It's not meant to set you apart. They are safe here, and it's because of you," Alagard says with a smile playing about his lips.

His amusement makes me feel a bit childish for panicking because, that's what I'm doing. Then again, I'm not exactly a social creature. My idea of socializing is watching a TV show, alone.

"I remember your mother being of the same mind." At his words I stop fiddling with my mashed potato disaster. "If memory serves, she spent a week hiding in her room when she was crowned. I had to bribe her with a brand-new sword to get her out of it."

"She was pretty good with them?" I ask.

There are bits and pieces of my mother's memories still floating around in my brain, but they're all around my brief time with her. I don't have any from before my birth.

Although I'll never admit it out loud I love hearing about her.

"Indeed. Nisha was my best student. I see a lot of her in you," he adds.

"I'm not a lady like her, Alagard." Waving my fork around I keep talking. "I wouldn't mind being your student too."

I shove a piece of steak in my mouth to shut up.

"That can be arranged." He studies me and then says, "Keep in mind that our people don't need a Lady, Iza. We need you."

"Do what?"

"Just be who you already are. Who only you are strong enough to be," he reassures me.

He smiles and, I give a little smile back. But not for the reason he thinks. Unfortunately I'm not feeling all gooey inside. It's more a baring of teeth than a happy one. Who I really am isn't something any of them have seen.

"I'm not sure they can handle the real me," I warn.

"They seem to be handling you just fine." He kind of laughs as he says it.

Chewing another piece of steak I stare out the window contemplating his words. Does he realize I'm working extra hard to—behave? Ha, behave. Be nice if that weren't the actual truth.

"I'm not used to being around other people." Other than Phobe. He is the only one I was comfortable with.

The kids are hit and miss but getting better.

There's also a good chance that Phobe is coming back. I'm not stupid. I know he was made to do some awful things to the Feyrie. Phobe is the boogeyman to most of them. A fair description, but still. That's more hassle I don't need.

If these people find out who he really is they will hate him.

"But you don't have to be on your own anymore, lass."

With a few exceptions I prefer it but, I can't tell Alagard that. It'll hurt his feelings. Wait. Since when do I care about hurting someone's feelings?

All right sharing time is done and I'm not the best at it. I think I've hit my hard limit. The need to help them is one I can't fight. Being their savior? Yeah, I can fight that all I want.

Pain shoots through my head so unexpectedly that I drop my plate and fall to my knees in it on the floor.

"Iza?" Alagard asks in concern, getting on the floor with me.

Agony rips through my poor brain. I grab my head and squeeze to try and make it stop. Distantly, I feel the impact of my upper body on the cold stone floor. I try to get up, but I don't have the ability to do it.

Instead my sight turns inward, yanking me down a long dark tunnel. Pain tears through my head again.

"Nika!" Distantly, I hear Alagard yell for the healer.

The tunnel ends abruptly and, I grunt with the impact. Blinking, I look around—no, it isn't me looking around. What the shit? The interior of a vehicle of some kind surrounds me.

Help me.

The words echo in my mind. It's a girl's voice, young. My gaze swings around of its own accord. I'm seeing through her eyes! Unable to control it, I focus on what I can, I'll remember if nothing else.

A man is leaning over me/her. A human man. I start yelling. No! Fight! But when I strike out with my arms they are much smaller than my own.

In vain, I try to send my Magiks down the connection between us. I try to tell her that I'll be there. I'll save her. I try everything I can think of and nothing works. She can't hear me.

Panicking, I latch onto the strongest thing inside of me. Phobe.

'Phobe! Save her!' I scream in my mind.

A flicker of something shiny fills my gaze with tears. It's a knife. No! No! I repeat over and over. Light floods the vehicle and I quickly file away everything I can about the car, the man, just as the light blinds me.

'I cannot, Iza. She is too far away.' Phobe's voice flits through my head.

The connection fractures and as my vision rights itself I find myself looking up from where I lay on the floor covered in mashed potatoes. Nika kneels on one side of me. Alagard on the other. Angry with myself, with the situation, I wave them off and slip and slide until I gain my footing.

Without a backward glance, I walk quickly towards my room. Right now I don't care about trying to look dignified. I break into a run.

CHAPTER TEN

za

ALMOST TO MY room I come to a jarring stop as every hair stands up on my body. My eyes rise from the floor to look up into the fiery eyes of the man who never leaves my thoughts—but left me.

The man I called out for and who couldn't help me. Help her.

Suddenly frozen all I can do is stand there and look at him. Six months he's been gone. Six fucking months. I also won't lie to myself—I missed him every second of it. Feeling him out there, somewhere in the world, but never knowing where he was.

As our eyes hold the world around us fades away and, it's just the two of us. Each breath syncing as step by step, we draw closer.

"You heard me, you jackass," I accuse, recognizing the stupid, angry words coming out of my mouth but, I can't stop them.

My anger is real wrong or not.

He stops so close to me I feel his breath on my face as he leans down to rest his forehead against mine. The mashed potatoes squish between our heads and, I don't care.

It's a struggle to hold onto the anger, and I try hard to, but the longer I look at him the more it fades. Logic is starting to take its place. It isn't his fault. None of this is his fault.

It's not just the logic, it's well… my brain is turning to fucking mush. All I can do is look at him. Drink him in with my gaze. Breathe in the scent that's uniquely Phobe and him alone.

"I will always hear you," he whispers, his breath warm against my mouth. "I am… apologetic that I could not help the child."

Like fingers grazing my scalp I feel him trying to sink into my mind like he always has. But unlike before I don't let him. Can't let him. As hard as it is things are different now. There is too much left unsaid, undone between us.

That doesn't stop me from throwing my arms around him and hugging him for all I'm worth. He might be a jackass, but I'm allowed to miss him. I pull away and plant a sloppy kiss right on his mouth.

He came back.

Pulling completely out of his embrace I step back and simply stare at him. He's standing there with his lips slightly parted, frowning, the most puzzled look in his eyes. I surprised him.

Taking his shock as an opportunity to study the changes in him. He's a little more filled out. He no longer having that hungry look he always had in prison. Which means he's eating more… people.

His hair is shorter. The long black strands I'm used to seeing touch his shoulders are tamed into a very cool looking, choppy style right down the middle of his head.

His ears are pierced. Two shiny opals sparkle in the low light. Phobe's been watching TV too. Wrapped in his plain black t-shirt and denim jeans he's quite a sight to see. All lean muscle and—power. I swear it looks like his skin is seeping black smoke. I blink. His skin is seeping black smoke.

Rolling my eyes I keep ogling the show-off.

Lean feet peek out from beneath the hem of his jeans. He isn't wearing shoes, but then again, he never did. The swirl of his Magiks along his tattoos is brighter, newer, but so are some of the tattoos. His power has grown, probably from the eating of all the people.

God, I missed him!

It only surprises me a little when I pull back and punch him as hard as I can in his pretty face. With a last look at him I whisper a request to the Sidhe and step through the door that appears on the wall. His laughter follows me into the darkness.

CHAPTER ELEVEN

 hobe

A LAUGH BUBBLES out of my rapidly healing, broken jaw as she disappears into the wall. Iza is already using the power of the Sidhe. Her power.

And she hits like a truck.

My tongue snakes out to lick my lips. The taste of her still lingers there—along with part of her dinner. Standing face to face with her after weeks of watching from the shadows feels good.

Tasting her feels better.

Studying the dispersing shadows where she disappeared I acknowledge that she is adapting to her new abilities well. I am not disappointed in her progress but, she still has a long way to go.

She is saturated in power. I can see it. Feel it. Want to explore it. *Will* explore it.

A whisper of words from my forlorn—my fiend counterparts— and I lose the stupid smile on my face. A dragon approaches. Shadows seep out of me and brush against the intruder. *Alagard.*

My skin tingles as my glamour locks more firmly into place. Dragons have better eyes than most. This old dragon does not need to know who I am. None of them do.

"Looks like she is happy to see you, lad," Alagard says with amusement. "Who might you be?"

I ignore him. None of these creatures have the right to demand anything of me, no matter how politely spoken. Iza distracts me too much and, I do not want them to see the reactions she causes. Those moments are private and, no one should intrude upon them. I flick a gaze to him then dismiss him. Alagard is right. She is happy to see me.

She is also angry with me.

Pulling shadows around me I step into the bits of the NetherRealm that exist in the Sidhe to pursue her. She is ahead of me but not by much. Iza might be able to traverse it here, in her seat of power, but there is no darkness in existence I cannot traverse.

A glimpse of her ahead of me and then she is gone. A leap and I am almost on her and then she is gone again. She is good. I will give her that. My claws swipe open air. I miss again. She is *exceptional*.

But I am better.

With a burst of speed, I run along the shadows of the wall to get ahead of her, watching her look behind her and smirk. Teeth bared I leap and cage her against the stone wall of the Sidhe.

She looks up at me anger swirling her eyes like pearls in the moonlight then, laughter slowly takes its place. Her sharp teeth flash in a smile that gradually fades as something else bleeds into them.

Desire.

I can see it, smell it, feel it and every cell inside of me reacts to it.

With a growl, I fight the urge to do the very thing I wanted to do since I stood face to face with her like *this* the first time.

Completely lose myself in her.

Using every ounce of self-control I possess I bury my nose in her neck. Smelling her skin to try and minimally satisfy the unbearable urge to *take* from her.

My need for her is primal. Our bond is deep and often confusing. Iza needs more than physical. I do not know what the more is yet.

Figuring it out is at the top of the list. I am not a creature of emotion… not until her.

Only with her.

"How long have you actually been back?"

My face hidden from her, I smile. "A while," I finally answer.

"I should punch you again."

I stay there unfazed by her threat. She can break my jaw ten times over if she wants to. I keep my nose against her skin.

"Creeper," she says softly.

She is teasing me. I lift my head to look at her.

Pulling back a little more I unabashedly study her from head to toe. Able to see past her glamour—with her awake and animated, I want to see the changes her ascension has indeed brought about.

Her medusa strands are alive writhing around her head towards me, blacker than the darkest night, with small white teeth flashing in those serpentine strands. Before they were subtle, the little poisonous devils, but no longer.

The corner of her red lip curls up and, I can see all those lovely sharp teeth. They are almost as long as mine and just as deadly.

Her face is slimmer, making her eyes appear even larger. As I watch the second lid—a trait she inherited entirely from her mother— blinks sideways exactly like I thought it would. Her body is still lean but, the bones are no longer as prominent beneath her skin. She looks healthy and monstrous and breathtaking.

"I missed you, Phobe." A breath and her arms encircle my waist again. Without a second thought I wrap mine around her and pull her tight against me. I inhale the scent of cinnamon.

'I missed you too,' I say to her with absolute truth.

The bond between us twangs as it tightens. This bond is a curious thing that I do not fully understand. But it is not unwelcome, this attachment to her. Not anymore.

The Magiks formed it, there is no doubt to that, but they do not make it grow stronger as it has been doing. That is all us. These emotions between us.

Death cannot even remove this bond.

45

And even if it could, I would not allow it. Through this bond I can feel her; feel what she feels. Find her anywhere. I dare anyone to try and take it.

CHAPTER TWELVE

Iza

MONDAY HAS BECOME movie night with the kids. With all the newness and *people* I'm more than okay with it. Honestly, I miss spending more time with them. They've made friends here. They fit in here.

I still don't feel like I do.

Knox is sitting beside me holding my hand like he's prone to do. At first it was a bit weird for me but, then I came to understand that he needed it. And since it isn't killing me...

"Is that your ninja you talked about?" he asks me in a loud whisper.

I smile at him as I answer. "Yeah, that's him."

I forgot about that conversation. I wonder what Phobe will think of me calling him a ninja? Probably tell me that he's scarier than a ninja. Which is true.

Hell, Phobe is back.

Somewhat successfully, I've managed to keep it together on the outside. Inside, I'm a freaking train wreck. My emotions are all over the place and, I now get the commercials talking about PMS and hormones even though it's not actually PMS. I think it's just part of being female.

Which is stupid. Why in the world would any woman choose to go through that?

'Iza, where is your mind going?'

I send him a mental eyeroll and say, *'Crazy.'*

'I regret to inform you that you hit that stage in your journey many years ago.'

'Oh look, you're a comedian.'

The jackass went and found a sense of humor while he was gone. Good for him, totally... not.

His chuckle isn't that big of a surprise. The reaction I have to it kind of is. Yeah, those stupid goosebumps are back.

"Iza, my head hurts." I frown down at Knox's words.

"Do you wanna go see Nika?" The idea of him in pain makes my stomach twist. He shakes his head and lays it on my lap. Well, if I can't get him to the mountain I whisper to the Sidhe.

"Why in the world am I here?" Nika says from the doorway.

I smile. There are some perks to this job.

"Knox has a headache. Can you check on him?" I ask.

"It is perfectly normal—" The look I give her shuts her right up. "Of course." She crosses the room to the bed and rests her hand on his forehead.

"I can't find anything amiss. Perhaps a growing pain of some type?" she says after a few minutes.

Frowning, I nod. She pats his cheek and leaves.

"He's jealous." Michael says from the beanbag chair he's sitting on.

My frown deepens. Is he? "I dunno Michael. He seems off." I stare down at his little face but, he's sleeping peacefully. If there was anything wrong with him Nika would've found it.

Physically, anyhow.

Rubbing his soft hair, I realize that Knox is asleep. He's at that age still where kids just drop off whenever. I've seen him to go to sleep in seconds much like he did now. Still frowning, I move him further up the bed and tuck him in. He can sleep in here tonight.

I won't be sleeping much anyhow. I don't want him separate from me.

After an hour or so Michael and Ruthie both fake yawn and leave within minutes of each other. Silly kids. I know they're going to go make goo-goo eyes at each other.

Standing up and stretching I check on Knox one last time. He's still sleeping peacefully. Something really is off with him. He doesn't feel the same to me. It's strange but, then again, there's a lot going on and everyone is adjusting. Why does thinking that feel like an excuse?

No, something is off. I'll talk to him tomorrow.

Turning I walk out the door and head towards the outside. It's cold outside so, the Sidhe won't open the door until I grab my coat off the coat rack. It's annoying and kind of sweet too even if I don't get cold.

Pacified it opens the door.

There isn't snow yet but, I can smell it in the air. The cold has this distinct... clean smell that I love. I'm looking forward to seeing the snow that's coming. To seeing the world blanketed in white, fluffy drifts.

I wonder if I can eat it?

'Yes, it is merely frozen water,' Phobe's voice drifts through my mind.

'You're following me, aren't you?'

'Of course.'

He appears beside me—still only wearing a t-shirt, jeans and no shoes.

'You don't get cold either, do you?'

'No.'

Impulsively I grab his hand and drag him along with me. He follows without a struggle and, his fingers curl around my hand. Well, then.

'When I was a kid, my Mom used to tell me stories about this place,' I share.

'The Sidhe?'

'Yes. You wanna hear the stories?'

'Yes.'

That answer surprises me in a good way.

Without looking at him I start talking. It feels good to talk to him; to share with him. As we walk and talk, I slowly start to relax. I realize for the first time since I got to this place that it feels right to be here.

Not just at the Sidhe… but with him.

hobe

"You're just too damned fast girl." Alagard chides Iza.

She glares at him from the ground—a place she is becoming overly familiar with. "If I'm too fast, then why the hell am I the one on the ground?" she bites out, her eyes flashing in the sunlight.

He pulls her to her feet. She dusts off her pants, complaining under her breath the entire time.

"Because the way I'm trying to teach you just isn't working. You fight dirty with no formal sword technique. I end up reacting to protect myself," he explains.

The Sidhe, sensing her needs created a training field. I watched the land essentially give birth to stone walls surrounding a large, dirt-covered area. A wooden fence also sprang to life, providing a place for weapons racks to hang. I'm currently using it for a place to sit and watch.

Watching the failure of her teacher.

He has been training her for the last week—or attempting to. He is incredibly frustrated with her lack of progress but, it is not lack of progress. It is a lack of his understanding of her and, her understanding of herself.

Iza remembers everything I taught her in prison and uses it but, I only gave her the basics. Basics that serve her well so far. But they will not be good enough for what is coming.

Alagard is a good swordsman for a dragon but, Iza is only half dragon. That half is not the dominant one.

He will never be able to teach her effectively.

She needs to learn to fight in a way that uses her unique genetic makeup. Iza is fast and incredibly strong with fiend weapons at her disposal. None of these can be incorporated by a dragon teacher.

Against unskilled half-breeds her skills are more than enough. But against a trained, armed opponent who can outmaneuver her she will lose every time. That is unacceptable.

"You really a ninja?" The soft words pull my attention away from Iza, and I look down at the little shifter standing there staring at me.

Knox.

Off and on since I sat on the fence he's watched me. He finally worked up the courage to speak. Commendable.

"Maybe," I answer, remembering the conversation I overheard before between him and Iza.

Knox squints up at me sizing me up. Smart child. My shadows brush him but, I receive nothing which is strange but not impossible. I sense no other Magiks around him. Some creatures have a natural resistance to mental intrusion. A very rare trait.

It is something I will remember.

"She said you could throw cars and have fire eyes. I just see blue." He squints even more.

Some foreign emotion touches me. I let my eyes flare—a little, letting the shifter see—but only my eyes change and only a peek. Instead of being afraid like I half expect he smiles.

"Goddamnit, Alagard, that hurt!" Iza's voice carries across the field loudly.

"Put your guard up and it won't hurt! Going straight for the kill won't always work, girl!" he yells back.

"You should teach her since you're a ninja," Knox suggests.

I look back down at him. In this, he and I are in a like state of mind. Hopping down off the fence I grab a sword from the rack and cross to them.

The dragon sees me coming first.

"Thank god. Someone else can get thumped on for a while," he says stepping back.

Iza turns to me. She starts to smile and, it fades as she studies my face. "You have that 'no bullshit' look on your face," she mutters.

Jumping towards her I aim the sword directly at her head. Halfway down I turn it sideways and smack her on the ass with it. Her shriek of outrage is oddly satisfying to hear.

"This is a no bullshit situation. Show me your guard stance," I order.

She falls into a sloppy stance. I smack her wrist with the side of the sword. She is not prepared enough to avoid it and, her sword clatters to the ground.

"Stop sucking," I say softly.

Her eyes light up then flash black. Good. She is pissed.

Glaring at me she picks up her sword. Annoyed now she charges at me and, I easily avoid every intended blow. She is fast but, I am faster. I am not gentle either. Several times I nick her or I smack her hard somewhere with the side of the sword. Most of the time on her ass. Those rile her up the most.

This goes on for quite some time.

"When you rush in without thought against someone better than you they will win," I critique.

Her response is to come at me faster. The clang of metal draws a crowd. I ignore them all because, they do not matter.

Abruptly I go on the attack and, then the real fun starts.

"Sloppy. Do it again." Nick on her arm. "Wide open." Deeper cut to the back of her hand. "Move the way I know you can move not the way you think you can." I almost smile the moment she starts to get it.

Iza is a very quick study.

As I swing the sword sideways, she bends backwards and avoids the blow that would have beheaded her. Just as fast I stab at her. She dances to the side and blocks me. Sparks jump from the force of the swords connecting. Unhooking our blades I stab her in the upper leg with the tip of the sword. I am not going to baby her. I did not before and, I will not start now.

This will save her life one day.

I push her harder. Finally, to my satisfaction, she pushes back. Her movements become smoother, her body more fluid. She comes at me with a flurry of blows and gets closer than anyone ever has to wounding me in a fight.

I will always be better than her but, there is nothing wrong with me making sure she is second to me.

"Too slow," I tease.

She growls at my taunt and lunges. I trip her and push with my foot. Mid-way down she turns her herself and aims her sword low at my legs. It is a good move but, I am already several steps away.

This is the best entertainment I have had since she and I fought the first time. That is... strange. I cannot recall the last time I was entertained by anything that was not related to her.

After several hours she is flagging. Iza is special. She is fast, strong and completely one of a kind. But she cannot go on forever.

"Okay, I'm cooked, Phobe." She steps back, sword pointed at the ground.

You can do better,' I say into her mind.

'You're pushy.' I can hear the irritation in her voice.

I fight the smile that wants to break free. Only she can make me smile this way.

'I'm the only one fast enough to teach you. Deal with it.'

'Jerk,' But she does not mean it.

Her eyes hold her humor and her weariness.

"See, you're learning," Alagard says coming up beside us.

Iza gives him a dirty look and stomps off.

He laughs. "You push her hard," the old dragon chastises me.

"Yes," I say. It is the truth.

He strokes his beard at my answer but does not say anything else. He may think I am being too hard on her but he is also an old soldier. He knows what will eventually find its way to her. To us.

Tossing him the sword, I follow Iza. I know where she is going.

CHAPTER FOURTEEN

 za

THE DRIP of water is the only thing breaking the silence of the hot spring room… cavern. Whatever it is. The Sidhe made it for me and, I love it. There are three large pools of steaming hot water of the absolute perfect temperature. There are also cushioned seats that are exactly the right height for me to sit on in the water.

They move if I want to go deeper in the water or higher too. How awesome is that?

I shiver.

His steps are silent but, I can feel him there. I feel every single molecule of his body. It's that stupid bond. The one I can't break. The one I'm not sure I want to break.

It's how Phobe found my hiding spot. The jerk.

But still I smile at my thoughts. He's a jerk, yeah, but I know that I'll be better from his teaching than anyone else's. It makes my freaking body hurt though. My healing abilities kicked in and took care of the actual injuries but, I feel every ache keenly.

Super-duper healing only does so much.

It's a good kind of ache at least. I understand what he's taught me so far while everything Alagard tried to teach me went right over my head.

While swinging the sword around with Alagard, I was starting to think I was a moron. Nothing he was explaining or showing me made any kind of sense. Then Phobe volunteered and, I started to understand. I think part of it is because he beat my ass. He left me no choice but to learn. He isn't a gentle or accommodating teacher. I need that.

Gentle and I don't fit in the same space together.

My gut tells me that this is only the beginning. He won't stop because I get tired of learning or because he hurts me. He won't stop until I understand it. Right now I suck. The good news is I won't suck after he gets done teaching me.

"Did you get what you went looking for?" I ask, breaking the silence.

I know he's right behind me now. I have those stupid goosebumps again.

"Yes," he says after a second of tension-filled silence.

"You going to share with the class what it was?" I snap out.

Apparently I'm still a bit miffed he left me. Understanding the reasons or not he still left. The silence continues for so long I turn my head and look behind me. He's less than a foot from me standing up to his waist in the water bare-chested.

For a moment all I can do is stare at him. At the trails of the water drops rolling down his skin. My eyes follow those trails until I force my eyes back to his face. Nope not just bare-chested. He's buck naked.

Boy does he do a number on my hormones. Which annoys me to no end.

"I had to be sure of no more shackles. I also had to be sure of you," he answers.

I blink. Uh. "I'm sorry, what?"

The water ripples around him as he takes a step forward. All the hair stands up on my body. Including the medusa strands which are straining to reach him. They *like* him. I'm being betrayed by my own hair. How does that even happen?

"I was a slave for a long time, Iza. Until you were brought there I had no hope of being anything more."

I open my mouth to speak then snap it shut. My gut tells me that if I interrupt him now he'll never finish saying what he needs to say. What I need to hear.

"One look at you and my entire world turned on its axis." His eyes pin me to my seat in the water. "You awoke this mess inside of me." He takes another step towards me closing the last remnants of distance between us. "I had to be sure that they were real. I had to know that these emotions—that I still do not completely understand—are genuine."

Stepping around me he sits on the cushioned seat before me the water almost reaching his nipples. He takes my hands in his.

"You will not accept anything less than everything from me. I know you well enough to say that." He tugs bringing my wet skin up against his own. "I am not a creature of kindness. I am not one of your gentle Feyrie. I am cruel, cold and unrelenting. I do not know the politics of romance. Nor do I care to. I am a monster, Iza. I can pledge my life, my loyalty and my respect... and these fucked-up emotions you make me feel. Is that enough?"

I'm speechless. I sit there with my mouth opening and closing like a fish for what feels like an eternity.

"That is the most I have ever heard you talk at once," I blurt out. Smooth, Iza.

It's then that I realize I'm straddling his lap completely naked. It isn't embarrassment that makes my skin suddenly burn hot. We've been well, I've been, naked most our time around each other. There's no embarrassment between us anymore.

This time is different.

'Let me in.'

Of its own accord, my mind opens to him at his demand. I feel him sink inside of me. Feel it lock something permanent into place, something right. My eyes close as I lean forward into him.

Just for a minute. That's all.

CHAPTER FIFTEEN

 hobe

MY HOLD SLACKENS enough for me to raise my hands to her back. To scrape my claws along her bare skin. I did not lie when I told her I am not a gentle creature. I can try my best with her but, in the end the animal inside of me will win.

Every time.

Sharp teeth trace my earlobe. Just hard enough to give me goose-bumps. She pulls back just a little and looks at me. Her claws leave trails of fire as they circle from my back to my shoulders then to my chest. I feel them sink into my skin, feel them make me bleed.

And I like it.

Only Iza will ever understand me in such a way.

Just one taste and I will stop. Just one.

I pull her flush to me pressing her against the proof of how much I want her. Hesitantly, I kiss her once then again. Testing her. Waiting. Her teeth bite, playfully rough, into my bottom lip. There is nothing remotely gentle in my next kiss. It is all teeth and tongues and ragged breaths. I devour her mouth unable to hold back the tide any longer.

My hands roam her body as I allow myself the privilege not allowed in the times I touched her before. I know I am bruising her but, I cannot stop. My clawed thumb trails down her stomach, dipping into her belly button before continuing its journey downward.

So hot. I cannot wait to—

"Iza, where in the hell are you? We have a problem. A lingire is here claiming to be the real Shepherd." Jameson's voice echoes in the chamber around us.

I am going to fucking kill him!

My forlorn explode into existence and, the cavern echoes with a girlish scream.

Iza takes a deep breath and pulls a little away from me. Her swollen lips part in a grin. *'So, you have some of those too, eh?'* she teases.

'The forlorn are the male counterparts of the fiends.'

She laughs in my mind. "Un-fucking-believable," Iza mutters.

'No, Iza. This is un-fucking-believable.' My thumb slides into her heat and, she moans in surprise. Mesmerized I watch her face as I move my thumb once, twice. Then she is gone, standing a foot away from me a frown on her face.

'I'll not be ruled by my hormones, Phobe.'

She is only delaying the inevitable and, she knows it.

'We will finish this,' I say into her mind as I appear next to Jameson who is clinging to the wall like it is a lifeline.

With a growl I punch him in the stomach, lightly for me, and disappear again.

Iza's laughter follows me.

CHAPTER SIXTEEN

za

I T TAKES LONGER than I expect to gather my composure and digest everything Phobe said to me, and underneath it, everything he did not. This is all on a whole new level of unknown. The depth of it freaks me out a bit but, at the same time it feels so damn right.

I just hate the feeling of fate mucking around in my life. It's better than admitting I ran away like a big weenie too.

Taking a deep breath I climb my pruned ass out of the pool and cross the massive room to my clothing. A fluffy towel sits neatly folded next to them. The goblins are a thoughtful bunch. Drying off quickly I dress in the plain jeans and black t-shirt just as quickly.

Walking down the hallway, I find that Jameson is still lying on the ground groaning, so I stop next to him. I don't even try to hide my amusement.

"I see Phobe is back," Jameson comments, as dryly as one can in his position.

"He said hello, didn't he?" I can't keep the laughter out of my tone not when Phobe did something I considered doing myself. Even though part of me is glad Jameson interrupted it.

In a weird form of thanks I put a hand out to help him up.

"What did I do to piss him off? What the hell were those big creepy things chasing me?" he asks, rubbing his stomach as he straightens and uses his Magiks to heal himself.

I shrug and begin walking.

"Wait, did I interrupt something?" There is a slyness in his voice that I don't like. The jackass. I should've left him on the floor—or better yet punched him too.

Ignoring him I keep walking.

Now that I can think about things that don't involve Phobe naked or Jameson bleeding I find I'm curious about a lingire showing up. They're rare and the closest thing to a schoth that exists in Feyrie.

Schoths are supposedly the top clan in my old world—the Juras Realm. The purest of the pure and all that crap. Humans call them elves here and, those legends aren't that far off. I've seen the movies most of which really is fiction. They don't run on snow and can't shoot bows at lightning speed. But the humans did get two facts right: they have Magiks and they're pretty.

Like the schoth, the lingire are also reputed to be a snotty bunch putting themselves above the normal Feyrie. All because they are humanoid and have cute little pointy ears.

In my eyes, it makes them closer to schoth than Feyrie.

I've only met one in person a long time ago. He didn't last long in the Mud Hole. He was a total prick and a complete wussy on top of it. Having an ego and no strength to back it up didn't work out for him in there.

I touch the Web within me and barely feel the lingire on it. More curious now I pick up my pace.

"Who is she saying she is?" I ask when Jameson catches up.

He pulls a notebook out which makes me smile. Nika insists that she can't stand him but, she told me that Jameson is the best steward she's seen. He's meticulous, OCD clean and good with people. Most importantly he likes the job.

I can't fault that he works hard at it.

The Sidhe picked him for it. That was something I didn't understand at first. I do now. Quite frankly, he can do the job better than anyone else.

"The imps who came in last week were servants of hers. They were not treated kindly either." Righteous anger laces his words.

Good, he is starting to feel the fire of a fighter.

I've seen the imps he's speaking about in the lunch hall several times. They look starved and damned near defeated. Jameson tells me they are the lingire's former bondservants and good with the earth. Jameson made them the groundskeepers.

At their request.

"Aha, her name is Lady Mirelle of the House Finley," he announces proudly.

Finally that big brain of his spit out something I can work with.

The sound of him flipping hastily through his notebook is entertaining. I need to get him a tablet. Not that the paper flipping isn't entertaining but, he could fit so much more in that handy device.

"She is the supposed great-great-great niece of one of the counselors of the Feyrie King. I could find no record of anyone from House Finley being on the council. I looked." Of course he did. It's Jameson after all.

"All of the dark king's loyal council members were beheaded. My father carefully documented all the executions." He pauses. "Personally, I think she's full of it, and the beginning of a long line of many. It always happens this way when there is a chance at power."

Jameson mentioned before that he was going to find out who was related to whom from the old king's counsel. Also what family members were still alive—if any are still alive. It's one of the reasons he gathered all the old records he could find in the Sidhe Library. He may not be a fighter, not yet, but he's a damn good sidekick.

I search again on the Web inside of me. This is all still new but, instincts guide me relatively well. And what I find is that she is born of the dark magiks but that's it. No kindness. No love for her people. This doesn't bode well for her.

She's Feyrie but not loyal to the dark. And that's something the Magiks don't like.

"Not much from them. Let's see what she's about because honestly, as much as I don't want this job—it's mine." My words ring with truth. It doesn't mean I like it but, I don't do anything half-assed.

Without shame I'll admit I have issues with aristocracy in general. This one probably came to tell me I'm not pure enough or royal enough for the job I didn't ask for.

Ha, this might be a fun conversation after all.

"You will need to set an example, Iza." I stop and look at Jameson. Jameson who never promotes violence but is right now.

"What kind of example, Jameson?"

"You know your kind." He waves his hands around then blushes.

"Jameson, I think I'm a bad influence on you," I tease and start walking again.

"No, my lady. You have been everything but." The shock of his words stops me once again in my tracks.

I look at him in surprise. He raises his chin a notch as I stare at him. Since when is he team Iza?

"They have no right to come in here and try to take what is yours. They need to be dealt with accordingly." As he speaks he puffs up a bit like a little chicken ruffling its feathers.

I smile and pat his cheek. People eat chickens.

"I knew there was a reason I talked Phobe out of eating you, Jameson." His smile broadens then, he frowns when my words sink in.

We start walking again. Well I start walking again and, he scrambles to catch up. I don't hate Jameson. I don't even dislike him, but sadly at this point, I don't fully trust him whether the Sidhe likes him or not.

Maybe one day soon, because he's working so hard and asking for nothing in return, I will.

"What else do you think? I'm sure there's more in that big brain of yours." There might not be a lot of trust but, I can use his knowledge. That I know he has in abundance.

God knows mine is sorely lacking in some areas.

"Well, her appearance seems planned. She wouldn't have had time to get this mess of people together that quickly and get here."

He has a very good point. I wonder who's plotting? I bet they're probably going to try and be the boss. Whoever it is has a valuable lesson to learn about the dark Magiks.

The web is *never* about the rulers. It's *always* about the Feyrie as a whole people. It reacts to love for those people; to the loyalty for those people. It has nothing to do with power, riches or fancy dresses.

Having the title doesn't get you the power.

Pausing in the doorway I take in the crowd of people in the entrance room. Something is holding their rapt attention. A quick look around shows me what.

It's a freaking parade of feathered, eye-watering crayons.

There's an entire busload of them. Each row of them passing through the door is dressed in more finery than the previous one. A Feyrie version of monster fashion week from the eighteen hundreds minus the cool music.

Just as I'm getting bored with it the last row of them enters the entrance room. The lingire that I'm waiting for is a purple eyesore right smack-dab in the middle.

Her head is held uncomfortably high and, she's dressed like the lady she's claiming to be. Staring straight ahead she strolls through the crowd of people refusing to meet the gaze of anyone she passes.

Isn't she a peach?

The woman is quite beautiful. There's no denying that but, something is missing. I can't quite put my finger on it yet but I will.

A Victorian hoop dress made from a gauzy, bright purple material sparkles like glitter in the brightly lit room covering her from neck to feet. Trimmed with gold that glitters in the light and makes the purple even more bright. The trim itself is designed to match the gemmed golden crown on her head.

Talk about counting chickens. She's gone a step farther and crowned herself a queen.

'She looks like a purple egg.' The comment floats through my head in a very familiar male voice. I bite my lip to hide my smile.

For the most part I don't want to be here—which everyone who knows me is fully aware of. But I am and that's all there is to it. So someone else coming in and wanting to take over can cause a big problem... for them.

My eyes follow the wanna-be shepherd. Seeing the disgust on the lingire's face as her gaze skims the other Feyrie gathered to see her makes me grit my teeth.

Oh this is going to be a big problem.

"You do what you must, and in that, you will make the right choices," a quiet voice speaks up from beside me.

I look down at Lidus the head goblin who serves the Sidhe and in turn its Shepherd. Who in this case is me, yay. Lidus introduced himself to me the day I woke up... as this Shepherd person. He also told me how he is helping Rubi readjust to be among his kind again.

All around he's the coolest butler ever.

"The dark knows its lady and it is not the imposter for she is not you." With that, he pops out of existence.

Would be nice to have that ability. Dad can do it too but not me. I have to do things the old-fashioned way and walk.

"Why thank you, Master Yoda," I mutter.

I fought this but, in the end I accepted it. I accepted it for the innocents who can't defend themselves. I did it to save them, to fight for them, to protect them from people like this gaggle of neon-colored geese.

One of the guardsman shoves someone out of his way. My eyes narrow. It's Jameson he shoved who puffs up and looks genuinely affronted.

"My lady will be joining us shortly." Jameson bellows out into the room.

"She is already here, servant. Now fetch her something to eat. She is famished," states an older imp woman who stands toe to toe with Jameson.

Her connection with the Dark is so deluded that it can't even tell me her name.

67

It's the first time I can say I've seen Jameson look menacing. His brown eyes flare with ire and, he steps right into her personal space.

Good boy.

"We will not be fetching you anything. But since *my* lady insists on us being courteous I will not stop you. If you wish to dine feed yourselves—there's the table." He waves a hand at the old wooden table that mysteriously appears.

The Sidhe really does like Jameson. A little anyhow.

I watch them set themselves up at the dining table. Their few servants struggle to keep up with all the demands of the heckling lingire and her obnoxious group.

The food is in golden dishes of all things.

The costs of those dishes would buy groceries for months for the starving refugees that showed up before them. Not to mention the fancy food that the snotty woman keeps turning her nose up at it like it's garbage. At least the wasteful bastards brought their own. There's no way I'm feeding any of them.

Looking around the room the lingire's gaze fastens on the chair. She can sense the Magiks in it. The chair is plain-looking but, it reeks of Magiks.

The witch in purple waves at one of her servants who tries to move the big old wooden chair from the middle of the room to the table. He pushes and pulls with everything he's got and, the chair won't budge. I smirk as another servant comes to help and then another. After the fifth attempt with no success they give up and look up to their 'Lady.' She raises her head and struts over to stand in front of the chair.

"Come, chair, obey your master." She waves her hands around in circles. Nothing happens.

She begins to glow as her Magiks rise. Again, she orders the chair to move. Again, nothing happens. Nothing will either. She can be a glow stick all day long and, nothing will move that chair unless it wants to move.

"Fine then. We will just move the table here," she proclaims, pretending like she doesn't look like a twit waving her hands around at an old chair.

She turns around to sit in the chair and hits nothing but floor. The chair is gone. A snort breaks the silence. I cover my mouth and nose to try and keep another one in.

"Who dares laugh at me!?" the woman screeches, like a stepped-on cat. "Find them," she orders her guards.

I snort again stepping out of the shadows to stand between the guards and the people I swore to protect. Enough is enough.

"I dared." When I speak the people in the room murmur amongst themselves. Knowing what's coming next.

"My Lady, the Shepherd, the WebRider!" Jameson announces loudly from somewhere in the room behind me. Good lord, he has a big mouth.

"This is your savior?" The lingire chuckles. "She is dressed as a peasant. Guards, put her in chains." The older imp woman beside Queen-y orders.

Every muscle in my body tenses. They've got another thing coming if they think to put me in chains. Up to this point it was amusing now it's becoming something else.

Annoying.

As one unit the people behind me step in front of me forming a wall of protection. Even Knox steps forward a growl coming from his throat. Now this, I can't have. Even if it does give me that warm, fuzzy feeling inside.

Casting a small smile over my shoulder, I move around them. My hands are out in front of me in a sign of peace. If a child can step in front of me to protect me the absolute least I can do is deal with the problem.

The woman will end up throwing a tantrum and try to have me beaten or something hopefully more creative.

Try.

Knox grabs onto my arm, and the closest guard shoves him backward. He hits the ground but not hard enough to hurt him. I kneel to make sure he's okay and then pass him to Alagard, who has smoke coming out of his nose.

Biting my cheek, I keep calm.

The only reason this room isn't erupting into chaos is because I did not. Do these idiots not understand the danger they are in? A tremor runs through the Sidhe as the anger runs through me. It doesn't like them either.

I can smell fear coming from some of those around me. Nothing will stay here that causes them fear. Especially Knox who is an incredible little boy who calls me beautiful and makes me necklaces out of crickets. He doesn't deserve any more mistreatment in his life from anyone. He will never, ever receive it again.

A shiver creeps up my spine as a familiar Darkness enters the room. Damnit, mister comedian himself decided to join the party.

"Pick on someone your own size." With those words I turn and punch the guard who shoved little Knox right in his sneering mouth. He flies backward. His mouth is now open in surprise.

"Kill the insolent lot of them, you idiots!" the imp woman orders.

With a horrified expressions on their face, the two guards moving towards me freeze. Darkness circles their necks in an iron grasp. Two fiery eyes meet mine from between the two men.

Hellllo, sexy.

Knowing these two won't cause any more trouble I turn to face the mouthy ones of the group. Queen-y and her sidekick.

"You know, when I first saw you strut in here like a giant purple peacock, I waited to see if maybe you needed help too or maybe wanted to help *our* people. Then I realized something is missing from you, something important." As I speak I clasp my hands behind my back and walk slowly towards them.

"It took me a few minutes to figure out what it is but, now I know." And I do.

She has absolutely no goodness in her. No loyalty, no love, no honor.

I let the mantle settle around my shoulders gladly because, the simple act of a child made me realize I'm tired of seeing others at the whims of people who mean them harm. This flock of morons means them harm.

No more innocent victims.

I lift my gaze to meet the contempt-filled one of the lingire. With a wave of my hand the chair appears. The wave is purely to make fun of her. I run a clawed finger up the arm of the throne, watching it change and come alive. Turning into swirling ebony bones. Dragon bones.

Walking slowly around the throne I watch the emotions chase themselves across the woman's face. Disgust, envy, anger and a flash of fear.

I like the last one.

"You are a no one. Some mutt who thinks herself important," she accuses.

I shrug at the words. Maybe I am a mutt, a no one. But these folks that chose to be here are someones. And I'll make sure people know that.

"Here is the throne, my lady." Gesturing towards the chair I bow mockingly.

The woman raises her head again and, I latch onto the contempt in her eyes.

"At least you have the manners to address me accordingly, mutt." With those biting words she turns and attempts to sit.

Once again the chair vanishes. Once more she ends up on her ass on the floor.

"Do you have a good view from down there, my lady?" I bare my teeth in an imitation of a smile.

"I will have you all beaten to death and mount your heads on stakes to rot outside these walls!" the woman screams, climbing to her feet.

Having grown bored of playing with her I move so fast it's a flicker and stand nose to nose with her.

"Try it," I whisper.

Magiks stir and a curse that should've knocked me unconscious hits me. My Magiks pulse and simply eat it. This time the woman's face does go pale. Fear is bright in her eyes. I grab the front of the fancy dress.

There's the emotion I like from her.

"I didn't want this, but I took it. Creatures like you leave me no choice." A sharp tug on my hair brings my head around. The plump Imp's hand is buried in my hair pulling with all her might.

My hair doesn't like it.

Grabbing it signs her death warrant. Hissing, the little monsters make themselves known and sink their teeth into the flesh of her hand. Screaming she falls to her knees. Her skin is decaying rapidly while she still draws breath.

There's no pity for her in me. In fact all I feel is power. The power that's still new to me—that I usually hold at bay—circles inside and around me, triumphant.

"Release the lady or this little bastard loses his head." At the guard's threat everything inside the room stills.

Even the screams of the dying woman fade into the background as I turn to the guard holding a knife to Knox's throat. Eyes still on him I grab the twat lingire by the hair and drag her towards them. The man sweats out his fear in waves. My eyes flick to Knox who stands bravely a little smile on his lips. Faith in his eyes.

Faith in me.

Some of my glamour drops. I can feel the stares as they see a glimpse of what I am. A face I show very few. I know my eyes are black as night. I know my hair waves around my head like the serpents they are. A growl passes my lips as the power rises, as all the power around me rises. The guard explodes like an overripe fruit.

This is my hoard!

CHAPTER SEVENTEEN

za

I SLING the lingire woman towards the rest of her party who stand there gaping at me. No one catches her and, she hits the table with a thud and another cringing screech.

She climbs to her feet, her crown lost somewhere in the room, her once perfectly coiffed hair a rat's nest around her head. Calling forth curse after curse, she hurls them at me. Crossing my arms, I stand there while my Magiks null each one of them out.

No dark Magiks in existence can hurt me so, I let her exhaust herself. It helps that she looks like she's throwing a big old tantrum. Sporadic giggles are a background noise to her screaming. They think she's funny too.

"I am pure blood! I am the ruler here! How dare any of you let a mutt treat me this way! He told me you would be weak!" Her screams continue even as people began to move away. Some are bored and, some are trying to distance themselves from her.

Her people are leaving her to her fate like rats abandoning a sinking ship.

When she finally runs out of steam and stands there glaring at me I speak. "I think they lied to you."

Walking towards her leisurely I make sure my glamour is once again firmly in place.

"He said that you held no power!" she starts screaming again.

He, huh? "Who is this he?" I stop less than a foot from the hem of the fancy dress that now has some kind of brown gravy caking the front of it.

She isn't loyal to the dark but, she is born to it. I can see into the heart of this woman, Mirelle. Can see the greed and malice and pettiness. Can see that she isn't and has ever been loyal to anything but herself. I lean forward just enough to put my face in hers.

"Who is this he?" I ask, for the last time. Her eyes widen and, she visibly swallows.

"You cannot harm me. I am... Feyrie," she sputters.

I smile and wait. My gaze never once wavers.

"It was a dragon... Romney or whatever his name is." The confidence she displayed during her tantrum is gone. She is seeing me for what I am for the very first time—just as I see her for exactly what she is. The notes of the Sidhe flare in my brain.

"How many did you betray to hold your wealth?" I ask quietly, leaning back to study a claw.

The wealth came from somewhere. The schoth took all that belonged to the dark king and his loyal vassals. So, it stands to reason that her family should be poor.

Not dining on golden dishes.

"My lady?" The quiet voice reaches me through the loud murmuring of the people in the room. I turn to look over my shoulder at the imp who stands hat in hand. It's one of Mirelle's former servants. Easily, I find his name.

This one is completely loyal.

"Yes, Val?" He casts a nervous glance to Mirelle and then squares his shoulders and raises his eyes once again to me.

"She sold my wife and youngest child to the blood locks." The silence is deafening.

Everyone knows what happens to those the locks take, or in this case given. I point at Mirelle. "This woman?"

He nods.

"It's how she bought—" His eyes water, but he fights them back. "—she sold them for a bloody carriage."

"They were servants. Mine to do with as I saw fit! I needed a new carriage…" Mirelle defends, her voice tapering off with the last sentence.

"Mercy?" I turn and ask the Feyrie that are now all gathered in the room.

The answer is silence. They want no mercy for her. As I'm about to turn and do what I decided to do the minute I heard the words blood locks someone speaks up.

"My lady! Mercy!" Jaw clenching, I watch Jake, a newly arrived shifter, makes his way to the front. I open my mouth to speak.

"Why should we show mercy to one who hasn't shown mercy themselves?" It's Knox who speaks.

My mouth snaps shut and, I wave my hands to encourage him to continue. He has a valid point and can probably say it better than I can.

Jake looks down at him only once before dismissing him. He turns to me instead. What a putz.

"Answer his question, *Jake*." It's not a request.

"A good leader leads by example. By sparing her you demonstrate that you are a kind, just leader." My eyes narrow on Jake.

A kind, just leader? This guy doesn't know me at all.

Awareness pulls at me and, I swing to face the door as Kael just strolls in Romiel in tow.

Now I have the *he*.

I remember Romiel—not well but I remember him. He's a gray dragon who has in his head he's a silver dragon and was always an arrogant little shit about it.

"He has a point, Iza. The Feyrie need an experienced, strong leader. Someone, who can guide them until the king becomes known. Someone strong to lead them out of the darkness. To work together with the schoth to form a lasting peace," Kael says, plastering on his best salesman face.

Kael is someone I remember from before, too. He's my uncle after all. A red dragon who always had a temper and a heavy hand towards people. Now he's the self-proclaimed dragon king. The throne didn't choose him.

There are no fond memories of him in the fog of my childhood. When I was a child he creeped me out and, I mostly avoided him. But my mother loved him and, because of that love for him she was blind to his true disposition.

My eyes narrow.

Since when do schoth and peace go in the same sentence together? Why in the world would Feyrie want to move out from the darkness? It's our birthright. I chew my lip thoughtfully and study my uncle.

I'm pretty sure that Kael is the plotter.

He's betting on causing dissension with his little lingire pet and his grandiose speech. Romiel... he's not too big of a concern. His own ego makes people dislike him. Jake is apparently in on it too, which is annoying, but no one really likes him either.

Wanting to gauge Kael's effect on the crowd, I cast a quick glance around the room at the faces of the Feyrie that are here. Some are still healing from atrocities committed against them. My eyes land on Alagard and the long scar dissecting his once handsome face. In some cases, those atrocities are committed by their own kind.

Anger stirs in my stomach.

"Do you think that's you, *Uncle*? Experienced and strong?" I ask out loud. Wanting to end his little tangent.

Pushing Knox behind me I move in front of him protectively. There won't be a repeat of earlier. I wipe my hand down my pants to remove the goop transferred from his shirt. Pretty sure there are some guts on him. Lots of guts.

I'll worry about that in a minute.

"I am too old for such an endeavor but, Romiel here—" He waves a hand at Romiel. "—at Mirelle's side can do just that. A dragon's strength is sure to give the people exactly what they need."

A dragon's strength got my mother murdered. Something I think Kael knows a lot about. He's definitely the plotter. But this time it's simpler. His 'grand' plan is that through Romiel, Kael can rule. If they wrote it on a piece of paper it can't be any more obvious.

Do they think I'm a complete moron?

I look at the way he's looking at me. The smug expression that's hiding underneath the false friendly on top. Oh yeah, he thinks I'm a total moron.

That's the reason he's trying such a silly thing.

He really should've taken some time to get to know the type of person I am now. I'm no longer a five-year-old girl that loves her mother too much to tell on him for being a creep and smacking her a time or two.

None of the Feyrie—loyal to the people—want a kind, just leader to make peace with the schoth. They don't want the schoth period. None of the Feyrie here want Romiel or his puppet master Kael leading either. Half of Kael's dragons abandoned his rule and came to the Sidhe with Nika and Alagard.

Kael moves forward his face all smiles and fake kindness. It's thick enough now I'm torn between laughing at him or throwing the table at his head.

Maybe I should laugh while I throw the table at his head?

"What you have done here is a wonderful thing." He sweeps his arms out to indicate the Feyrie who are staring at him like he smells bad. "Pulling these Feyrie together wasn't easy but you did it. But they are not soldiers. They cannot fight a war. No one can under such an inexperienced girl." There goes that smug smile again as he continues blathering.

"Peace with them is the only way. The peace that you will never be able to see past your prejudices to negotiate," Kael continues, looking around the room to try and beseech support from the gathered Feyrie.

His smile starts to fade when their faces don't change. They won't accept him or his puppets. Which I think he's starting to see—he isn't blind.

The Magiks won't accept them either. It chose me for a reason whether I'm reluctant or not. Until I die it's a done deal.

Darkness steps to my side. I flick a glance to him tasting his glamour in the air. Phobe's up to something. The glamour around him is thicker than normal. That's a sign of intent for sure.

'Repeat what I say, word for word,' Phobe's voice whispers through my mind.

Phobe has a plan and, I trust him. There's going to be so much shit in the future that I don't mind making it a little less cluttered, anti-climactic or not. So I do as bid. As his voice floats through my head I repeat it word for word.

"Peace, you say? Does that peace include the wingless children you gave to the humans as payment for your anonymity? Or the deal you have with the schoth to keep your own pockets lined with gold so your hoard stays full?" I ask as I let the disgust show on my face.

There are gasps of shock from several people in the crowd. Phobe's words are enlightening to all of us. I know Kael is a dick but the fact that he did it for money won't go over well with his own kind. It doesn't go over well with me either.

Kael's connection with the dark is so spelled that I can't feel much about him. Spell after spell is woven around him protecting him from my inner gaze. It's then that the worst suspicion swirling in my head solidifies. He betrayed my mother. I know it down to my core.

Why hide so thoroughly if you're not guilty of something?

The smile on his face falls and, he looks at me with his real emotions. Contempt and anger, mixed with a little bit of hatred.

"I do what I must to protect my people." As he speaks, he smiles again. It's not a nice smile this time.

Phobe's next words make my hands shake and, I tuck them into my pocket to try and look nonchalant as I accuse, "You do what you must to protect yourself, Uncle. Like you did when you trapped my mother, Magikless, to be slain by the fucking schoth king."

"I did what my foolish sister would not! I saved our people from extinction at the hands of the schoth! I kept them safe and comfortable for years after her silly romance almost cost us everything! She deserved what she received!" Kael bellows, his voice is deepening as his dragon swims close to the surface.

His red hair glints in the lights of the room, his green eyes that are so like my mother's lighten.

Hate. I fill with hate.

I grit my teeth and continue saying Phobe's words carefully. "Finally, you admit you are a pawn to the schoth, Kael." The rage and pain courses through me at his admission. To be betrayed by one so close to you, by your sibling. My poor mother.

"I am no one's pawn, little girl. I am a king and, you will show me respect!"

"Respect? On your knees, bawling like the pussy you are, you begged the schoth king to spare your life. In place of yours, you offered my mother's. So yes, you are a pawn, Kael." My voice is thick with amusement. Not the nice kind either.

'Dad, you need to be here,' I call out into the nether of existence. In a cold blast of air he appears behind the false dragon king. His eyes are black and shiny in the light of the room and, his rage so profound it coats my skin like a blanket.

'Can you kill him, Dad?' I ask quietly in my mind.

His black eyes meet my own. *'Not unless he admits to killing her directly, Dove,'* he answers, his voice sounding like he is speaking through gritted teeth.

Kael isn't dumb enough to do that. My dad blows me a kiss and gives one final look of death to Kael.

"There is nothing you can do about it, you insolent brat. Only the strong can rule and—" Kael 's speech cuts off, his finger pointing at me accusingly. I just smile.

"You are no longer welcome here. Remove him." My words echo as the room begins to shake and rumble.

Kael stares at me angrily as he starts to change but, it's too late. A bubble of Magiks surrounds him trapping him within them. With a shout of surprise he is gone leaving only a spattering of ash.

"What in the hell was that?" Romiel demands, turning with his shiny glowing sword in hand.

"That was Kael getting kicked out." My heart is heavy as I answer.

"She is the *Shepherd*, you stupid lizard. The Sidhe reacts to her will alone," Jameson pipes up from somewhere in the crowd.

There is a single chuckle, followed by another and then another until everyone follows suit. Well, everyone but Romiel and his group.

Romiel is standing there frowning, his long gray hair swinging around him in a way that the girl I hide deep inside of me envies. He's looking around like he just lost his keys instead of realizing they're laughing at him.

My Magiks try to touch him only to be instantly repelled. Light Magiks suffuse him. He's coated in it. Just like Kael if, not more so.

Maybe everything isn't as cut and dried as it seems?

"I'm not sure where the Sidhe dumped him so you might wanna go look." I comment.

He stops spinning in place to look for Kael and puffs up like a rooster. What is up with men mimicking poultry?

"His wish is for Mirelle and me to take over as the Feyrie rulers. It is best for everyone involved. We have experience with servants and negotiations with the schoth. Whereas your experience is limited to the unclean." It's entirely possible he's as stupid as I first thought but, some people can fool anyone. I truly hope he doesn't pass those genes on to any mini-dummies either way.

If nothing else he's an arrogant shit. He's just as "unclean" as the rest of us, the moron.

"There is only one way to try and take her place, hatchling. Trial by combat," Phobe says, speaking out loud for the first time.

The sneaky bastard planned that all along. Phobe's also lying because, winning combat will not pass on the power.

"That's acceptable. I am the best swordsman in the kingdom so, whoever is pitted against me will lose. Who shall you name as champion from the rabble assembled, half-breed?" He looks around him as he speaks. His eyes full of arrogance as they skim right over Phobe.

"Is he blind or did the fact that you kicked his boss out not sink in?" someone calls from the crowd.

"That was merely a cheap trick cast by a mage. I am too wise to fall for such antics," Romiel defends.

"Romney, I'm not sure this is such a good idea," Mirelle speaks up from where she hides behind him.

He looks at her like she has grown three heads.

"There is no one here strong enough to defeat me in combat, woman. Alagard is too old and, that imp standing next to her doesn't possess a drop of Magiks." He points at Phobe and then he points at me. "She cannot fight me herself because she is 'chosen' so, she has no choice but to pick from this group."

I want to reach over and smack the stupid out of him.

Mirelle looks at me and, I can't help but smirk a little. I already got to smack it out of her.

"Jameson, what are the rules concerning a champion?" I ask my walking encyclopedia.

"You can pick anyone you wish as long as they are pure blood." Jameson supplies, a smile on his face.

In the end, there isn't really a choice to be made.

"Phobe shall be my champion," I announce.

'Had fun with that, did you?' I ask in his mind.

Phobe knew all along, the smart bastard, and simply waited for his chance. I'm a little curious why he made it a goal to kill Romiel in this particular way because, there's no doubt he'll kill him.

'A little,' Phobe answers, a blank look on his face.

"That imp? Accepted." Romiel sheaves his sword—the one that didn't concern me at all, at any point. Shows how much of a threat I think he is. "Come, Mirelle, Kael wants to prepare our people for the news that I will soon be taking the dark throne."

Wait, dark throne? Does this idiot think he's the king?

"See you after Harvest Moon," Jameson calls out as Romiel, Mirelle and her gaggle leave the Sidhe—out the actual door this time. Jameson steps out of the crowd and stands beside me, a satisfied smirk on his face.

"When is the Harvest Moon, Jameson?" I lean towards him and kind of whisper.

"October fifth, Iza," he loudly whispers back.

So there are a few weeks to go before then and, the humans have a great holiday in October, too. Halloween! It's our kind of holiday. Monsters and Magiks and candy. Lots of candy!

My stomach rumbles. "So, now that the excitement is over who's ready for dinner? I'm starving."

The people in room laugh as a group. The tension is gone; one part of it handled. Smiling people do the back-pat thing, laugh and chatter as they file into the dining hall. I slip away.

As I walk I ask the Sidhe to have someone bathe poor Knox. His back is covered in gore. Then I push my mind away from the "chosen" crap and let my thoughts settle on one of the reasons I slipped away.

'He follows you,' Phobe cautions.

'I knew he would. He's not as smart as he thinks he is. He played his hand tonight, thinking the outcome was going to be different.'

'He is torn between his lust for you and his lust for power.' Is that a little irritation I hear in his voice? *'Yes. It is an uncomfortable emotion. I plan on killing him regardless.'* That answers that question.

'You can't just kill someone you're irritated with, Phobe.' I try for a scolding voice but, my heart isn't in it. Right now I feel like killing someone.

'Why not? He causes me discomfort and, now he has betrayed you. It is what you call a win-win situation.'

I hate when he uses logic against me.

As we walk I tell him why I led Jake away versus killing him right there in front of everyone. *'I figured you might be hungry but, I wasn't sure if you needed to eat that kind of food still.'*

'It is still how I feed. What do you call it? Milkshake them?'

I fight the laugh that bubbles up. If I laugh, Jake will hear and be suspicious so, I decide to take advantage of the good mood Phobe seems to be in.

'Do you want to pounce before or after I kiss him?' Maybe he just needs a little poke now and then?

"Do you wish to kiss him?' That's not the answer I expect but, with Phobe you don't get what you expect very often.

"Maybe. Depends on if he brought tic tacs to cover up the doggy breath.'

Phobe's chuckle floating through my mind is so surprising I stumble. That chuckle catches me in a place near my heart and stirs up feelings I'm still trying to understand.

Feelings I think both of us are struggling to understand.

Also, I need to fully grasp how his place in my life is different and is now going in a direction I know nothing about. If that kiss in the bathing pool is any indication things are changing.

Dealing with this isn't going to be easy. I need to work through my crap and move forward. He's my best friend but more than that. I didn't understand it when we were in prison but I'm starting to.

There are just so many other things to deal with too. The schoth, the Light Fey as a whole, and of course, the humans.

'They grow curious.' Phobe's voice is knowing.

The bastard is always snooping in my brain.

'That's not too big of a shock. We are growing in number daily. Numbers attract attention.'

'They will make a move soon,' he adds.

Well, that'll be fun and, a chance for me to get some information I need. *'Good. Then I might be able to find the wingless.'*

The fact he gave them to humans is now known and, it explains why Kael is left alone by those humans to do whatever he wants. A bartered favor. Something right up his alley.

"Iza, wait up!" Jake calls from behind. I stop walking and turn to face him.

'If you do kiss him he will die more slowly,' Phobe adds quietly.

'You say the sweetest things, Phobe. Especially about things you have no say in.' I can't help but add that and throw my mental shields up. He doesn't need to keep snooping. That little spiteful part of me is still a bit stung. No one, not even Phobe, can tell me who I can or can't put my lips on.

Not that they will go on Jake but still.

That unexpected chuckle floats through my mind again.

I had my shields up, how the hell did he get past them?

'Do not forget that I learn very quickly, Iza.'

That mother—

"Iza, I must speak with you about what happened," Jake says, coming to a halt at my side.

Standing uncomfortably close to me he positions himself between me and the wall. So close I'm overwhelmed by the smell of the detergent he uses for his laundry. The instinct to remove the threat is hard to fight but I do.

For the moment I will play along.

"What exactly is there to speak about, Jake? Phobe will face him and that's the end of it." I raise an eyebrow when he smiles.

"It doesn't have to be. When Romiel defeats your elf there are still many good things you can do. Things I'd like to help you do."

Jake fancies himself a helper does he? This is the first time he's tried to 'help' with anything. As far as I know.

And how in the world did he get the elf thing?

"I didn't realize you want to be proactive in our little community here. I was told you haven't shown interest in helping," I say.

In fact Jameson said Jake goes out of his way to avoid doing anything other than annoying people. He refuses to work with the rest at any job. He refuses to go out and help bring people in. Other than sleeping all day in the crappy room the Sidhe provided for him he doesn't do much of anything.

Now he's pestering me but, this is the first time he's gotten the balls up to speak to me. The lust thing Phobe mentioned is a bit beyond me. How can you want someone you know nothing about?

"Well I figured I'm working more from the sidelines. Kael promised me a small ranch outside of town for helping him. You can stay there with me while they take care of the others," he says, smiling.

My eyes narrow. Do what? Did he just blatantly admit his betrayal so openly and, then invite me to be his girlfriend at the same time?

Is it an attack of the stupid day?

He caresses my face which is something he should be smart enough not to do. I don't exactly exude the teddy bear vibe. If I didn't need information from him I'd rip his arm off and beat him to death with it. This time I ignore the desire to hurt him. I need more information. The way Phobe explained his ability works is that he needs the idiot here thinking about the subject matter to get it.

Jake touches me again and, it makes me shiver in repulsion. I'm not surprised when he takes it to mean something else, men like him always do.

"What do you mean? Take care of the others?" I ask, pushing down the urge to puke in his face. Or rip it off and stomp on it. Either thing would make me happy.

"Give them to the schoth king as a gift for negotiating. They're wanted traitors. Kael said it will be enough to secure the treaties." It takes every ounce of self-control I possess not to eviscerate him.

Every ounce.

"Have you and Kael been friends for a while then, Jake?" I say through gritted teeth.

He nods as he kisses my cheek.

Slowly I wipe the kiss germs off my face. I sincerely regret making the joke about him kissing me. *'Phobe, you better be getting a lot of info right now.'*

"We've been acquaintances for years. He's told me all about your illness. He said that when you have episodes we can just chain you and, it will help with the transition—"

I can't handle anything else coming out of his mouth. I interrupt, "Are there more of your friends hanging around?"

He's frowning at me now and, starting to see through the very transparent ruse. "You have no interest in me at all, do you?"

I raise an eyebrow at his question. Duh. At no point in time since I came here did I show any sign of interest in him or anyone else. He came up with that all on his own.

"Nope. Especially considering how you betrayed us all for a house. While idiotically believing that Kael will stick to any kind of deal with you demonstrates how bad a case of the stupid you have."

"Betrayed you? I want to survive this. Someone like you should understand that. You're not going to succeed and, I don't want to die along with the rest."

Maybe we won't succeed but, it won't be him that stops us.

Patience at an end I mumble, "Please kill him before I do."

Jake's frown deepens as, abruptly, a large clawed hand digs itself into his brown hair and pulls him away from me. I watch Jake's face and try to find pity for the shifter, but I can't. He speaks of the others as if they're insignificant thinking only of himself.

"I told you it would be slower if he kissed you." Phobe's voice is a hiss in the darkness gathering around the shifter he holds in an unbreakable grasp. They both disappear.

CHAPTER EIGHTEEN

za

"Iza, can I talk to you a minute?"

At the sound of Ruthie's voice I pause while toweling dry my hair to look at her. I wave towards the bed.

With a look of dejection on her face she flops onto my bed. "I need advice."

"I'm flattered you're asking me but, I'm horrible at advice," I tease. Tossing the towel over the drying rack I sit next to her, leaning against the headboard. I suspect that the advice she is looking for is of the romantic kind and, I'm certainly not good with that. But for her I'll try.

"See, I kinda sort of—" She twists her fingers around each other nervously.

"Have a crush on Michael? Yes, we all know. So what's the problem?"

She rolls her eyes at my question. I warned her I'm not the best person for this. "What if he doesn't like me back the same way?" Her big brown eyes look at me imploring and cutely pitiful.

I laugh. I can't help it. This is hilarious. "Why in the world would you think that?"

"Well, when I try to talk to him he turns all red and stares at the floor." At her answer, I laugh harder. "What is so funny about that?"

Laughing for another solid minute, I wait until I can breathe right before I say, "Does he bring you meat in butcher paper?"

She frowns and nods her head.

"Does he also give you weeds that sort of look like flowers?"

She nods again.

"Did he take you on a picnic and pee on a tree?"

When she nods this time I start laughing all over again. Now I know where that internet search on romancing a werewolf came from on Jameson's computer. Here I thought I would have something to tease Jameson about.

Now I have something to tease Michael about instead.

"Ruthie, just tell him that you like him. Maybe he'll stop peeing on trees," I say, giggling in between words.

"What if—"

I cut her off. "Ruthie, he's peeing on trees because he thinks that's how the internet told him that you court a werewolf."

Her mouth falls open and, she blinks a couple of times. Then she giggles and giggles again. Within a few seconds she's laughing so hard she's holding her sides.

Suddenly she hugs me and hops off the bed.

"I'm going to get cleaned up and then tell him." She leans over, hugging me again, and kisses my cheek. "Love you, Iza," she calls as she runs out the door.

"Love you too," I whisper, knowing it to be the truth. I'd die for these kids in a hot minute.

Shaking my head I stand and head towards the closet to look for some shoes. A chime of music in my head from the Sidhe brings my gaze around to the door.

I'll be damned.

"Iza, I need to talk to you," Michael says from my doorway.

Turning towards him, I smile and ask, "Does it have to do with you peeing on trees?" The look on his face makes me break into laughter again.

"How do you know about that?" he demands in a fierce whisper as he shuts the door behind him.

"Something I have learned about the Google God is that it isn't always honest. Why in the world would you search on there for ways to romance a shifter?" I ask, sitting back down on the bed.

"I'unno," he mumbles.

Lifting his chin with my finger I look into his blue eyes.

"Just tell her, Michael. Sometimes the most direct way is the best way to deal with these kinds of things. Saves you all kinds of anxiety and teenage angst."

He blushes and smirks. "I am irresistible."

Well that escalated quickly.

"Yeah not trying to crush your dreams of stardom or anything but, no you're not. However, you just might be to her. Now shoo. Go talk to her."

Leaning forward he too kisses my cheek and practically skips from the room. I handled that better than expected. Maybe this advice thing isn't so bad?

My stomach growls.

Now it's time to deal with other things. Heading towards my closet I pause at the door for a few seconds just in case. When no one comes I grab my shoes and head towards the kitchen stopping to put them on while on the way there.

The sound of heated voices raised in an argument stops me in my tracks outside of the kitchen. Nika and Jameson. Stepping closer to the door, I wait to see what it's all about.

"I can't believe you were talking to the new imps in their bathing chambers!" Nika says in a rather shrill voice.

"Oh my god! You singed my hair! What's the big deal? They're nice and I figured this was all right since I spent four fucking hours washing dishes." Wow, he sounds mad.

Washing dishes for four hours would make me mad too. I think Nika is taking advantage of Jameson's reformation. I like it.

"You should be out there raking leaves," Nika says with that haughty tone to her voice that I hate.

"Raking seems pointless. They just keep falling down. Why not turn into your fat dragon form and use your meaty man hands to shake the leaves out of the tree?"

Oh, he totally went there. I'm surprised she didn't smack him. Meaty man hands. I giggle, unable to help myself.

"Get out there and rake right now before I toast you like a kabob," she threatens.

The door swings open and I step aside into the shadows. Jameson is so mad as he stomps past he doesn't see me. Nika, slower to exit, does.

"When are you going to admit you want to do him and stop being a jealous twit?" I ask as I brush past her into the kitchen. I agree that Jameson needs to prove himself but, I don't agree with her being mean to him because she's petty. This is something she needs to stop doing before I stop it. Jameson doesn't deserve it.

"My lady, I am—"

"So jealous it's turning you bitter. Jameson loves women and, if you'd stop being a bitch you might have a chance with him," I say as I start searching the cabinets for food.

"Jameson is not the type of mate I would seek out."

"We both know that the destined mate shit is crap. That's only in books. Dragons can mate with whomever they want to. My Mom proved that."

"And look what happened."

Her words stop me dead in my tracks. Turning slowly to face her, I squeeze the can of fruit in my hand until it pops. It's the only thing that stops me from doing that to her head.

"You know I think for the most part you're a sweet, kind person. But other times you're a self-righteous bitch and, it makes me want to make a pair of boots out of your lizard ass. Stop being an asshole to

Jameson. Either tell him you like him or stop liking him. It's that damn simple. Now, is there anything else?"

Her green eyes hold mine and two spots of red are on her cheeks. She nods and inclines her head and leaves the kitchen.

Shrugging, I keep looking for food. I spoke the truth and, she knows it. Hopefully it gets through to her. She and Jameson actually kind of fit. He'd remove the stick in her ass and, she'll keep him from trying to stick things up every other woman's ass.

Looks like a good match to me.

CHAPTER NINETEEN

*I*za

MY NIGHTMARES ARE no longer just my own. They are quickly becoming the nightmares of others. The ones suffering. The ones in pain. The ones who will not make it here.

I see it all.

They're in many different worlds, all different ages and races. Some are trying in vain to get here. They won't make it. Some died while I slept. There aren't enough people to send after them. The fiends are limited in what they can do and, they can't talk to people. They can only witness.

Fuck.

Holding my face in my hands my heart weeps for them. I feel every second of their pain. There isn't a fucking thing I can do about it. So many live a life of poverty and abuse. So many of them are hurt by others.

Feyrie have become insignificant to everyone.

They are in even more danger because I called them. Did I make things better or worse for them? That question now haunts me and, if you throw in the anger and crap about my mother, sleep is not my friend. Not that we've ever been friends.

"You are troubled by things you cannot control." I shouldn't be surprised by his voice in the dark but I am.

Since when did he start lurking in my bedroom at night? Oh, wait. This isn't a new thing.

Yesterday, I spent the entire evening building up my mental shields to keep snoopy pants out. I check them and see they're still intact so, how does he know? Oh, there's that thing he said about learning too. How obnoxious of him.

"This lady gig is shit." Rubbing my eyes with the heels of my hands, I swing my feet to rest on the cold floor.

"You seem to be doing a good job with it."

"I didn't peg you as a self-esteem coach," I snap out.

"I am not but, I am your friend?"

My lips twitch. He sounds so uncomfortable using that word.

The weight of him sitting on the bed next to me brings my body up against his. I rest my elbows on my knees and look over at him. His eyes are bright in the dark as they stare at me. The feeling of his body heat soaking through my shirt gives me a strange sort of comfort.

"I feel it all and, part of me doesn't want to," I say into the silence.

"Stop being a pussy."

At his no-nonsense tone a surprised chuckle barks out of me. And just like that some of the grief fades away. At least for now.

"Do not let yourself fall victim to guilt that is not yours to carry, Iza. You can understand their suffering and that is something that is meant to be but, you do not have to live it. You have already lived your own." He sounds all logical and Phobe-like. I can't argue with it.

Still, don't like it.

"Fucking prophecy," I mutter.

At the mention of it, he shifts a little in his seat. Is Phobe uncomfortable? The idea of that completely amuses me and makes me suspicious at the same time.

"Iza, has anyone told you more than your specific part of the prophecy?"

Frowning, I stare at him and think about it. No. I can't say they have.

"You need to know the entire thing."

"Okay, since you know how it goes enlighten me, oh great one," I tease.

He starts to speak, and as he does, my smile fades.

Sonofabitch.

After he gets done talking I sit there a moment and digest everything. It's a lot to take in and I feel like I've been deceived my entire life. Well, I was but, now it's worse.

"So the version I've heard my entire life is the wrong version?" He nods at my question. "How does everyone know the prophecy anyhow? They teach it in school or something?"

"Actually, yes."

That's stupid. Why would you teach your kids something ridiculous like that?

"Because they believe in it, Iza."

"Why did the dark king never sit on the throne, Phobe?"

He stares at me for a while before answering, "The original king did not need a throne. He *is* the throne."

"So, I can sit on him?" I ask, only half-joking.

The smile that breaks out on his too-pretty face makes me smile in return. Those damn dimples.

Which makes me think of another face with a dimple. "Is Knox acting strange to you?" The smile instantly fades and, I almost regret asking. Almost.

"Why do you ask that?"

"I dunno. Something is off with him. I just can't figure out what. Have you picked anything out of his brain?"

"Iza, I cannot read Knox."

"Do what?"

"Sometimes creatures possess natural shields that keep me out.

Unless I want to hurt them to get in." He pauses. "I assumed you did not want me hurting Knox to read his mind."

"No, no I don't. Did you get anything off him?"

Phobe shakes his head. "Iza, I will watch him and see."

Chewing on my bottom lip I nod. I'm also going to take my own advice. I'm going to ask him. I stand up and the digital clock on the wall reminds me that it's three o'clock in the morning.

Tomorrow. I'll ask him tomorrow.

Plopping back down on the bed I come to rest against Phobe once again. When his arm slides around my back and he rests his hand against my side I say nothing.

It feels too damn good to mess it up. Resting my head against his shoulder, I sit there and let him hold me.

CHAPTER TWENTY

hobe

I AM unsure why talking about the prophecy with Iza makes me feel this emotion she calls 'uncomfortable.' Her ignorance of it left a bad taste in my mouth. The entire situation does. Iza was kept in the dark about her place in things. I too kept her in the dark—but no longer.

And with the knowledge of the entire prophecy she will eventually figure it out.

There is no hurry for her to do so at least for tonight. I like sitting here holding her. If her relaxed state is any indication she likes it too.

"So basically, no matter what I do—war is coming?"

I nod, watching her face and thoughts—those I can see. She built her shields up again—so I cannot see everything in her mind only bits and pieces of it.

These shields are better than before. I do not like it. I will remove them but, it will take time. Suspicion burns in my gut. I do not believe that is the only conclusion she came to. Iza is full of shit.

Jake gave me some insight after I ate him. He had a 'crush' on her, an unhealthy one, but there were other people he genuinely cared about. I looked closely at a few of these feelings because, it has been so long since I ate a creature that cared for anything besides themselves, it is enlightening.

"Cool. Want some icecream?"

Her abrupt topic change can mean many things and, although we are deeply bonded, I cannot easily discover this. Something I will remedy. As I stand up and walk towards the door, in the back of my mind, I go to work on her shields again. Iza should know I will always get in.

"Can I eat it off you?" I say, knowing the reaction I will get from her.

Instantly her face flushes and, I feel her skin heat up from across the room. Serves her right. I pause in the doorway. "Are you coming?"

A breeze ruffles my hair as she runs right by me. Mention food and Iza will always be the first one at the party. Plus, my mentioning anything sexual makes her run like a scalded cat.

One day I will do more than mention. Soon.

CHAPTER TWENTY-ONE

 hobe

THE FOLLOWING WEEKEND her group of misfits decides to have a special dinner for Iza. They are scurrying back and forth like merry little ants between the Sidhe and the lake outside of it.

Iza's triumph over the usurper gave them the idea for it. What the lingire did not realize was that Iza intended to feed the woman to the people she treated poorly.

Iza's people know what she planned to do. She is a practical person. She knows the ancient customs of the Feyrie: enemies are eaten. This barbecue is symbolic.

Although it is not her dinner plans that concern me. Yes, I admit I am concerned about her. Her nights are more restless than before. Since she started sharing the dreams—the pain, the suffering of the Feyrie—sleep eludes her.

Not that she slept restfully before but now there is nothing more than brief naps. Instead of sleeping she talks to me or watches TV. Or explains why people wear socks and use the 'facedbook.' Those two I still do not understand.

But she is helping me understand other things.

Sometimes we take walks in the woods outside the Sidhe and, she pulls me along by my hand smiling while she tells me stories about the people in the Sidhe.

At first I felt awkward and was not sure what reactions to have.

At some point, I started liking these moments with her. Seeking them out when before I would have hidden in the darkness. There but not, watching and not participating.

Like I am watching now. She looks there... but not.

On wooden but persistent feet I cross to her letting the darkness hiding me drop away. Quickly, before I can change my mind, I sit in the chair beside her at the table. Her small hand sliding into mine is a comfort to us both.

Iza is nervous. Suddenly she smiles and looks at me.

'It'll be a while before things are ready. Come with me,' she says.

Pulling me by the hand, we cross through the backyard to where the forest is thickest. I am curious what she is up to because, she is absolutely up to something. I cannot breach her barriers fully—yet— to determine the exact nature of her thoughts.

The feeling of her mind fully opening to me is like a blast of heat on my body. I rush in. I do not like her blocking me out. Sinking into the familiar comfort of her chaotic mind, the very essence of her, I smile when I see what is there.

The Sidhe communicates with her exclusively. This land is just as much a part of it as the inside of it's heart—the house.

'You have dimples. Did you know that?' She pokes one with her finger.

Then she too smiles exposing a single dimple in her right cheek that I am now suddenly curious about. Then she is just gone before I can act on that impulse leaving her laughter echoing in my mind.

Chit.

Feeling the rush of the hunt hit me I wait prepared to move. I give her a head start because, she wants to hunt. This time her prey are the people camped just inside the borders of the Sidhe. This is because she is worried about my appetites not being met.

Iza wants to feed me.

Feeling the distance between us growing I pursue her.

We hunt together well, perfectly coordinated. She goes left and, I go right without a word being spoken between us. To be so in tune… is rather incredible.

And something to think on.

She is standing, staring at a dead tree, a puzzled expression on her face.

'This tree shouldn't be dead. Something is wrong.'

'Perhaps it is the fault of our prey?' I ask her, knowing what it is we hunt.

'No, they couldn't do this kind of damage to the Sidhe. Something else did it but, it doesn't know what.' By the it, I am assuming she means the Sidhe. *'Can you sense anything about it?'*

I shake my head. The Sidhe and I are alike but also very different. The Sidhe is hers.

'I'll have to do some research. Something is definitely off but, it doesn't feel like an emergency. I'll deal with it after we have a bit of fun.' She smiles that toothy smile I like so much and jerks her head towards the reason we are out here.

Dinner.

Our prey is close. Seven heartbeats. Six owners of those heartbeats are practically Magikless, so, they must be the guards. The seventh one is the only one of any concern. At least for Iza.

The guards are easy. They do not see me coming and, the blood lock is too preoccupied with Iza to notice me. Iza, who is standing there out in the open, looking at him—studying him. Knowing him.

"I smell my kind on you. How many Feyrie lives have you claimed for the small bits of power you have?" She is not wrong; it is how a blood lock sustains their power. Blood, death. "Well, let's see how you like it."

I walk up behind him. The darkness inside me is salivating for the Magikal essence.

With a smile she continues, "I'm sure you remember the magistrate's former slave, the one they called Beast? That's not his name, but I thought you might recognize him that way. You see, I recognize you. You've seen my back flayed to the bone, haven't you, monocle man?"

This makes it even better.

The second he looks over his shoulder at me, his face pale with fear, I strike.

CHAPTER TWENTY-TWO

za

"It's going to be a long road, isn't it? I mean, seriously, we can't go longer than a couple of days before someone tries to kill us," I say to my companions.

"Tell me more about how I'm supposed to do this prophecy shit." My dad laughs and points in front of us at Jameson and, Phobe looks away to hide a small smile.

"What?" I don't get the funny. I feel left out.

"Why didn't you say you wanted to know about the prophecy, Iza? I would've gladly given you my notes!" Jameson exclaims, coming to sit on the bench across from us.

Oh, now I see their amusement. Jameson. He's so damn excited about it, the weirdo.

"Sure, Jameson, let's have it," I say, knowing he'll tell me regardless.

"Your part in the prophecy, simply put, is to be the shepherd of the people. You are to gather them, heal them and unite them. Then you prepare them for the coming of the dark king. One of your titles is also the Heart of Darkness, or better known as the heart of the king—the original one." He takes a breath. "Anyway, as it states, you will awaken the king who will fight for the Feyrie in a war of massive proportion." He speaks so fast I'm not sure he's even breathing while he talks.

But I still catch something.

"Wait. What does it mean awaken?"

Jameson ignores my question and continues.

"Your role has predominantly been a role delegated to a wise woman. A much older wise woman. Besides pulling the people together to some degree she played no large role in the scheme of things." A flip of the notebook page.

He continues, "Now it's different. You aren't a queen. You're more important than that. When the king awakens you will stand at his side with your guard, the Nightmares, and your people. But—"

I hate buts. At least this kind.

"If you die the king will kill everyone. Not just our enemies."

"So, you're telling me, if I die—everyone does?"

Jameson nods exuberantly.

I look at Phobe, really look at him. Because call me crazy—which is true too—I think he's the king. After a moment of looking at me with those eyes that make my stomach do flips he nods confirming it.

Sonofabitch.

Surprised but not surprised, I lean my elbows in the table. Phobe mentioned a war before but, what kind of war are we talking here? Like a hundred against a hundred or, are we talking a full-on world war? The shit we're doing now is annoying but small. Incredibly small in the scheme of things. I don't like admitting it, but that lingire bitch is right, most of the people here aren't soldiers.

I look at Phobe again.

'Just how much damage are you capable of doing, Phobe?'

'Enough.'

That isn't an answer, and he knows it, but it says a lot. There's got to be a way to protect these people from certain death.

"Jameson, didn't you say that the schoth were preparing for an invasion or something before we got out of there?"

"Yes, they were talking about trying to conquer another realm. The reasons I don't understand. It's one that has no Magikal significance so, you'd think they wouldn't worry about it," he answers.

But they are which means I need to know why. Mentally, I add it to an ever-growing list.

"When?"

"Not for like ten years or so. The high king is supposedly losing power so, they are all squabbling over that. That will take time. The schoth don't move quickly at anything."

That's the truth.

"How long do you think it will take them to come after us here?" I ask, thinking—and maybe hoping, that it's going to be at least a few years. Precious time that we need.

"It's hard to give any kind of specific time frame. Anyone with a chance at the throne cannot leave their base defenseless. That gives us quite a while," he answers.

Yeah, just what I hoped.

I go deep inside myself to the pulse of the Sidhe and ask it a single question. How strong does Phobe need to be? The web rings with its musical answer.

Stronger than he is now, much stronger.

"You know rumor has it that a few former council members are floating about from the last king. Not just those pretending to be relatives. I'll hazard a guess that we will meet them one day soon," Jameson muses.

'I'm assuming these are the ones that sold him out?' I ask Phobe in my mind.

'Of course.'

"Interesting," I murmur.

It won't be a pretty sight when I meet them. If they'll betray their most loyal protector they will betray anyone. It will make some things simpler to take care of them before they can wiggle their way in and destroy people like the cancer they are.

'Your mind surprises me at times, Iza. I see great compassion in you. You have this huge streak of practicality and then a small line of viciousness that matches my own.' At his words, I slowly turn to look at Phobe.

He needs to feed more to get stronger and be at the peak of his power. I'm not sure how the prophecy translates the way it does or how I ended up in it. I can see him being some long-lost king— which I'm going to ask him about later—but me being his heart I'm not sure of that. I know I mean something to him, just like he does me, but I don't know what that means.

We're best friends, more than that. Not lovers—but so close. I have a feeling he's waiting for me. If that's the case, I need to get on that. I snort at my thought.

'Anytime.' The amusement in his tone is overshadowed by the promise.

Shit! Eavesdropping bastard, who's suddenly developed a sense of humor. Though it's mostly bad humor or in this case pervy.

Blushing, I stare at the tip of a fingernail and picture a wall of singing smurfs. Why the hell am I blushing? Oh right, I know— because I have no idea how to have a semi-normal relationship with anyone. Because I'm a relationship moron.

I wager he doesn't know either.

"You two are so awkward together. How entertaining," my dad teases.

In response I elbow him in the ribs.

"I know why Mom called you Captain Wonderpants and, unless you want me to tell everyone you'll hush," I threaten.

My dad, showing where I get some of my sense of humor, throws his head back and belly laughs.

"It'll work out. I know he wasn't honest with me about everything but, for some reason he wanted you to make it this far," Dad says, patting my hand.

"Who is this he?" I ask suspiciously.

"The All-Father."

"Oh, him. Do you still believe in anything he tells you?"

"He did make us, Iza. I imagine he only wants what is best for us."

"Actually, he didn't make you," Phobe corrects.

Frowning, my Dad turns a little to face him, and I feel distinctly like a bone between two dogs.

"Of course he made us. He's the One God," Dad insists.

Automatically my head turns to Phobe for his input.

"He was there for your creation but, the eldest are all creatures of the darkness." That's something I didn't know. Going by the look of shock on my dad's face neither did he.

Oh, shit.

"You're telling me that my entire belief system is a lie?" Dad demands.

"Complete and utter bullshit," Phobe clarifies.

Wow, this is good. I wish I had popcorn or beef jerky to enjoy with this show. Suddenly, his face clears as if he realized or accepted something.

"I'm off, Dove. Have a good barbeque. Save me some ribs; anyone's will do." Laughing at his own joke my dad drops a quick kiss on my cheek and disappears into nothing.

That explains my wonky logic. I inherited it honestly.

I hope he'll be okay with the news. Dad is pretty dedicated to his 'job' even if he hates it half the time. I didn't feel anger coming from him and, I can definitely feel it when he's angry.

More like calm.

The web inside of me chimes reminding me of how busy today is going to be. Searching inside myself I touch it. So many are coming. It'll take weeks for all the Feyrie I called to get here to the Sidhe. Even as I sit here there are several on their way including some that are legendary.

Wouldn't Jameson shit a dragon?

Not all of those that show up will be about saving our people. Some will come because the summons is strong and, they can't resist it. Others because they see a way to get some power or wealth.

Idiots. Those ones should be worried about coming here.

I'll be their judge, jury and executioner. This I know without a doubt. Only those deserving compassion will get it. I'm not Snow

White surrounded by singing dwarves. I'm the bad guy that will eat Snow White like a chicken wing and use the dwarves to mop up the gravy.

The Feyrie need strong people, fighters. Phobe and I are two of those fighters. Some of the dragons, including Alagard, are fighters as well. That number, compared to what's coming, is so insignificant—it causes me concern.

Even if it kills me, which it probably will, I'll fight for them. This has nothing to do with the stupid prophecy. It has to do with these people needing someone willing to defend them especially the ones that have no one else.

I feel his eyes on me and look over my shoulder at him. I thought I was blocking him but given the brighter orange color of his eyes, I'm not so sure. I think he has an issue with me dying. His eyes flash to lava. Ha, so, he does have a problem with it.

The wall of singing smurfs returns. It doesn't hurt to make him work a little. Damn mind reader. I'd kill to know what his thoughts are.

A bit of mischief enters me.

Letting the wall drop I picture us kissing. Then I throw the wall back up again. Let it drop again picturing my arms around his neck and my legs around his waist. Wall up. Wall back down. Picture his hands moving up to cup my face…. the wall falls for the final time. His hands move down my body over my breasts. His mouth…

The sound of wood splintering draws me out of my daydream. Surprised, I look at the portion of the table in front of Phobe. It's now in pieces some of which are still in his clawed hands. He's staring at me like I'm a giant piece of steak and he's starving.

The web within me twangs saving me from my own stupidity and, giving me a well-timed excuse to run away. Thank god.

"Guests are here," I squeak out.

Soon he and I need to talk about this. Just not today. I poke the tip of his nose and, then climb to my feet and head to the edge of the trees.

Looking at the web, I can see that there are others on Sidhe land now too. Keeping their distance, watching. Even more of them will be here within the hour.

The next few weeks will be busy.

'I am going to look,' he says coming to my side. I look up at him.

'Be careful,' I tell him.

He rubs his thumb across the small cleft in my chin a quick caress that's barely a touch. It's an interesting sign of affection and, I like it. Although I won't tell him that. Honestly, who likes saying, 'Oh, by the way, you touch my chin and it kind of makes me wanna see you naked?'

I frown. Okay, I've watched a lot of TV here so there might, in fact, be someone who thinks that way.

'I am not the one you should be worrying for, Iza.' Then he wraps himself in shadow and is gone.

"Jerk," I mutter, turning back to speak with Jameson.

CHAPTER TWENTY-THREE

 hobe

AT THE LAST MINUTE, I detour to see the nearby Nightmares. They are not a threat to her so, I let my thoughts wander. The little shit pulled a stunt back there. If not for eons of control I would have fucked her on the table spectators be damned.

To tease one such as I is a dangerous game to play. Especially for her. Because the next time I get my hands on her I will not stop.

My thoughts turn to more serious things. In her short life she has survived and excelled at it overcoming everything thrown in her path. The thought of her dying—permanently—makes my stomach churn.

Before this moment I was already willing to destroy Death himself —my rage now will be apocalyptic. The realms-wide kind of apocalypse. I will destroy them all. The prophecy is not wrong about that.

Then I will aim higher.

Iza is significant to me. No, that word does not begin to do it justice. I dig in the memories of those that are part of me; I dig deep.

Love? No, not enough. Obsessed, entranced, completely charmed? All of them?

Frustrated, I shove the words aside.

In my existence I have had no need for such words or feelings. I have no idea how to use them or understand them. I absolutely cannot articulate them because, before her I did not feel them.

And now they refuse to cease existence.

The Nightmares move closer pulling me out of my thoughts.

It has been a long time since this many journeyed out of the Dead Lands. In fact, not since they sought refuge there after the death of the first dark king who enslaved them.

Iza's call packs a punch.

I can hear them just ahead of me, barely. That says a lot about their stealth. Sneaking up on me is hard, and until a certain distraction came into my life, impossible.

She tends to distract me to the degree that can be dangerous in certain circumstances.

Looking to the treetops I see the massive shape moving above me. This I did not expect: the original Nightmare herself. She stops above me as if sensing me. Part of her probably does. I drop my Magikal cloak and allow myself to be truly seen.

The massive shape above me morphs and shrinks, changing from the shape that is identical to the tattoo on Iza's back to something more humanoid. A rustle of leaves and then a woman, the Mother of all Nightmares, drops down in front of me. A strand of silver spider's silk is her rope.

I have not seen her for hundreds of years, and unexpectedly, she shows every one of those years. Her once lustrous flaming hair is streaked with gray and, her face bears wrinkles of the passage of time. Her skin is paper-thin and translucent each spidery vein visible through its paleness. Her red glowing eyes are not as bright as they were with Magiks but still sharp with intelligence.

Why has she aged in such a way?

"It is true," she says softly, her words spoken slowly.

I nod to her knowing, the meaning behind her words. Why else am I free otherwise?

She smiles and it transforms her entire face. Once upon a time she was dazzling and, her legendary beauty lingers in that smile. "We have waited so long and had almost given up until I felt her awaken the web. The dark is strong in her." Her voice gains strength as she speaks.

Keeping my attention on her face I let my other senses seek out the additional creatures watching me from the shadows. Her children mostly. Their Magiks are muted, almost nonexistent. My enslavement hurt them.

Her aging? That is not so easily explained.

"Tell me, creator, does she bear the mark? Is she the Heart of our Darkness?"

I nod again.

"It is very good then, very good. We have brought her tribute and hope she will welcome us as her guard. As we are destined to be."

It says a lot of things that they came to a world not their own to serve her willingly. The first king kept them by force until his death. The others were too afraid to summon them.

The Nightmares were fanatics at protecting the first King. Iza, their destined charge? They will burn down worlds for her.

"You will not need to provide tribute. She is not like others," I assure her.

Auryn, the first Nightmare created, watches me with a stillness that hints at the spider she truly is. "She will get it just the same. It is meant to be given to her." She makes a clicking sound with her mouth, and the others step into view.

There are eleven of them of every shape and sizes but, one familiar face is missing.

"Auryn, where is Licar?" I have a suspicion but, I do not voice it. Only one thing would keep him from her side.

Her face grows solemn as her eyes fill with pain. "The schoth king sent blood locks. He was alone and lead into a trap." Her eyes flash a bright red and then dim.

That explains the aging. I study her closely. She is dying without him. It is amazing she survived this long. They were bonded by blood, by love. Their souls were intertwined.

"Before you meet her... she has two rules. Kill no innocents and give mercy only to those who deserve it," I caution.

"We are the Guard to the Heart of Darkness, the WebRider. We live for her will," Auryn proclaims, her fist on her heart.

My head dips with respect. What she is proclaiming is important. Nightmares are exceptional fighters—dirty ones, too—loyal to a fault once it is given.

Iza is going to love them.

"She is awaiting your arrival. They have barbeque."

Auryn inclines her head and shoots upwards.

Once again, the sound of a large body moving overhead breaks the silence. Iza has a soft spot for spiders. She saved them more than once in prison. That is the only bug she has any kindness for. Any other insect and she tried to climb me like a ladder while screaming like a banshee the entire time.

I bite back a smile. But the humor is brief.

Now it is time to check on the shifters.

The shifters are easy enough to find. They make enough noise to be heard for miles. Obviously not professionals in surveillance, most are sitting in cars listening to music and talking loudly.

An annoyance.

A quick count nets thirteen. This large a number is a little surprising but, their idiocy is not. All the vehicles hold occupants that are relaxed and uncaring, save one. I look closer at the car he is in.

The man sitting in driver's seat looks aggrieved. Easily explained by the woman beside him who is vehemently nagging about how uncomfortable the car is. I can hear every single word coming out of her mouth as clearly as if she stands beside me. He has more tolerance than me. They must be sexual partners. Why else would he deal with her?

It will be unfortunate if she comes with him. If I spend too much time in her company, will either cut her tongue out or eat her.

I stay back in the shadows of the trees.

My eyes are drawn back to the male who is looking straight in Iza's direction. This shifter feels the call more strongly than the others. Perhaps he is more pure blood than the others? It explains his behavior.

My shadows creep out and slip through cracks and openings in the vehicles to touch each one of them. A smile tickles the corner of my mouth. Iza will not be happy about the lot of them. They are here to spy, to gather intelligence.

Other than the single male the rest do not care about Iza or her misfits. Instead they are simply making a mess and a lot of noise. The ground is littered with their discarded food wrappers and drink bottles.

No, she will not be happy at all.

There is only one thing to do about it. Stepping out of the cover of the trees I walk towards the cars. As I stop in the front of the car with the most rubbish around it the conversations around me cease. Noses in the air they are trying in vain to figure out what I am.

Without a word I bend down and grab the bumper of the car and flip the car backward. The sound of screeching metal and screams fills the air as it hits the ground on its top.

"You have five minutes to clean up your mess before I beat you all to death with this car."

Iza is rubbing off on me.

CHAPTER TWENTY-FOUR

za

BEHIND ME, where I stand with my hands in my pockets like a ninny head, they're firing up the grills and cleaning and setting more tables. The goblins had the foresight to bring roasting sticks and the stuff we need for making 'smores.'

I have no idea what they are but, one of the main ingredients is chocolate. Which means I'll adore them. My stomach growls at the thought.

It's still early in the evening, leaving plenty of time for everyone to enjoy themselves. The entire population of the Sidhe is out here. Our little group of children is running around, chasing each other and laughing, some of them are free for the first time in their lives. Little Knox, my alpha puppy, among them.

Too few of them, really. The Feyrie don't have many children anymore.

"Can I help?" I ask Kay, an imp who has been here for a lot longer than I have.

Smiling, she ignores me and keeps busy, which translates to a big fat no. But I'm stubborn so, I keep trying to help. After taking my now —melted kitchen utensil away from me, she shoos me off so, I give up and plop myself on the tailgate of a truck to watch.

"You break things. They all know this. But you're their lady so, that on top of your wanton destruction of anything from the kitchen, they want you to not help," Jameson supplies as he sits down on the tailgate with me.

"Do all 'Ladies' get this?"

He nods, stuffing a marshmallow in his mouth.

The Nightmares will be arriving within a few minutes,' Phobe's voice floats through my mind.

'And the shifters?' I smile. I'm not about to tell him I can eavesdrop on him using the Sidhe as my ears. Well, sometimes—it doesn't always work. And it's an idea versus an actual insight.

It's frustratingly vague.

'You are learning to work with the Sidhe but, you still have far to go,' he says, not even bothering to hide the snark in his voice.

I felt him doing something with those shifters. I'm not sure what but, I have a feeling it was entertaining.

'The shifters at the borders are terrible at their jobs but, at least one seems to hear the call.'

Then I feel the tingling of his presence in front of me. I look up into his eyes and frown.

'I need to find out more information on this group,' I muse.

'For now they are just watching you but, ultimately, they will do something that is going to piss you off.'

I roll my eyes at him. *'You're such a... realist.'*

'Someone needs to be with you,' he shoots back.

Okay so he has a point. I'll let him get away with it this time. *'Anything else?'*

He leans over me and steals a marshmallow out the bag Jameson is trying to hide behind his butt. Until recently Phobe didn't eat much food but I got him hooked on sugar.

'If their ruler refuses to follow you they will probably try to get rid of you.'
He says it so nonchalantly that I know he isn't worried about it.

I am and it annoys me. I'm getting tired of people trying to kill me when I've only been at this for a few weeks.

'It is a fact. Accept that and you will not feel any more anger about it,' Phobe chastises, wiping the crushed marshmallow off my hand with a napkin.

I didn't realize I smooshed it.

'Kinda like when you broke the table earlier?'

'I would say touché but, I want them to be afraid of how I react to things.' The snark is back in his voice.

Damnit.

'I'm still learning how to control the Magiks so, it still influences my emotions. It sucks.' Do I sound whiny? It's possible because I feel whiny.

He leans close to me. His face is a breath from mine. Butterflies go crazy in my stomach. Just like that all my anger and irritation banks itself placed on the back burner by the straight lust that takes its place.

It's not fair that he can make me feel like this so easily.

His eyes flare and he closes that small space between us. His lips are cool and soft when they meet mine. Instantly, I feel like I'm on fire. His tongue dips into my mouth and, then it's over barely a meeting of lips. Part of me is disappointed it's over if the thumping of my heart is any indication. It's not even that it was a passionate kiss; it's that there was a lot of passion in it.

I open my eyes and smile sheepishly. "I hate you," I tease, mostly.

'You taste good.' His voice is more than just a voice in my mind. It's a caress to my soul, more intimate than any touch. Did I really just think that shit? Gah, this gooshie romance shit is going to kill me.

Phobe chokes on his marshmallow.

My amusement fades when I smell them, feel them. Ancient Magiks. Almost like family.

"They're here," I mumble under my breath. Nothing wrong with trying to bolster myself.

I go to the edge of the forest knowing Phobe is behind me. An older woman, her long orange hair streaked with gray, walks out of the trees, head held high her shoulders straight and proud.

Quickly I process my scattered knowledge.

Auryn is the first Nightmare, supposedly created by an obscure god, enslaved by the first mortal dark king. I cast a gaze over my shoulder and then back to her. It's her true shape that's tattooed on my back.

But she shouldn't be an older woman.

She smiles at me, and it takes my breath away. Why is an immortal creature like her aged? Frowning, I look at her life thread carefully: no disease, no bad Magiks.

Wait. There is something.

"We have come to pay tribute to our long-awaited Heart of Darkness," Auryn states in a strong voice.

More Nightmares come out of the trees to stand in a half circle behind her.

"There is no need for that. I should give you tribute for coming," I say just as formally.

"I am honored you think that, my lady but, this is something destined to be yours," Auryn says, waving forward a rather good-looking brown-haired man holding a burlap-wrapped bundle in his hands.

He passes it to Auryn and then bows at the waist, first to me and then to her, before stepping back. Studying each one of their faces I frown. Each one of them has the same look of respect. How can these fierce creatures of renown respect me in any way when they've never met me before?

It's something I'll ask later, that's for sure.

Snapping myself back to the moment at hand, I unwrap the package. It's a weapon, a sword to be exact. The blade is the bleached white of manipulated bone with a super sharp black metal edge. This sword was not crafted by mortal hands.

The handle is unadorned save for the blood red gem mounted in it. The handle swirls with the Magiks used to create it but, it's not overly done or too fancy. This sword is beautiful in its simplicity.

"This was made from a bone of my husband. Magiks shaped it into what it is now, and I have kept it safe, waiting for your arrival."

This time I bow my head to her. Immediately I access the web again. That's what's missing! Licar, her mate. His life thread is still there, though, but faint. Curious, I caress the blade and, something in it caresses me back. Taken aback I do it again.

Something's in this sword.

"I am proud to be right. This is meant to be yours," Auryn's amused voice pulls me out of my thoughts.

"Honestly I'm just learning how to use swords, but, Phobe is teaching me. So, in a couple of hundred years, I might have some skill," I say with a smile of self-mockery.

Auryn looks at me with glowing red eyes and then laughs. Blackness crawls up my forearm on my right wrist and engulfs the sword. It vanishes as the darkness receded.

Well, that's a neat trick.

"I doubt it will take so much time as that." Auryn's eyes bore into me. "You are so much more than I had hoped, my lady." She crosses her hand over her heart and, I jump to catch her before she goes to her knees.

"You should kneel to no one ever, Auryn," I say, holding her arm to make sure she doesn't try to kneel again.

She pats my hand, her eyes slightly moist, and then bows at the waist. From someone like her this is a lifetime pledge of loyalty. My gut tells me that much. "You have given me a great honor, my lady. I will never forget it and neither shall my children."

"It is an honor I will always give you, Auryn." It's the truth.

Movement in the woods catches my attention. Something is hiding just out of sight watching me. My eyes narrow. I can feel him in my web, but, he can almost make his physical presence invisible. Almost.

Not nearly as good as Phobe, but better than the others.

Intrigued, I walk towards him with determined steps. I can smell him now. His smell is somewhat like dragons, that deep earthy dirt smell. But it's different in a way I'm not quite sure of.

My Magiks move forward to touch his.

Unlike most of the other Nightmares his Magiks run deeper. Almost as deep as his mother's. Perhaps one day even more than hers.

"Come out," I urge. If he doesn't then I'm going in to get him.

There's a rustle of branches and leaves as something big moves around and, then a slim, dark-haired man steps into the clearing. He looks at me intently, with reptilian green eyes. As he blinks his eyelid moves sideways.

"Why were you hiding?"

At my question he moves closer to me. I think he's used to people running away and is surprised I'm not. "I cannot completely hide like the others. I don't want to scare you."

I snort letting him see my special eyelids. "I don't scare easily. What's your name?" I already know it, but I'm learning that people like to be asked.

I like him instantly. He's young looking like most Feyrie are but, he has a sinewy look to him, stronger—older in the way he carries himself.

He's firstborn.

His face is gorgeous. Only a blind person wouldn't notice. Strongly resembling that 'ocean-man' actor in the movies, the mouthwatering one, Jason something. That isn't what makes him stand out although it doesn't hurt either.

Those eyes, even if you take away the impossible green color, stand out. His eyes lashes are longer than mine giving him that dark, brooding look that women fall all over themselves for. Such a good-looking little devil.

He stops in front of me. I look up. Way up. Well maybe not so little but definitely a devil.

"I am Adriem." He smiles as he speaks, exposing one perfect dimple in his left cheek.

"I'm Iza. Nice to meet you," I answer, amused despite myself.

That smile of his is dangerous. Luckily for me I'm hooked on two dimples not just one.

The smell of food overrules any thoughts I consider randomly sharing. Saved by my stomach again. I pat it in appreciation.

"We are all monsters here, Adriem. Let's go eat." I walk back towards the lake and wave for them to follow me.

There's a lot to think about and eating usually helps me think quite well. Maybe it's the chewing that gives me that extra bit of thought processing power. The feeling of everyone staring at me drags me out of my thoughts. I sigh. I bet I'm talking out loud again.

"What?" I ask all of those around me who are staring with amused expressions. I eye a grill that's full of ribs, not self-conscious, just impatient to eat. "I'm hungry," I say in explanation of my moment of crazy.

"That's the dragon in her," Alagard says proudly as Auryn regally walks past me to sit at the same table as him.

Auryn's brow arches up as she ponders him but then, the facade of cool elegance disappears as a plate of still-bloody beef is placed in front of her. Her eyes flash red as she dives in.

Oh, I'm going to like her. A lot.

Seeking out Ruthie, Michael, and Knox, I plop down next to Knox, who has sauce all over his cheeks. He smiles and hands me a rib.

We fall into conversation as easily as if it's been happening every day for years. Alagard and Nika regale me with stories of my parent's mishaps and some of my own. That amuses the kids quite a bit.

Apparently me setting a courtier on fire is funny.

My mother was quite the rebel too and, I can see where I get some of my quirks and stubbornness.

Auryn, quiet at first, starts to share her own stories. Soon her children join in even the reserved Adriem. It's the first time since I was a kid that I can remember feeling this sort of contentment. It takes me a moment to put a name to it.

Family. This is my family.

I smile—I can't help it. This is a marvelous thing to behold.

Beaming I look around at all the Feyrie present, happy with my world, with barbecue sauce on my chin. I like this and, I'll gladly get used to it.

'*You are happy?*' Phobe's tone is questioning.

'*I gotta take it when I get it, ya know?*'

'*They love you and will follow you anywhere.*'

'*I think it's because you scare everyone into submission,*' I tease, partially. There's no doubt in my mind there'll be instances where Phobe being scary is exactly what I'll need.

Plus it's hot.

'*It is not me they are afraid of.*"

I giggle. I can't help it. I'm fully aware of who the scary one is between the two of us. Besides, I'm not scary at all.

CHAPTER TWENTY-FIVE

za

THE SECOND THEY hit Sidhe land I know. A few minutes later I look over my shoulder to watch the three vans pull into the driveway between the house and the lake. I figure they'll approach when they're ready to approach. I stay seated and keep eating while encouraging everyone else to do so as well.

Maybe they're hungry and will grab some food?

"Why are the servants eating at the only tables in this awful place?" The raised voice cuts right through the laughter.

Frowning, I look up at the speaker.

Silence falls heavily throughout and several sets of eyes turn to look at the imp woman standing with her nose in the air like she's surrounded by smelly garbage. If the woman puts her petite nose any further into the air she'll pull a muscle in her neck.

Crap, it's another snotty one. Sighing, I let the rib in my hand fall to my paper plate. My Magiks push out and touch the newcomers.

"Perhaps the shepherd is away, Jiquelle. Servants are notorious for taking advantage of their betters," says a rather plump man stepping up beside her.

Schoth and lingire seem to have a thing for looking like walking candy. This one is wearing horizontal stripes—bright pink and green ones. I bite my lip to keep from saying one of the many smart-ass remarks floating around in my head. With my luck, one comment and they'll throw a fit about it and give me a headache.

Like the whole thing with the lingire.

The web pulls me inwards. The dark isn't connected to either one of them as deeply as it should be. Which is strange because I sensed them approaching.

Or perhaps the assumption it's from these two idiots is wrong.

'The male is Montgomery,' Phobe supplies in my mind.

Phobe knows them. This isn't a good sign.

A third man steps up beside them looking decidedly uncomfortable. Without hesitation his eyes go right to me. He's a little more clever than his companions. This one I can feel completely—his strand on the web is bright and shining. The web's notes of emotion float through my mind rapidly and, I work to decipher them as quickly as possible.

Ducard's one of the ones I sense but, somewhere in this group there's more. I climb to my feet and, his eyes widen. Apprehension is stamped all over his face. I can feel it, smell it. The imp moves to the side away from his traveling companions, his eyes staying on me.

"Remove yourselves so we can break our fast, servants," Montgomery orders the occupants at the table in front of him.

Oh, the headache is building already. It's another one talking about servants and shit. This is going to put me straight into a bad mood. Jameson shoves a napkin in my hand and, I take the hint and wipe off my face and hands while watching Montgomery with curiosity.

No one at the table moves which isn't surprising. No one knows who the hell he is.

Montgomery's face reddens with anger. "Guards, remove them."

At his words, I step in between him and the table.

These imps aren't deeply connected to the web either. When your service is bought and paid for your only loyalty is money. I'm seeing a trend with some of these people. One I don't like.

A: they're mostly cowards hiding behind guards. B: somehow, they have money in a world full of poverty to afford said guards.

Yep, there goes my good mood.

A dozen men walk towards us with their intentions expressed clearly on their faces. These guys don't look like they're going to say, 'pass the ketchup.' They're going to try and physically remove my family—yes, *my* family—from their tables.

Phobe vanishes from my side and reappears in the center of the group. Immediately two men fall onto the ground. They won't be getting up. I wonder what's was on their minds for him to kill them that quickly? I raise a brow at him.

He just looks at me. That bad, huh?

The rest turn towards him weapons drawn. Well, look there—they have guns. I cross my arms. They're still not going to last long guns or not. As I walk towards him, two more fall just as quickly as the first ones. Approaching the group, I pause only long enough to toe one of the fallen men.

Oh yeah, dead as a doornail.

'Don't let them shoot. I don't want them to hit someone with a stray bullet,' I ask.

He doesn't answer again.

Walking around the men left alive I ignore their presence entirely. Life is now a temporary state for them. My attention is completely focused on the imp I can feel.

Ducard La Rounte, whose father was a member of the inner council before the Dark Kingdom fell. His father was executed for his loyalty to the Crown and refusing to abandon or betray his king.

Very honorable, and in this case, the son did not fall far from the tree.

As I near him something else tickles my Magikal senses. My eyes move past him to the middle van. It's more beat up than the others but, there's this big blank spot where it sits. One that shouldn't be there. My Magiks feel around it with caution, and to my irritation, find that it's saturated in light Magiks.

Now, why are a bunch of imps traveling with a van saturated with light Magiks?

"What's in the van?" I ask quietly, knowing in my gut it's going to be something bad.

Ducard is the only one of three standing in front of me that knows who I am. He alone knows what I can do to him if he lies or at least has an idea. He straightens his shoulders, showing he does have some pride and, then bows his head respectfully.

"I am not sure, my lady. I am not allowed near it."

I stare hard at him looking deeper than his skin.

"Whatever it is he sends food and water to it occasionally." He speaks the truth. I'd know a lie from him a mile away.

So the contents of the van are alive.

Looking at him just long enough to make him uncomfortable I walk past him heading for the van. I can't see through the Magiks hiding whatever is in it. Those are strong spells for a something so innocuous looking. The best money can buy I'm sure.

Dark Magiks do not affect me. In fact I null them out which isn't normal by any means. I also discovered, by trial and error, that I can absorb some light Magiks—change them but at a cost. It hurts like a sonofabitch and, too much will probably kill me.

This much light Magiks at once—yeah, I'll need some aspirin after this mess. If I can get through it. Big if.

Putting my hand out in front of me, inches from the van, I concentrate on the invisible shield that covers every inch of it. A flare of pain races through my entire arm when I connect with it. Gritting my teeth I pull the Magiks into myself. The backlash is more painful than I expected.

Within a few minutes I'm sweating a bit but feeling good enough to keep going. I need to keep going. Something inside of it is calling to me. I'm on my knees by the time I reach the last bit of barrier. Pain wrenches my stomach so hard that I can taste vomit in the back of my throat.

There's a loud pop, and with the sudden relief of pressure, I'm through.

The pain is awful but, the protective shield is gone.

Climbing stiffly to my feet I pull the side door open staring into the dimly lit van. Instantly, I notice that the seats are missing and, in their place sit three small beings.

Three bedraggled heads lift to look at me their eyes lighting with recognition. Bright blue eyes, unnaturally bright, in small bruised dirty faces—two girls and one boy. The oldest one not a day over twelve. Hell, they're children. I crawl into the van uncaring of the mess and filth around them.

Their little faces are gaunt from hunger. Tiny bodies bruised and cut from repeated beatings. What's left of their clothes are torn and stained with god knows what. In them I see the child I was and, it absolutely infuriates me.

Why is it always the children that suffer so much in our world?

Pushing the anger off my face I replace it with the gentlest look I can manage. I have very few soft spots and children are the biggest one.

Dirty bastard abused them… in many ways. The evidence is on their little bodies and in the ghosts now haunting their eyes. I clench my jaw harder.

I'm going to kill someone.

"Hello there, lovelies. I'm Iza and if you give me just a few minutes —I'll get these chains off you, okay?"

They nod solemnly at my words.

I focus on the chains holding them but, the pain forces a hiss from between my teeth. A clawed hand moves past me and grabs the chains which simply dissolve at his touch.

'You are not taking on any more pain from this fat fuck today, Iza.' Phobe sounds angry.

Leaning forward, I give him a wet kiss right on the cheek and, then continue talking to the children. Reassuring them, treating them as gently as possible. I hold my hands out for the smallest child, a little boy. He's two but so skinny that anyone will believe he's younger. He looks up at me with eyes as blue as the brightest sky and smiles, displaying four very prominent canines.

"Hungry," he demands quietly.

My heart melts into a puddle.

Sliding out of the van I grab the door and rip it off. I fling it towards Montgomery who's cursing Auryn over his men being killed. So intent is he on her that he didn't notice me at the van.

That was her intention.

"What would you like to eat, buddy?" I ask, moving his dirty hair out of his eyes.

He pats my cheek as only a child does and smiles. "Fat man."

I smile at that. Then he looks at me all serious, his brows drawn down in concentration. "Mama?" he questions, and I feel the bottom of my stomach fall out.

Where is their mama?

"He will eat anything including the fat man." I look down at the oldest of the trio, who is now standing supporting her sister's weight. "You are our Lady." She says it in that voice all children use when confronted with something they are awed by.

She's adorable.

The child's beautiful face is marred with scars and bruises. Her head is bald, which is the equivalent of cutting off a limb to her kind. Blinking, I fight back the tears. Now that the Light Magiks are gone I can feel them strongly. And because they are young and have no guard against me, I can feel what's come to pass.

All of it.

"Would you like some barbecue?" I carefully keep my voice low, letting my anger burn in my gut instead of my words.

I bounce the baby on my hip. It's something I've seen women on TV do. He seems to like it. To keep my head cool I focus on their faces. I know their names already but, I want them to tell me. It will help them feel a little better. People get uncomfortable when you know their name without asking them.

"What are your names?" I ask the trio.

"I am Lissa, she's Louise and he's Cadey." Lissa's got a strong presence to her. I can see how she's struggling to have a calmness and maturity that she shouldn't have at this age. "Our mother used to say that we're named after our warrior ancestors."

"Used to?" I ask, looking around at the condition of the van.

It's disgusting. There's a bucket in between the two front seats they used for personal needs—I can smell it. No sign of any food or water. The bedding is a single dirty blanket, and their clothes are stiff with filth and probably their waste.

"They killed her when they took us." I don't miss the glistening of tears in her eyes that she quickly blinks away.

Searching my brain, I remember there there's no male parent. Fathers are chosen randomly from whatever creature the mother chooses to procreate with. Men are not kept on as mates; they are discarded after being used as sperm donors. Gorgons mate with other females of their kind for life.

Normally, though, they live in large family groups.

"Aunts?"

Lissa shakes her head no to my question.

"Mommy was the last of her clan."

I pat her shoulder at those words. This child is too grown up for her age. I have to fix that.

My hair is playing with Cadey. It likes him. Then again, his hair has personality too. Mixed in with greasy, brown strands, little snakes are writhing around his head. None of them more than a couple inches long. They are similar to mine but look more like snakes than long bodies with teeth like mine do. I smile at him and, when he smiles back dimples appear on his cheeks. Man, he's a beautiful baby.

He's also one of the rarest Feyrie in existence, a male gorgon.

Gorgons are few and far between, even more so than lingires. Gorgon males are a myth. Here I stand holding one in my arms with two little girls standing beside me.

I don't even mind that he just peed on me.

"I tell you what, let's get you a snack to tide you over while we get you cleaned up. Then we'll have some yummy barbecue and roast some smores. How's that?" I say, with a smile planted firmly on my face while walking towards Nika who I know will take them and get them cleaned up.

"Put them down this instant! Those slaves are my property!" Montgomery's angry voice filters in through my chatter with the children as Phobe—mister monster himself—is helping me make sure they walk okay.

Dad chooses to pop in right at that moment.

"Never a dull moment, eh, Dove?" His eyes flash black when he looks at the kids. "I had a strong sense that you needed me."

"Yeah, good instincts."

"Okay, Cadey, this is my Dad. Will you go with him?" His lower lip pops out and, his blue eyes fill with fear. I smile in reassurance. "He's a very nice man and, he can do Magikal stuff. Can you keep a secret?"

All three of the kids lean closer. Children love secrets, even children as scarred as these. "I bet if you go with him and, let him get you bathed and fed, he will show you how to make lightning."

All three sets of identical blue eyes grow wide. "Boom!" Cadey exclaims, his little arms reaching out for Dad who takes him with a soft look in his black eyes.

"Goblins, I want them to have whatever their little hearts desire. They need to be bathe—they're filthy, Nika," I call to the dragon who's mended my wounds and, I know can mend theirs.

She's been standing wringing her hands since the children's presence was made known. Nika can be a bit bitchy but, she can't stand to see a child hurt. Being a healing dragon anything in pain near her causes her stress.

At least anything that she's kin to.

"My lord and I will care for them, my lady," Nika says, taking the hand of the youngest girl, Louise.

The oldest surprisingly looks at me for guidance. Leaning down I cup her soft cheek. A cheek with a big purple bruise covering it.

"You're going to hurt them, aren't you?" Lissa asks somberly.

Staring deep into her eyes, I remember a little bit more about gorgons. She smiles, exposing her sharp teeth. They're bloodthirsty things even at this age.

"Oh yes, sweetheart. I'm going to hurt them a lot." Gently, I rub her bald head. I'm also going to try to find a way to get her hair to grow back.

Lissa leans forward and kisses my cheek then hurries to catch up with dad, Nika and her siblings. I watch them all go noting the limp the smallest girl Louise has. Once they are out of sight, tucked into someone's safe arms on their way to the house, I turn. The happiness fades off my face replaced by fury. The Darkness wakes up.

I unleash the rage I've been holding in with a control I didn't know I possessed.

My power fans out from me. Every Feyrie, except the children I carefully protect, can feel its burn. Feel it building more. This time I let them. I want them to. In Lissa's haunted eyes I saw pain, horrors inflicted upon the child's body and soul. Just like Knox, like Louise, like Cadey. The little girl that died while I was linked with her. All the ones I can't save.

The hope in her eyes… it's not the first time a child has looked at me like that. A wishful part of me hopes it's the last time but it won't be.

I meet Phobe's eyes and his burn hot. He feels my rage the most, the strongest and, he will respond to it. And he will celebrate it.

Slowly, I turn around. Montgomery is so occupied with me, he hasn't noticed the half-circle forming around him. Nor does he understand the anger I know he can feel.

My Feyrie stand silently, watching me, waiting for my judgment. Their angry eyes are a kaleidoscope of colors on cold and impassive faces. Even Ducard stands next to Alagard in the front his face holding his fury.

"Your property?" I ask finally, responding to his demand from several minutes before.

His female companion struts up to me and stops a less than a foot away. I cross my arms and raise my chin. No spoiled twat is going to intimidate me, ever.

"Yes, our property. Bought and paid for," she proclaims.

The bruise on Lissa's face flashes through my mind. The size makes me pause. It's too small to come from a man's fist. My gaze falls on the riding crop in the woman's hand. I remember the welts I saw on little Cadey's arm.

I don't think it was just daddy dearest being a dick.

"Who are you exactly?" I ask forcing my face and voice calm.

"I am Lady Jiquelle de York, Daughter of Lord Montgomery de York, a senior council member. I am, quite frankly, your better and I expect my demands to be met this instant."

I take a step towards her. Her demands?!

"I did try to warn you, Montgomery but, you refused to listen to me," Ducard says, breaking the silence.

"This rabble cannot be the lady. She has food on her shirt for God's sake. Her hair is moving with lice." She dares let her hand get close to my moving hair.

She screams as her hand is engulfed in its bloodthirsty, black tendrils. She panics and her crop catches me right across the cheek. There's a brief, biting sting and a few drops of warm blood trickle down my cheek.

It's a minor irritation, nothing more—but not to Phobe. I feel *his* anger. She makes a choking sound as she's lifted off her feet with his hand around her throat. She'll die either way. My hair is venomous in whatever way it chooses to be.

"What are these foul Magiks? Release her!" Montgomery orders, but is ignored. I notice he does not attempt to help his flailing daughter. In fact no one does.

I consider her bulging brown eyes. There's nothing but greed and avarice in the woman, nothing in her to redeem. She's beaten children for no other reason than she can. There's simply no excuse for it and no mercy.

"You have a history of turning on your own, the both of you. I see that it doesn't matter that you betrayed your King and enslaved the children of Feyrie," I say, walking around Phobe. My eyes are on Jiquelle, my words for both father and daughter.

"I made a decision that saved my life and the life of my family," Montgomery protests.

"Is that what you told yourself as you watched them executed, Monty?" He remains silent, his eyes watching me, full of anger. "Your former king was tortured because, he refused to give out the names of his council members. You rewarded his loyalty by spying for the schoth king."

"Council members were being executed with him!" he argues vehemently.

"Then you should have been loyal and died," I reply quietly, studying Jiquelle intently.

The woman's brown eyes are full of fear but, it isn't enough to sway me. I can picture the children's eyes filling with something worse as they were beaten by this same woman. Beaten because they're smaller and unable to fight back.

Phobe whispers information in my mind, showing how much he does indeed know this man.

"Your property was rather poor, your family line old but by no means wealthy. When the dark king fell you suddenly had riches galore. You didn't do it to save your family. You did it to line your pockets and keep yourself in comfort." There's no redemption for traitors who betray for riches. None for their traitorous offspring either. "No mercy! Her life is forfeit," I announce, knowing exactly what her fate will be.

Phobe's eyes darken to a more orangish color. I know for certain he won't turn the woman's life down. It calls him. This idiot girl has Magiks. Not much but enough.

"Go. Doughboy can't hurt me and you know it," I reassure him.

His eyes soften just a little. Hunger then fills them and, with a chilling smile directed at Jiquelle he vanishes. I know by the taste of his glamour that no one has else seen or heard us. Sneaky man but right. Now is not the time for everyone to know who and what he is. Not yet. How did I not see it? It's the main reason he didn't feed on the guards.

The bastard is so smart sometimes.

"You can prove nothing." Montgomery protests.

I turn to face him. "I don't need to prove anything," I say blandly, stepping closer to him. Walking in a small circle around him I ask, "How did you get those children?" I poke at the mint green bowtie he's wearing.

He has the nerve to insult my clothing and, he looks like someone from a cartoon. I snort.

In a shaky voice he answers, "I bought them fair and square. It is not illegal to purchase servants."

I raise an eyebrow.

No, it's not illegal to purchase a servant's Bond Debt if they've given it to someone as payment for something. But that's not what he's done at all. Children are forbidden from selling a Bond Debt.

"They're children." Which should say enough—but not for Montgomery. I watch it go right over his head.

"They are inferior."

I lean towards him standing on my tip toes to get in his face. "Inferior to you?"

He nods and his second chin jiggles.

My temper's very close to snapping but, I need information from him. And Phobe isn't here to read his mind.

"So, tell me who did you buy them from? An associate that's a Light Fey?" Montgomery's now looking at me with a little fear in his beady brown eyes.

Just for a little longer, I tell my temper, fighting to keep myself calm.

"No, but his partner is," he answers after a moment.

"Give me his name." I bite out, my patience at an end.

Montgomery takes a step back from me tripping over a basket. He hits the ground hard enough to jar him. As he sits there on his butt, looking stunned, he begins to sweat nervously as he swivels his head side to side looking for help.

Help won't be coming for Monty.

I inhale loudly through my nose and say, "Can you all smell that?" I inhale again, smiling my toothy smile. "You smell like bacon cooking."

I clasp my hands behind my back, looking down at him. All traces of niceness gone from me, all I can feel is that dark anger that's causing my blood to heat, causing my hands to itch to strangle the very life out of the man at my feet.

"Now give me his name." This time my voice deepens, and I let the scary Iza out. His eyes widen.

"His name is Henry. He is an imp who works with some schoth named Rickher or something like that. He's gone into hiding because he heard your summons." The words tumble out of him in a rush.

I file the name of the imp away for later—the schoth I already know well. I can't wait to see him again too. This time I'm not a prisoner.

"Are you not going to ask about the welfare of your daughter?" I ask, not surprised he's a shitty parent too.

"She can take care of herself." In other words, he doesn't care.

"Really? Way to be the father of the year, Monty."

"The real Lady would not treat nobility in this fashion."

I laugh at that statement unable to help myself. Then my face sobers again. Nobility will be treated the same as every other Feyrie who comes. Of course a good Feyrie wouldn't be on the ground sweating in fear. In fact I'd still be eating barbecue.

But Monty isn't that kind of Feyrie.

"Have you ever met a Nightmare, scaredy piggy?"

He shakes his head no. Sweat pours down his face and soaks the front of his shirt. "They don't exist." His voice is small, unsure.

"Adriem, what's your favorite food?" I ask the silent presence directly behind me. The youthful-looking Nightmare comes to stand beside me, watching Montgomery with a hungry look in his reptile green eyes.

"Bacon, my lady." Adriem answers, with a toothy smile.

Montgomery's face pales, going straight to white. I can see he remembers my bacon comment.

"You—you're the real Lady?" Monty stutters, seeing the truth of it now, feeling it.

"Why yes, yes I am. Do you wanna know what you are Monty?" He nods his head, hesitantly. "For the rape of that little girl you're dinner."

I look at Adriem, who is practically salivating. The clearing is full of carnivores none who are above or below eating an imp. Some traditions you should stick with. There are those that will call us evil creatures. They will judge us for their ways, our beliefs. But each one of the Feyrie around me, except Montgomery, holds children sacred; very sacred. The gorgon kid's faces come to mind.

I let more of the darkness out.

My claws grow and I hear the hum of my hair because it's wanting to taste his blood. Yes to some we are savages, but not to me. My Feyrie, my monsters, are beautiful. Lashing out with my hand I feel his skin part beneath them and feel the hot blood hit my face.

He screams.

Staring down at his face, smiling, I can see all the way to the bone. The crowd moves closer as the smell of fresh blood hits the air.

"I condemn you to death, Montgomery De Yuck, death by Feyrie."

Beside me Adriem's shape starts to morph and twist. And in his place… well, all over the place stands a freaking dinosaur.

A Tyrannosaurus Rex to be exact. Ha, I knew he smelled kind of like a dragon.

"All right, big guy you get a bite but, save some for the others."

Lowering his head he sniffs at the sniveling Monty. I swear Adriem is laughing when he bites him in half.

CHAPTER TWENTY-SIX

hobe

"SHE'S BEEN like that for well over an hour," Auryn answers the question in my gaze as it rests on Iza.

She is sitting at the edge of the dock with her feet dangling over the water staring out into its depths. Her thoughts are completely hidden from me and, I know she is deliberately keeping them that way. She is putting considerable effort into it.

It always makes me nervous when she does it. Since she died I do not trust it. Paranoid is the term they use—she makes me paranoid.

I slip silently down beside her and slide towards her sitting close enough to feel her body heat. All the chaotic emotions rolling around in me calm at this small contact with her.

"You are keeping me out," I say aloud.

She tosses a pebble into the water causing small ripples. "When you're in my head with me it's hard to work things out for myself. This is something I need to work out alone." She sighs.

"Do you want to talk the old-fashioned way, then?" I ask.

The paranoia is not the only reason. I will admit if only to myself I miss the intimate contact of her mind when she kicks me out. I have gotten used to it and to be cut off from it... bothers me. But I am not quite ready to admit this by demanding the return of it.

Instead I go to work, once again, on her shields.

"You mean out loud?" She gives a small humorless laugh then nods. "It boils down to one thing, Phobe. I feel bad for how these people have suffered. Like those children." She looks over at me and the lost look in her beautiful eyes pulls on strings I did not know existed until her.

"It is not your fault they endured such things." Not her fault she did as well.

"When I look at them I see myself." She tosses another pebble in the water. "Can I do this?" Her voice is small, quiet.

She leans her head on my shoulder and, after a moment of being unsure what to do, I lean my head against hers. The smell of her herbal shampoo fills my nose as her hair stirs beneath my face, tickling my cheek.

"You are already doing it," I say, kissing her head. Allowing myself this—emotional moment with her.

She slides her other arm through mine hugging it to her. She is hugging it so tight that I can feel her heartbeat beating like a small drum against my arm. She is more upset than she is admitting.

She has been through much, Iza. If she were human I am not sure she would still be alive. Humans are such fragile things. Iza is not fragile, most of the time.

"This isn't the last like him. Feyrie or not they'll be treated the same as Montgomery was."

I nod at her words. Men like Montgomery destroy others. Something I am familiar with—I destroy lives too. Before I met Iza, destruction was the only thing I was capable of.

I am learning to do more. Slowly.

"It is how things have to be." She nods against my arm.

She looks at these Feyrie with her soul. She does not judge them unfairly.

"He was an evil asshole even by our terms. He violated children… imprisoned them for power they didn't have. I'd kill him again if I could." Her voice is so quiet, it is barely more than a whisper.

After a thoughtful, silent moment she sighs and relaxes against me. It does not indicate that whatever is bothering her is gone. It simply means she has a new way to look at. Iza has peculiar perspectives on things, but she has a very analytical mind.

It took me time to see that. It will take others even longer.

"There aren't many Feyrie children. Do you know why?" she asks.

I opt to tell her the partial truth. "With the dark Magiks fading the Feyrie started losing their ability to have many children."

In fact children are so rare that most are teenagers or older. The gorgon children are the youngest true blood Feyrie I have seen in many years.

"But the gorgons?"

"They are an exception. It is not well known but they can share Magiks with family members to have enough to make children. Or sacrifice themselves to give their sisters children."

Which the aunts of the three gorgon children did. It is why the mother was the last one in the group, and why the small family was so vulnerable. Had her sisters lived, those children would not be here. Not in the way they arrived.

Iza's shields drop a little allowing me to peek into her mind. Her thoughts whiz through her head, a twisted mess of past and present and all possibilities to come. I admire the chaos that is her mind.

Carefully, I peel back another layer exposing more of her thoughts.

How did she ever believe she had human in her? There is nothing human about her thought processes. Parts of it are comprised of simpler thoughts—food, clothing, and home. The rest of it is as complex as anyone I have encountered and downright intriguing at times.

Her information processing abilities are odd, perhaps, but effective. She weighs each possibility and works them out in every direction. Iza sees their reactions and behavior from a place of experience and sometimes pure imagination. And responds to it. But she is not infallible.

Just a clever, clever woman.

"So, if the Magiks grow stronger, they can have children again?"

"Yes. Already it is strengthening them. Before you know it there will be babies everywhere for you to coddle," I assure her.

It is the truth and, there is no reason to not share it with her.

Children are a soft spot for her. Iza is fully aware she cannot have children of her own which makes all children more precious to her. Something she does not know that I know about her.

This I discovered while she slept. I do not have any qualms about eavesdropping in her mind while she is vulnerable.

"It's very strange caring about people and having people care about me," she muses.

I read the thoughts that prompt that comment. She is not used to having the closeness and support of family or even friends. In between the age of eight and now there has been no one to care.

Except me. That surprises me a little.

"You have gotten their loyalty and respect simply by being your-self. Continue to do this, Iza, and you will be successful."

She turns her face to look at me. "*We* will, Phobe," she corrects.

A small part of me likes that correction.

"You do not mind the stains on my soul, Iza?" I surprise myself by asking.

She smiles her sharp smile her eyes soft and full of something I cannot define. Something that makes my heart beat faster in my chest.

"You don't mind the scars on mine?" she asks, then kisses my chin.

This kissing thing is still new to me. My memories say it is an expression of affection that's not sexual.

I like it.

CHAPTER TWENTY-SEVEN

*I*za

WHEN I WAKE up in the back of a truck I'm only a little surprised. I fell asleep against his shoulder on the dock. And I'm assuming he put me to bed like a little kid. Right now I'm toasty and comfortable and not in a hurry to get up. Around me I can hear the murmur of voices and muted laughter. The clearing flickers with the lights of fires and lanterns.

I vaguely remember a warm body behind me but, he's no longer there. If he was to begin with.

"He went on patrol, my lady." Auryn's quiet voice precedes her poking her head over the side of the truck.

"You're not a mind reader too, are you? Because I've got enough of those in my life."

"No, no. I merely heard you stirring."

Thank god. Another freaking mind reader might put me in a bad mood. Running a hand down my face I sit up. It feels like I haven't slept for days which isn't completely wrong. But I did just wake up from a nap.

"Do you need anything?" Auryn asks, sitting on the tailgate at my feet. I stare at her, frowning. "Like a drink or some food?"

Oh.

"Sure. But I can—" I start to say, but Adriem steps out of the shadows and nods to his mother. He is gone before I can call him back. Well I guess that means I can sit here in this nest for a little while longer.

Auryn stays quiet while I eat the barbecue Adriem brings me. She's watching me with a small smile playing about her mouth. I'm curious about it but not enough to ask.

Finally full I set the plate aside, chug a cold soda and, lean back against the back of the truck bed and stare right back at her.

"I have served rulers before but, never in all of my years have I met someone quite like you." I remain quiet while she speaks. "Phobe said that you do not wish for all the formality. We have agreed to be more relaxed around you."

Well, thank you, Phobe.

"Yeah, this 'my lady' shit freaks me out. Tell me about youself, Auryn. I know all the folklore but, I want to know the real story."

"When I was a girl I worked for the king as a milk-maid."

"Milk-maid? That was an actual thing?" I can't help but ask. I mean, seriously, milk-maid?

"Yes, it was. My job was to milk the cows twice a day and deliver the milk to the castle. But one day the king saw me and being noticed by the him was never good."

I tucked my feet further into the blanket. I love a good story.

"My father wanted sons but had all girls. Still, he made sure to teach us how to use a sword..."

CHAPTER TWENTY-EIGHT

hobe

A WHILE ago the children crawled up in the truck with her and, now Iza is reading a bedtime story to them. Knox and Cadey are both currently asleep with their heads on her lap.

The older ones, including Ruthie and Michael, are looking at Iza in rapt attention. She is reading them their history and, they have not realized it yet because she is making it so entertaining.

Clever. It is not something I imagined her doing.

My eyes linger a moment longer then move to the other man watching from the shadows. Adriem. His green eyes are only on one person. Iza.

My stomach tenses but I fight the emotion. I know it for what it is now— jealousy. It is not something I enjoy feeling nor is it something I will let myself continue to feel.

My shadows brush against him. There is no reason for jealousy.

I understand my place in things and, he understands his.

Knowing she is safe, especially guarded by the Nightmares, I turn away and head towards the human town. My skin tingles as the glamour coats me.

I am wearing an unrecognizable face. After putting some thought into it I opted for one that no one has seen: a child, or at least a form that looks like a child. He was male with black hair and blue eyes. He looked about Michael's age. Now I do too.

This form was a lange. A shapeshifter of sorts. They favor inanimate objects like trees and shrubs that they use to entangle their victims while feeding on their essences. They do not age past puberty. The body of this one was over a thousand years old when I ate him.

So long ago.

Choosing to walk, instead of taking on a form I can move more quickly with, I find myself enjoying the night. I cannot recall the last time I did so. For a few moments I admire the brightness of the moon in the sky, the stars twinkling brightly in the background and the smell of the the crisp night air.

Soon this place will be blanketed in white when the snow that I can smell in the air finally reaches here. Within a month. Iza's children will like the snow. Some of them have not seen it before.

I am not sure how she will feel about snow. She takes wonder in the strangest things though. I know she is looking forward to the human holidays.

Humans have many holidays… some of which make no sense—or are based off obscure gods who never existed to begin with. Although they did get one thing right.

There is a god here. A creator. There were three at the beginning of it all. The creator is one of them. Iza calls him the One God.

Ahead of me a human steps out of the shadows. "Kid, are you lost?"

The smell of gun oil is carried on the breeze towards me. His clothes are too clean, in too good of condition, to belong to the dredge he is trying to portray.

This is one of the humans that are watching Iza.

"My friends kicked me out of their car up the road," I say in a voice much younger than my own. I take on the mannerisms of this form.

My forlorn prowl the shadows around him, looking for others but, this man is alone.

"Anything I can help you with?"

My shadows brush him, and I say, "Oh, yes sir. Do you have a phone I can borrow?"

"I don't but, why don't you come on over here and get warm. I have some hot chocolate."

The man thinks I am vulnerable. He knows I came from the Sidhe. He does not know what it is. He and his superiors do know that it is not humans that reside there.

Kael has been telling tales.

The human plans to lure me further into the shadows and incapacitate me. It is a trick that has worked for him before.

"It is pretty cold." I feign snuggling down into the light jacket I am wearing and follow behind him. I do not miss his sly smile either.

"I might have something to eat, too. Let's have a look." He waves me past him.

Oh, he has something I can eat. Him.

CHAPTER TWENTY-NINE

Iza

I STARE up into the night sky. The stars are bright, shining like gemstones on the pitch-black backdrop. The moon is a beacon to my gaze and is already half-full. I shiver but not from the cold. The cold isn't what's bothering me.

What does bother me is the emotion-filled bubble—full of all the junk I keep locked up inside—rising quickly to the surface. I wondered when it would happen. I expected it sooner. I hate it regardless.

The Sidhe made this tower room for me on a whim. It looks just like one out of storybook. The ledge I'm perched on is the perfect size for me to sit on—another tweak by the Sidhe.

I move a little closer to the corner of the stone ledge and brace myself for emotional impact. It hits me with the force of a tsunami. I close my eyes as wave after wave of grief, fear, sadness and pain tear at that those soft spots left in my heart.

This shit sucks.

"Foolish clutter in your brain, Dove." My father's voice pulls me from my emotional self-punishment.

I turn to look towards him, blinking rapidly to clear my blurry vision. Seeing him in living color I hurry and wipe my face. He surprises me by crawling in the small cubby hole on the ledge with me. He puts his crossed legs underneath mine and rubs my knees to comfort me.

"I still don't see the flaw in my thinking process foolish or not," I finally say. A handkerchief appears in front of me and, I use it to wipe my face and blow my nose.

"You're not a human, Iza, so stop punishing yourself like one. This war is something you can fight but only as the creature you are." As he talks, he rubs my legs until all the tears stop. "You've seen things in your life so dark and awful that—" He takes a deep breath. "Use that rage inside of you, Dove. Let it free." Exhaling, his voice more gentle he says, "You're doing better than you think you are."

"It's very hard to go from who I was to who I am to who I'll become—whatever that will be."

Truthfully, I'm afraid of losing who I am now.

"Silly girl, you're blooming. I bet you've laughed and smiled more since you met Phobe and those kids than you have in the last 21 years combined."

I nod, it's the truth. "Don't forget you too, Dad."

His smile flashes big and bright and then he continues, "You can't change the events unfolding in your life. You can only shape them."

It's not your typical father-daughter speech but, the father and daughter aren't exactly typical either.

I sigh.

"It's going to get worse before it gets better. I won't demean you and what you're doing by telling you otherwise. But your enemy? They can only be defeated by someone who can meet them equally. You're that someone. Don't ever think you're not."

I lean forward and hug my father.

"Thanks, Dad." I feel him smile against my cheek. Wearing one of my own I say, "So… about your girlfriend situation."

CHAPTER THIRTY

Iza

A FEW DAYS LATER, the mood in the Sidhe is lighter. The children are running around causing a ruckus everywhere. Ruthie is on their shirt-tails a smile on her face. The gorgons have practically transformed overnight. Amazing what good food and safety can do for a child's disposition.

Nika and Jameson also spent hours healing their injuries. Some were from abuse and some from malnutrition. Good food will fix the latter. The soft growth of hair that has appeared on Lissa's head is nice to see especially when its moving around.

Now that is fantastic.

Standing at the entrance to the dining room, with an oddly shy Knox hanging at my side, I watch Cadey giggle as he tries to hide behind a tapestry from my dad who's pretending like he can't see the little taloned feet sticking out at the bottom.

"Where did Cadey go? Anyone see him?" he calls, winking at me as he passes.

Lissa and Louise come to stand on either side of Knox, who blushes adorably, and even the solemn Lissa is laughing at her brother's antics.

"What do you guys want for breakfast? I'm starving." I pat my stomach and, taking a page out of my Dad's book, wink at Lissa who dares to wink back.

I laugh, unable to help myself. She's going to be a force to reckon with when she's grown. Probably before.

"Bacon," Cadey exclaims running straight for me from his hiding place.

I stare at him a moment, finding it weird he said bacon, all things considering. Intelligence is a bright sparkle in the blue depths of his eyes. I raise an eyebrow at him. He puts his arms out to be picked up, and I snatch him up, spinning him around.

"Bacon it is. Let us ask the goblins if they can make us some." I walk into the dining room and greet people as we pass by their tables.

"Good morn, my lady. How is your day so far?" Jameson asks coming to stand just to the side. I wish he, at least, would stop the 'my lady' shit.

"Cadey wants bacon."

He turns to study the children, who solemnly study him back. "Look there. An entire plateful just appeared at your table," he says, pointing at the steaming platter of perfectly crisp bacon.

"Pawpaw!" Cadey yells, putting his hands out towards dad as he joins us.

I hide a smile at the look on my dad's face. He hesitates only a moment and then takes the child into his arms. My father is as charmed as I am.

"You seem to draw the oddest things to you, daughter," he says after a moment turning to talk to Cadey about what he wants to play after breakfast.

I have a feeling there is a deeper meaning to his words, but I'll think on it later, and the answer will come.

Auryn and Adriem join me. The gray in her hair draws a quick gaze from me. The reasons for it still bothers me. It's stuck in my brain and, I can't let it go. There's got to be a way to fix it.

Gray hair is a completely unnatural state for someone like her.

"I do not know how anyone rides around in those things all day long," Auryn says.

Still foggy from being lost in my thoughts I frown. What's she talking about? Then my brain kicks in. Auryn is not a fan of cars. They went with Jameson, earlier in the morning, to the store to get clothing. We can't have them walking around in stuff from two hundred years ago. That would draw even more unwanted attention. We've already got enough eyes on us.

"You guys want to join us for breakfast?" I ask, snagging a piece of bacon.

"Not this morning, my lady. We're meeting Phobe at the practice field. We are learning how to use those metal gadgets," Adriem says from his mother's side.

Metal gadgets? Does he mean guns?

"The guns I'm guessing?" He nods at my words. "You guys have fun. They aren't so bad once you get used to them." With that they both bow and leave the room.

They really need to stop the bowing.

I sit at a table with the kids and my dad and help dish out food. Conversation flows and so does laughter. Now is the time to enjoy these little moments of happiness because, I know that in the coming months—years—they will be the most precious memories.

The sound of giggles keeps the smile firmly on my face. I can worry about that after I have a nice breakfast with them.

Knox slides into the seat beside me. I glance down at his face as I shove more bacon in mine. The look on his face is solemn and way more serious than I'm used to seeing.

"You doing okay, Knox? Everything going all right?" I ask.

He turns to look up at me and for a split second I'm looking at a stranger. Then he smiles and charms the bacon right out of my hand. That smile is one hundred percent Knox as he snags the piece I was going to eat with an indulgent smile from me.

Right this second he looks happy as he munches on the bacon stri with a spot of grease on his chin. I still can't shake the feeling something is off with him.

I follow his gaze to a child I don't recognize. He's blonde, slightly older than Knox, and he has the flattest brown eyes I've ever seen on a kid. The scar that mars the left side of that baby face hits me in the gut. Half his face is a mass of scar tissue.

The horrors this child has seen.

My Magiks reach out to him and, I get the normal feedback. A shifter. One of the kids I took from Boobs. But nothing personal. This kid is locked down.

"Who's that?" I whisper to Knox.

"My friend, Peter." Without another word Knox climbs to his feet, runs to Peter and with their heads close together they leave the room.

I think it's sweet Knox made a friend. Is that why he's been so weird? Have I been worrying over nothing? Frowning, I stare at the empty doorway.

No, my gut says there's something going on there.

A sour note strums through the song of the web and, then a shout sounds across the hall. I jerk my head around just in time to see someone collapse. Shit. Shit. Shit.

CHAPTER THIRTY-ONE

*I*za

AFTER VAL'S COLLAPSE, which he seems to have mostly recovered
from, the peace lasts for two blessed days. Val is recovering nicely and,
although no one can figure out what happened, he doesn't seem to be
experiencing any side-effects.

So I put everyone to work.

The cosmetic stuff outside I asked the Sidhe not to fix. This many
people with nothing to do is not a good idea and, I like keeping busy.
So now I'm up to my elbows in paint as we work on the fence
surrounding the house. When a large limousine pulls past us to the
front of the house, with a beat-up looking multicolored van right
behind it, I sigh. Right off the bat I know who and what at least one
set of my 'guests' are.

The limo holds more lingires, but, they're not alone. The van
behind them is full of imps. I look over at Adriem, who looks at me
with paint on his nose.

I sense a headache coming on.

At least some of them are nobility. I've got a bad track record with nobility so far. Resigned, I put my paintbrush in the brush can. The temptation to send someone else to deal with it is strong but, my gut tells me it's something I must do myself.

My gut had never failed me so, there's no point in ignoring it.

For half a second I'm concerned with my appearance. My hair is wrapped in a bandanna for protection. It doesn't like the paint at all. The bandanna is black with crossbones on it. I love it. My hair gives me an excuse to wear it. I'm wearing a pair of too-big jean bibs and a t-shirt with some local band on it topped off with a pair of black chucks.

I look fabulous for painting. Not so much for meeting new people.

Why the hell am I worrying about my clothes? Hell, I need to pull my head out of my ass. It isn't my clothing that needs to make an impression. It's me.

'Oh, you will make an impression, Iza.' I roll my eyes at Phobe's words.

He thinks he's a comedian lately.

"Oh well," I mumble, heading inside. My little group of fence painters was overlooked by the newcomers.

Pausing in the doorway I turn back to look at Phobe who's wearing a plain black t-shirt and a pair of those incredible jeans that hug him in all the right places. He stops beside me his bare feet silent as always. Looking down at the paint covering me, and then looking pointedly at his spotless clothes, I make a face.

The bastard was painting just like everyone else. How the hell does he always manage to remain clean?

"Showoff." I stick my tongue out at him.

The sound of raised voices can be heard outside over the sounds of saws and hammers. Not good. I pick up my step.

What meets my arrival inside is a screaming woman wearing some old dress with peacock feathers sticking out of an incredibly ugly hat. Her face an inch from Jameson's. Poor Jameson looks like he wants to strangle her.

Behind her stands a younger version of the screaming woman and several armored men. Off to the other side of the room are some very dirty, poorly dressed imps. Why are they hunkering down in fear while the obnoxious woman is not?

I'll find out, as soon as I dealt with this mess—a mess that better not be a repeat of the Montgomery fiasco.

"I will not live in the same place as those despicable creatures. They are filthy! Nobility does not house with the peasants!"

I stand there a minute. What's with the I'm better than you bullshit? It's getting on my nerves.

"Enough!" My voice cuts through the argument, silencing the room.

Everyone turns to look at me. The woman's eyes rake me from head to toe speculatively. This one is ignoring her gut instincts. She really shouldn't. I find her thread easily. Snotty she may be but, she's loyal. This makes everything more difficult.

"I demand to see the Lady about this atrocity." She uses a voice that I imagine is quite effective on servants.

Gently I strum the thread connecting me to, Florenta, the widow of one Hieran De Salve who was executed with the former dark king.

The shock on her face is something I can't help but smirk at.

"You're looking at her, Florenta. How may I be of service?"

Several chairs appear for the weary ones to sit. It doesn't escape my notice that only the ones with Florenta sit. The tired ones remain standing there, staring at me.

"You're the Lady?"

I fight the urge to reach over and shut her gaping mouth. Is it that big of a shock? I shrug. "Yep, that's why I said I was."

Someone snorts in amusement. The throne poofs into existence beside me. I've been on my feet all day it won't hurt for me to sit down for a few.

When I sit the the poor imps do too. So that's the trick. Refreshments for the guests would be—they poof into existence. The goblins are busy at work. They like being busy again as I can see in the polished look of things around the Sidhe. Now and then you can hear whistling echoing through the halls. I can feel their contentment.

"But you're dressed like a peasant covered in paint." Florenta comments in disbelief.

At least she shut her mouth.

"And you're wearing a dead bird on your head. I think that makes us even." I'm not one to mince words and, I'm horrible at the 'eloquent' speeches I've seen on TV.

"Why, I never!" she sputters out.

"I suggest you get used to it. I do it all the time." I turn to study the group accompanying her.

Using my inner sight and outer sight, I carefully take in their reactions to me. Some hold amusement, some the same look as Florent and some hold assessment. One of them holds look of hope clear as day.

"So what's the problem? I was busy."

Florenta squares her shoulders. Oh god, here it comes. I ready myself to hear something I'm not going to like.

Be calm. Be calm. Be calm.

"This steward informed me that I have to reside in the same wing as the peasants," she finally says.

I raise an eyebrow. Peasants? I can't believe how often they use that word. Hell, add a letter, and it's a bird.

Like her hat, ha.

"Well Jameson has the right of it. All will share the wings assigned. We have many to accommodate and, the Sidhe will shape itself to satisfy your particular needs in your set of rooms." The woman hasn't considered that has she? Snotty old biddy. I'll take care of this quickly.

"But they will be given the same status as I. My family is—"

I interrupt her. "Times have changed, Florenta. There are not very many of us left. Over the last few centuries we've been brought almost to the point of extinction yet, you're complaining about rooms."

I watch the guardsman next to Florenta looking at the gold and silver lining the walls in front of him. He's not interested in who I am because, he's too busy imagining the money from selling the valuables.

I almost feel sorry for him. He's another of those Feyrie who don't carry any loyalty for our kind in his heart. He carries only the greed for more money. The brief satisfaction having a full pocket gets you.

Speaking of pockets. "It won't fit in your pocket. Shame you didn't bring a bag in with you. It might fit in there," I say dryly.

His eyes jerk up at my words His hand going to the hilt of his sword.

"If you pull that weapon you'll die," I warn.

The man looks around him seeing no one protecting me. He smirks. I'm in the Sidhe. I'm never alone here.

'I must do this myself,' I say quietly in my mind to Phobe, the unseen presence in the shadows to my right.

"Who will kill him?" another of the guardsmen asks.

Two out of fifteen that's not so bad. The only ones left out of Montgomery's group are Ducard and the gorgons. Briefly, I glance at Florenta's face. She's now watching me with a bit of caution. She felt my flare of power on the Web.

The first one pulls the weapon from its sheath.

The thing about stupid people is they can never see past themselves. He's in the Sidhe. For fuck's sake—does he think he can kill me and take off with the silverware? I don't understand how stupid people survive in the world.

"She must be an imposter, my lady," he says more to justify his actions than he cares whether or not I am.

He's also under the impression that everyone else in the room is as greedy as he and his peanut gallery are. He takes one step and, I move.

The sword that Auryn gifted me with materializes in my hand. It slides easily through his neck splattering blood all over poor Florenta's ugly dress. I turn to look at her knowing my eyes are midnight black.

"Like I said—" I swing around before Florenta can even blink and punch the second one in the face, hard. He falls sideways, his sword clattering loudly to the ground. "—Times have changed. You are loyal to your people, Florenta. I respect that but, you will obey the rules we have, understand?"

Florenta nods her blood-spattered face. There it isn't disgust in her eyes. There is fear mingled with respect.

My sword vanishes in dark smoke up my arm.

Florenta drops down into a full curtsy. "My apologies my lady, for bringing vermin such as them into your home and, for disrespecting you in such a fashion." She's being truthful. I'd feel a lie from her.

I pluck the damp towel out of thin air and remove the blood from my hands and right arm. The the towel vanishes again, along with the dead man.

My fiends are hungry.

They aren't the only ones. The still breathing guard slides into a particular kind of darkness that I haven't seen in a while.

Phobe.

"Now, once you and the rest of the nobility get over yourselves, we'll get along just fine. Until then I imagine most of you will be pissed off about one thing or another. This isn't an acceptable way to be to each other. Not while I'm here." I stare pointedly into each face with equal measure.

"Those peasants, as you put it so nicely, are the lifeblood of our people. They're willing to do the things that need to be done without complaint. If you respected them more you might have discovered that before." I stare at Florenta pointedly. "Now I expect all of you to eat, rest and then get your paint brushes. There is work to be done."

Work I feel everyone should pitch in on.

With that said I leave the front room heading back outside to finish the top posts on the side fence. A fence that has grown since I went inside.

The Sidhe senses the need for people to be busy.

Luckily for everyone my dad and Jameson convinced me that we need to fit in. I was already picking out neon pink paint. Well, after some grumbling, they convinced me to use white paint for the fence.

How very normal looking it is. Unless I look deeper. That's when I see the different kinds of Feyrie walking around on eight legs or flapping by on clear-membraned wings. The large blue trees that move

156

and sway to the Sidhe's music—some of which are alive in a more Magikal sense.

When I look inside of the Sidhe no castle in the world can compare to it.

To the non-Magikal, or anyone it doesn't want to see, it will look like any normal house. Only to the Magikals does it look like its name the Dark Sidhe.

A chord of warning. It's going to be a long month.

'Iza.' At my name, spoken with caution, I stop to look at Phobe, but he's gone.

Shit, while I was lost in la la land, I missed something.

'Full Glamour.'

Those words, whispering through my mind, bring my glamour fully active. Someone is standing behind me. I sigh again. I want to get the freaking fence painted. Turning, I throw on my poker face.

Before me stands someone connected to the web faintly but still connected. He's a decent-sized guy not tall like Phobe but big like a linebacker. He's attractive but, not my type. I cock my head to the side paying attention to my other senses.

No Magiks other than what they call the 'physical' kind. He's a few steps genetically below a Feyrie. A shifter but not as watered down as some of the others I've come across.

There are hundreds of different species of them on the planet. They're all half-breeds from one type of Feyrie or another. This one is some kind of canine. I can smell it but, can't quite put my finger on it yet.

Shifters are strong, fast, and capable of doing some pretty heavy damage in a short amount of time. Jameson's still gathering information on the power structure of the ones here in this realm.

I need to know who is who and where they are.

I ignore his three buddies hidden ten feet away in the shadows of the tall oak trees that surround the property. The ground is already coated with one layer of dusty-colored leaves. A rather pretty picture to see considering the circumstances.

I'd rather they not destroy this natural artwork with their blood and guts and such.

"Can I help you?" I ask, breaking the silence and his intent study of me.

His eyes flash green then back to a dark shade of brown.

"We have been summoned here." His voice is deep and accented with an unfamiliar slow drawl. "Our alpha has asked me to inform you of his arrival."

Okay, so why send men ahead? Wouldn't it be easier to just show up with the lot of them?

"Let me ask you something, dude." I pause for effect mainly to gauge his reaction. I'm betting he's hyena or possibly a wolf. "Why didn't he come himself instead of sending a puppy to inform us?"

"We don't know your Feyrie master's customs well nor, do we trust them. All we know is that we heard a call that some of us could not resist."

So obviously my glamour works well. He thinks I'm human.

"Where is this alpha right now?" my curiosity makes me ask. I've never met a legitimate alpha before. I know he's the head honcho of a pack in the shifter world.

I wonder if these shifters realize that standing just behind the hiding ones are some of their forefathers. Auryn and Adriem are completely hidden from their view waiting for them to do something threatening to me.

"He is across town in a hotel because, the trip was tiring," the shifter explains.

Eh? He doesn't expect me to believe that bullshit does he? He hands me a plain white business card that I tuck in my front pocket without reading it. His alpha is connected with me to the same degree as the shifter standing in front of me.

Barely a whisper. For now.

The connections are weird like that with shifters. I have to awaken their Marks. Initially, they're not nearly as strong as the other Feyrie. Even the shifters in the shadows are dormant—although not all the shifters are really what they're claiming to be. But I'll deal with those when I get to them.

'Iza.'

Oh, my attention wandered. I refocus on the shifter.

"All right, then. So he's too fucking lazy to come here?" I ask.

He barely hides his surprise.

Good, I hit a button. I learned over the years if you hit the right buttons you get the right information. Or a fistfight. Depends on whose buttons you push and how hard.

I'm good with either.

The shifter gathers his composure quickly and says, "Since he's the alpha he will expect appropriate accommodations to be made."

Squinting at his face I finally see the beast just under his skin. Definitely a wolf.

"Well, hate to tell you but, he'll receive the same accommodations as every other person coming here." My answer once again surprises him.

This is too fun.

"You will not give him the special treatment he ranks as Alpha?" his asks, his voice thick.

"As I said, he'll get the same as every other."

Smelling leather, I look at his clothing for the first time. I have been dazing out. He's wearing a leather tie and a cowboy hat. Oh, hell, they're that type—good old boys.

Chewing on my lip to hide my smile, I fight to keep the serious face on. This is going to be entertaining.

"Would it not be better if I speak to her myself?" he asks.

Oh, so he's trying to see me in person—probably to try and see how big a threat I am. Wouldn't it be a riot if he knew he's talking to me now? I have to fight harder to keep the smile off my face. This glamour thing is wonderful.

"I don't think so. But I'll make sure the message gets passed on as soon I go inside," I say, keeping the humor out of my voice, or at least trying to.

His frustration is clear in his eyes and body posture.

"He is to come to your Lady equal to everyone else?"

Chewing on my cheek to keep a straight face, I nod. Wow, he is having a really hard time with accepting that. I see on his face the minute he does... at least enough to pass on the message.

He nods his big head and steps back then turns and walks calmly away. I watch, unsurprised, as other shadows detach themselves and follow closely behind him. Good I managed to handle that rather well. No one died or insulted me. It also helps that I was talking to someone who knows when the conversation is over.

I watch them until they disappear into the trees.

"You do like to push them, Iza." Phobe's softly spoken words pull me out of my thoughts.

Thoughts he eavesdropped on. The wall of blue doesn't work anymore. Nothing works anymore. Jerk.

"I'm not dancing to their tune. He's no different than any other Feyrie." I made up my mind about it and, I'm not planning on changing it anytime soon.

"You are choosing to handle the shifters with aggression," he points out.

I frown, thinking about it. Perhaps I am indeed.

"I don't think they'd respect me at all if I turned belly up and tried to ass-kiss them to death. My gut tells me this is the right way."

I look at him through my lashes and say, *Would you like some aggression?*

He chuckles at my words and tosses a paintbrush at my head that I barely catch.

CHAPTER THIRTY-TWO

*J*za

I've gotten into the habit of sneaking out at night, alone. Or mostly alone. I can't say I'm ever truly alone but, I need room to breathe. I need to think.

So, I used every trick I possess to ditch my wannabe guards and Phobe. I can't feel him out there so, I'm assuming I pulled it off.

Tonight, my mood is morose and, since sleep isn't happening, I wanted to walk.

My brilliant idea didn't include an actual destination. After walking around aimlessly for hours I ended up parking myself on a bench in the park. I sit watching TV on my phone which isn't helping at all.

Humans are just as cruel as the schoth.

When I first woke on Earth I assumed that humans were delicate and fragile like the ones I met in prison. They are but that doesn't stop them from being monsters in their own right.

Horrible ones. The TV and the Google God show me everything

on them. The atrocities they've visited upon each other are just as bad as any the schoth have perpetuated. Here they have bombs that can wipe out entire countries. All it takes is a button push and boom everyone is dead. Where is the honor in that? I wouldn't even do that to the schoth and, everyone knows how I feel about them.

I turn the phone off and slump down on the bench. Did I call people to a doomed world? Did I—god, what the hell am I doing? Why did I start looking at my phone anyhow?! It made my mood worse.

"They don't sell drugs here anymore." The voice pulls me out of my thoughts.

On the bench, across the walkway from me, sits a man dressed in a fluffy orange coat covered in layers of dirt. The smell of him informs me it's not just dirt. His brown hair is a tangled and messy crown around his head with what looks like clumps of dirt in it. His beard is scraggly and grayed in some places.

But those eyes of his are a vivid blue that reminds me of the sky early in the morning. Familiar eyes—but I'm pretty sure I've never met him before.

"Drugs? What drugs?" I answer, after staring at him for far too long.

I know the literal meaning of the word but, why would I come to the park to get drugs? Humans make no sense. Drugs are used to treat illnesses. I have no illnesses.

"You don't wanna get high?"

High? Frowning I stare at him what can he—oh, I get it now.

"No, I'm not here for drugs. I came here to look at the stars."

"So, you're a hippy?" he says, digging around in the garbage can beside him. He pulls out a food container of some type.

"No. I just like the sky. I wasn't able to see it for a long time." I don't know why I share this with him but, there's no real harm in it. He's not going to tell anyone, I mean, he's going to eat an old salad he got out of the garbage can.

"They lock you away in the loony bin too? I spent five weeks in there last year," he asks.

"Something like that."

He smiles at me exposing the fact he is missing several of his front teeth. Which makes me smile back at him. He doesn't care about superficial things. What an interesting human.

"What's so heavy on your mind?" he asks, sniffing his dinner. Then he takes a big bite of the goop.

I opt for honesty. "I'm the Shepherd to a Magikal race of creatures from another realm. They came here to grow and build an army to stand up to the schoth when they come here. I'm totally not equipped to do this shit but, it's my supposed destiny, and it sucks balls." After my speech, I take a drink of the bottled water sitting beside me on the bench.

He stares at me a minute, chewing his browned lettuce, then laughs.

"You sure you're not here for drugs?"

"If they'd work I'd probably take them. So why do you live out here?"

"Drugs, of course. But I've been clean for ten years now. Just can't climb your way back out sometimes." He begins to lick the container the salad was in.

I know what it's like to be that hungry. I stand up and stretch and walk over to him.

"So, no more drugs? What about booze?" He shakes his head at my questions. I toss a wad of cash at him. "Go get a proper coat and some real food. No reason for you to be cold tonight, right?"

"I've learned in my life that people are chosen to do things for a reason so, remember that nothing is ever as bad as it seems. People surprise you. I hope you win your war," he says, as he grabs the money and shuffles off.

Yeah, buddy, me too.

CHAPTER THIRTY-THREE

*T*za

WAITING on the crosswalk light to turn green to cross the street I stare at the name of the store lit up in red neon lettering across from me.

Moleville Exterminators.

The name of this town always amuses me. There are a bunch of supernatural creatures living in a town called Moleville. They should change their high school football team to Moleville Monsters. It has a ring to it—versus their current one, the Moleville Diggers. I get the play on words and all, but aren't their sports teams supposed to be intimidating?

Speaking of school… the kids need a teacher to homeschool them. I can't risk sending them to a real school. In this world all kids are required to have schooling. The last thing in the world I need is to draw more attention from the—speaking of humans.

The bag getting pulled over my head is only a little bit of a surprise. The smell of garlic coming from the man wielding it kind of gave it away a little early.

Oh, this is fantastic! I'm being kidnapped like in the movies! The canvas bag over my head even smells.

At the last second I decide to let them take me without a fight. It's not too hard of a decision. They enacted this elaborate kidnapping for a reason. Besides the fact that someone closer than Kael or fluff brains betrayed me and knew I snuck out alone.

Unless they don't know who they have? That's entirely possible. And it makes things more fun—for me anyhow. I'm never actually alone. The Fiends, my constant companions, are very unhappy with my current situation.

I grunt as I'm tossed into some vehicle. I hope it's a van which will add to the experience. I can tell Phobe—uh-oh. A sudden sharp prick of pain right in my upper hip draws a curse word out of me. Did they just stick me with a needle?

My lips go numb. Sweating, I push my body to fight the sedative. Because I've seen enough TV to know that's what it is. Wow, it has a bit of a bite to it. But their human drugs won't work on me like they're supposed to.

Distractedly, I feel the vehicle moving and, I allow myself to go limp and feign unconsciousness.

There's a chance that they snatched me because I'm alone not because of my title. If it's because of my title the rat doesn't know me on a personal level. If that's the case, then when I get out of this, they're going to get to know me extremely well.

Calloused hands lift me up roughly, I'm tossed over one of their shoulders. My first instinct is to nail the guy with my knee but I don't. Last time I checked unconscious people don't knee men in the balls.

Unceremoniously, I'm dropped into a hard chair and, the bag is yanked off my head. Watching through my lashes, I see at the cuffs they snap around my wrists. I allow my body to remain limp. I even go so far as to start sliding sideways off the chair.

The man behind me mutters a curse and quick dives to catch me which is hilarious.

Now that the bag is off my head I can see the men—some shady government agency like in the movies. They're wearing minor Magiks wards too. I can smell them in the room as well.

A lot of Feyrie could be contained with them. I'm not most.

Tired of playing possum I pop my eyes open and sit up leaning my elbows on the table. I'm connected to it by the handcuffs which are annoying but not a hindrance. Cadey could break them.

They all jump back. Pussies.

"Did you sedate her, Eric?" the big blonde one in front of me asks one of the ones behind me.

"Yes, Greg. I gave her the max dose."

"Give her another one," Greg insists. That's not a good idea.

Greg—better be glad I'm curious. They want something either from Feyrie or me in general. I look down at the handcuffs annoyed. I scratch two words into the metal table with a claw.

Fuck you. It suits the moment.

The door opens. Another human man, wearing a cheap black polyester suit, joins me at the table. Clearing his throat he rests his elbows on the table and regards me.

Am I supposed to be intimidated?

"Name?" he asks after a quick glance at the words I scratched into the table.

Humans aren't completely stupid. But they aren't prepared either. Good.

"I have one, yes," I answer, staring right back at him.

Lifting my upper lip, I test the air. He's well-armed. I smell two guns, at least, one knife and—I inhale again—an electronic device of some kind that isn't a cell phone. A taser I think they call them?

Taking in his whole person I get the info I can. Blonde hair with graying around the edges standard military cut. He's even somewhat handsome by human standards. Tan skin, light blue eyes with crow's feet in the corners possibly from spending a lot of time outside. Hiding in the jungle, Rambo-style, probably.

No wedding ring but he smells faintly of sex.

"Get lucky this morning, eh?" Other than the slight widening of his eyes and the speeding up of his pulse in the vein in his forehead there are no other reactions. Tilting my head to the side, I say, "I suggest you hurry this along because, I'm getting bored and you won't like me that way."

"What do you know about vampires and shifters?" He's a direct kind of guy. A not very informed one, too.

"That I'm neither because they aren't real?"

"We'll be doing some blood work shortly to determine your exact species," he continues in that dull, monotone voice of his.

Obviously he doesn't believe me not that I care. They won't be doing their blood work on me.

"Time's a-ticking," I say, feigning a glance at the non-existent watch on my wrist.

"This building is completely secure against your kind. You will not be leaving." His voice is serious, sounding almost bored.

I snort. This fella thinks he's way more informed than he is.

"I allowed you to bring me here, bud. So you gonna tell me why you snatched me up?" My glamour is good—I know for a fact it is. They can't pierce it with their gadgets and such. So yeah, someone either gave them pictures or is following me.

I'm distracted a lot lately. It won't surprise me to find out I was followed.

Taking a quick glance around, I roll my eyes. This is the perfect setup for dealing with a young vampire, shifter or a lower Magikally skilled Feyrie. The sedative would work on any of them. The wards can keep the vampires from using any form of coercion, the shifters from going partially zoo on them and the Feyrie from doing whatever that particular kind does.

Be interesting to find out what else they know. Something Magikal, that's for sure. They don't have these types of Magiks here— well, the vampires and shifters don't. A full-blood Feyrie might.

Really good chance they got their info from a Feyrie.

"We have sufficient experience keeping your kind here." He says it with such arrogance I kind of want to rip out his tongue. I might before all is said and done.

He's also wrong but, I'm not going to point it out. He shuffles through papers in a manila folder and says, "Our informant tells us that you are some type of leader. Is this fact?"

Some type of leader, eh? Yeah, they were after me specifically. And there's no point in playing human anymore either.

"It sounds like your informant has already answered all of your questions."

Letting my Magiks peek out a little the hair on my arms stands up. There are Feyrie in this building—I can feel them. Barely. I try to look for them on the web but, something is blocking me. Apparently the warding wherever they are being kept is a bit better than this room.

Up close and personal I can deal with the wards but, I can't do anything from here.

Find them. A few of the Fiends peel off from the swelling number of them to search. There are so many now that the G-man across from me is looking over his shoulder.

Yeah you should be nervous, blondie.

"We are going to see how big of a threat you are to national security. You are at this moment remanded into scientific custody for your species and purpose to be determined," he goes on in that robotic voice I'm starting to intensely dislike.

This gets my full attention. This is not the first time he's given that speech.

"You mean to cut me open and see what makes me tick?"

He nods at my question.

Leaning my elbows on the table, I move closer to him. "You okay with them cutting up people like me for scientific study?" I watch his face carefully for his answer.

"Protecting mankind is my only concern."

I laugh and it startles him. He's full of crap. I saw the flash of guilt on his face. He's good at schooling his emotions but, I'm just as good at reading them.

"I can understand wanting to protect your kind really well. And if you release *my* kind from your dungeon or whatever you have here, I'm not a threat to your kind."

My words are met with a stone wall. I can tell by the look on his face that it's not an option. Shame.

The force of me standing disconnects the shackles from the table. The links ping loudly off the floor in the sudden stillness of the room. Holding my bound wrists up in front of him I pull them apart—amused when he ducks to avoid flying metal bits.

Jumping to his feet, he draws a gun and aims it at me.

"You gonna shoot me?" I ask, watching him closely, almost hoping he does so I have an excuse to beat the shit out of him. Not that I don't already have one.

A trickle of sweat winds its way down his face. He's thinking about it. "They will kill you if you leave this room," he threatens.

"I'll kill you if I stay in it."

The sound of running feet draws part of my attention to the door. Reinforcements. My eyes catch the blinking red light of the camera in the upper corner of the room.

Is their informant watching? I stare straight at it and mouth three words: I'll find you.

The whispers of the fiends send my temper straight to lost. Before my brain registers my movement I have the human by his throat against the wall. His gun is now a mangled mess of metal on the floor.

"You have children as prisoners?" I demand with a growl. How dare they!

Satisfyingly, fear bleeds into his eyes.

"How can—" He swallows against my grip, the one that isn't quite tight enough to choke the life out of him yet. "—you possibly know that?"

"Where are they?" I hiss out between clenched teeth.

There is no patience left in me for a human, or any person, who captures and experiments on children. Seeing the refusal in his eye, I use the one thing against him that even the strongest creatures fear. Their mortality.

"If you don't tell me I will kill everyone here to get to them, including you. Choose."

I watch the decision form in his eyes; he believes I'll do it. Smart of him because I will.

"They're on level one." Growling at his answer, I drop him. "You will never get to them."

"The next time we meet it'll be on my terms. If you capture any more of mine you won't need to run tests. I'll show you what I am." I pause then turn back to him, "One day you'll need my kind to save your stupid asses. Pray that I'm in a giving mood when you come begging."

With those parting words I head towards the door. Gripping the handle I yank the door right off its hinges and fling it behind me. The entire hallway is filled with humans, all fully armed, with those guns aimed right at me.

My Magiks roar awake.

The humans open fire.

Bullet after bullet slams into me flinging me around like a puppet. The impact of them drives me to my knees. After what feels like an eternity the gunfire stops leaving the hallway choked with the smell of sulfur and human sweat. I raise my head to look at them, smiling. As one, the fired bullets fall to the ground.

My Magiks caught them all.

"My turn." Darkness engulfs the hallways as the fiends let loose. I run forward and dive into the men slashing out with the daggers that materialize in my hands. Easily, I dodge in and out of the chaos, trying to disable without killing them.

The fiend's roars have the humans panicking and screaming as they're pulled into the darkness for seconds knocking them unconscious. A trip through the NetherRealm will do that to a human.

I don't want to kill any more of them than necessary. I just want to get my people out.

At the other end of the hallway I stop and look back over my shoulder at the path I took. Most of them are out like a light but, some are awake and moaning in pain. All of them are alive.

Blondie is standing in the doorway of the room I left eyes wide in surprise. Just to be a dick I blow him a kiss and duck into the next hallway at a run.

If I'm correct I have three floors to get through. My path takes me into a lobby where another group of armed men waits for me. There are three times as many this time. I grit my teeth and run at them because, they aren't getting the chance to fire first this time.

Make sure there's none of my blood left, I ask the fiends. I hate to exhaust them for something so trivial but, it's important they don't get to run their tests. I watch science fiction movies. Blood samples always lead to bad things.

Wading into the men, knives flashing, I push myself to hurry. Sliding across the floor on my knee I grab an earpiece off a fallen man. Won't hurt to know what's going on. I shove it in my ear and duck between the legs of another guy. It's comical how he looks between his legs for me—even more so when I grab him by his hair and pull him through.

Grabbing a keycard from a belt of another man I run towards the elevators. God, I'm totally glad I'm a TV addict.

The fiends can finish with the rest of them. The elevator opens, and I hurry inside. Now there should be buttons…. where are the buttons? I push the down arrow and nothing happens. Oh, the card. I scan the card and exhale in relief when the doors shut.

"More reinforcements are inbound. They have the mages with them. Headquarters thinks they can get her under control. They want the package at all costs, over?" The voice in the earpiece makes me glad I stole the thing. The main question right now is where did they get mages? And what is this package? Me?

"Clearance denied. Please scan the correct badge for admittance to lower floors," the robotic voice informs me.

This won't do. Hastily, I study the floor impatience winning out. I punch my hand through it. With a groan of tearing metal, I make the hole bigger. Without hesitation, I drop down through it.

And as I fall my pride gives up. I call out, *'Phobe, I kind of got myself in a pickle.'*

It's not a big surprise when I get no answer. This place is warded more heavily the lower I get.

The concrete buckles when I land with my knees bent one hand on the floor to steady me. Jumping to my feet I shove through the closed elevator doors landing on the floor.

Ouch.

But now I can feel them. Feyrie. So fragile. Some barely alive. Some already dead.

Angrier now I climb to my feet and run at the next set of double doors. Leaping I take them to the ground and stay on my feet. Time is running out. If they do, in fact, have people here who can wield light or blood Magiks they can hurt me, a lot. But more importantly, they can injure the other Feyrie that are already hurting enough.

Men and women in lab coats yell at me as I pass and, soldiers sporadically fire guns at me. I will not be dissuaded. The bullets aren't hitting me. The fiends guard my back sacrificing their limited energy to take on physical form.

Feeling the urgency, I pick up my speed until the walls blur.

I don't stop running until I find myself in a corridor lined with doors. No, cells. All with wards on them. Without thought, I let the Magiks out, ripping through the wards as quickly as I can. Each one hurts but, thankfully I've got a pretty high tolerance to pain.

There are so many of them. I can only stare as they come to stand in the doorway with their eyes on me. The ones that can walk are carrying the ones that can't. But there are more. Yanking on the doors still closed I run from room to room, helping when I can, but there is something—something is calling me.

I find it towards the end of the hallway. I ignore the humans in lab coats clustering around it. This is the one.

Yanking the door open I look inside and find myself wishing I had killed them all. A sterile white crib sits alone in the room surrounded by beeping machines and tubes snaking into the bed. Reaching outside the door, I grab the closest human.

"What have you done to him?" I demand, giving her a little shake.

"He is sedated," she answers in a wobbly voice.

172

"Unhook him from all of this shit." When she hesitates I put my face right up next to her face and yell, "NOW!"

She hastens to do as ordered.

Heart in my throat I walk towards the bed.

Inside lies a teeny, tiny baby. A Nightmare. He's naked with no diaper or blanket for warmth. So small and delicate. Gently, I touch his little forehead letting out the breath I didn't realize I'm holding when his little red eyes shoot open.

As the grogginess clears from them they zero in on me. Minos— his name is Minos. He lets out a little mewl of sound and, my heart constricts.

It's always the children that suffer.

He cooes up at me. Emaciated, each one of his bones sticks out in vivid details through the scales of his skin. What did this poor baby do to deserve this from them? The adults I can see them tinkering with but a baby?

I can't grasp the reasons why.

"Hey there, bud." I smile as I say it feeling the flare of him on the Web.

This little guy is a strong one. I motion for the human to undo the rest of the tubes and wires as I grab the sheet off the bed making a sling to lay Minos in carefully. I tie it securely and turn to leave before I kill them all.

"My lady, let me help you." At the voice, another strand pulls to life within me. I raise my eyes to meet those of a dragon but not the wing-less. Behind her stand others. As I look at each one, in turn, the web twangs. It's almost overwhelming.

"I've got him. Let's just get the hell out of here. We're not leaving anyone behind."

She – Arista, her name is Arista – nods at my words looking nervously behind her. "Most will need to be carried. We cannot fight, my lady."

The earpiece squawks from my hair. I shove it back in my ear.

"We are—" Heavy gunfire. "—under attack from an unknown entity." My heart rate increases. "Sir! We need orders now!Nothing is stopping it. SIR, respond!"

"We have to go, now." I hurry from the room cradling my precious burden carefully and head for the stairs since I broke the elevator. It's the only way up. As I walk, I count. There are a total of twenty prisoners counting Minos.

Miraculously no one lags behind even with the bad shape some are in. When we hit the main floor I don't waste any time trying to be gentle with the humans anymore. Using the last of the fiends I clear the way to the front door. My Magiks are running on empty; all the light Magiks drained the shit out of me.

The good thing is I'm pissed.

"Anyone know how to drive?" I yell, blowing the glass front doors out. I don't even have time to gape at the black claws my Magiks form to tear through it.

"I do," Arista answers.

I spot a large truck not too far away and I lead them towards it. Luckily something else is holding most of the human's attention. Or should I say someone else?

Someone that can sling an armored truck at least fifteen feet in the air.

Yanking open the tailgate I usher everyone in. After the last one I hand the baby up.

"You keep them safe—do you understand me, Arista?"

She nods solemnly and goes around to the front of the truck.

"Go to the Sidhe. Let your Magiks guide you," I yell, turning back towards the carnage behind me.

Thankfully someone left the keys in the ignition and, I hear the truck rumble off. Coming around the corner of the building I stop.

Before me stand several Schoth, in chains, and even more soldiers. My kind aren't the only prisoners here.

A human man steps forward. He's round in the middle and wearing a suit that is a size too small. His head is completely bald and, he looks harmless. But I don't miss that edge of intelligence in his eyes.

174

Or the small barreled gun that's leveled at me. It's still smoking from being recently fired. Shit. My eyes flick down to the dart sticking out of my chest.

Pulling it out I throw it at him. For a minute I get a little woozy, but, I can feel my body already ridding itself of the drugs.

They've got to do better than that.

"If you come peacefully I won't blow up the truck," the little bald man says with a smug smile.

There's him doing better. I believe he'll do it too—children or not.

A helicopter races over our heads going in the same direction as the truck. The fiends are exhausted and, I can't take on rockets. I just don't have enough left to try and catch up with the truck.

My Magikal muscles aren't strong enough yet.

What choice do I honestly have? This asshole will kill them. Clenching my jaw I nod my head reluctantly.

He raises a cell phone to his ear and says, "Package secure. Deal with the other problem and meet us back at headquarters. Jarvis out."

A familiar darkness reaches out to me. I almost want to cry from the relief of it. I'm smiling as they cuff me and lead me back towards the building. Already the schoth are chanting their spells and tightening the Magiks on the cuffs holding me.

"I expected you to be more difficult considering all of the damage you've caused. It will take me weeks to get things running again because of you," Jarvis complains while pulling me roughly by my arm.

As we come to the front of the building I laugh a little. There is devastation everywhere. Smashed vehicles, small fires and dead people. I didn't cause this damage, but I know who did.

Several of them yell out in surprise as something crashes into the building. A fiery ball of mashed metal—or what was known a few minutes ago as the helicopter he sent after my people.

I laugh louder, unable to help myself. Jarvis just lost his ace in the hole.

Inside I start picking at the light Magiks holding me prisoner keeping me from calling out to the man I know is close by. A dark form lands in a spray of concrete between us and what's left of the front of the building.

"What the hell happened to the helicopter?" Jarvis yells at his phone.

Several military grade vehicles pull up behind us. Armed humans pile out to face a threat. That threat is standing there, swords in hand, with black smoke rolling off his body. He raises his burning eyes and looks at me.

"He happened to it," I answer Jarvis's question.

Phobe's upper lips curls as a spray of bullets hit him. He blurs as he moves. I watch, somewhat mesmerized, as his fist comes down on the hood of the car the bullets came from.

"What in the hell is that?" Jarvis demands in his phone again, hiding a little behind me. The chicken.

Phobe looks at the little bald man and then me. Jumping in the air he comes down on another car. The screech of metal panics the soldiers standing around us. They run for cover from the man standing in a small crater that was a car staring at me.

"God, that's—that's…run, run!" one of the schoth yells.

I look over at him. He's trying to drag the other ones that he's shackled to terrified eyes on Phobe. Either he knows him or he knows that a Feyrie doing what Phobe is doing is dangerous.

Either way, he's smarter than the rest of them.

"Put her down," Jarvis orders the frightened schoth.

Light Magiks flare around me the pain rolling in my stomach drops me to my knees. They lock around me like a steel trap. Teeth clenched I try to use my poor Magiks to fight it but, I expended way too much getting out of the building.

"Do you know what that creature is?" Jarvis asks, leaning down to look me in the face. He shakes me when I don't answer.

"You should run," I grit out to the schoth, even though their Magiks are tightening around me like a vice stealing my breath. They're in shackles too.

"We cannot, Feyrie. Our king ordered us so," the solo female answers, right before feeding more power into the spell holding me.

Their choice.

"Human, we should leave her and go. That creature will kill us all," that same male schoth encourages. He's staring at me with horror.

Frowning, I look down.

Darkness swirls around my knees and slowly starts climbing up my body. As it progresses and thickens, the pain eases.

"We are not leaving without her. Do your goddamn jobs before I throw you in a cell with the others," Jarvis orders.

My eyes drift closed as they start chanting again. A hand slides up my hip to rest on my stomach. I know that hand. My eyes fly open as I'm pulled to my feet and against a warm, hard body. Then he's gone.

"Death is your champion, Feyrie," one of the female schoth says, right before her head disappears off her shoulders to bounce across the pavement.

That's a good statement right there. Off with their heads.

"Where did he go? Does anyone have eyes on him?" Jarvis is yelling into his phone again.

The other two schoth open their eyes in surprise at the same time and both disappear into the darkness. Phobe apparently needs snacks.

The sad thing is Jarvis doesn't notice their disappearance at all. Or the head sitting right next to his foot.

The release of my body from the light Magiks is the highlight of my day. Shaking out my arms I break the cuffs holding me. While I was busy with my internal struggle, and the crap with Jarvis here, Phobe was busy.

There are bodies everywhere. Another vehicle pulls up and, the driver is yanked into darkness door and all.

Show off.

"I will kill all of your little pets if you don't—" Jarvis begins what I'm sure will be a lovely tirade on killing my family if I don't cooperate.

I'm tired but a point needs to be made.

Taking a step forward I punch Jarvis in the face. He flies backward into a car leaving a dent in the door. He's not dead but, he's going to hurt when he wakes up. It's only fair.

Rotating my shoulders I force the weariness to take a backseat. I've got a little more in me. Inky black smoke crawls down my hands to form the fiend daggers.

A group of men circle me, guns pointed, yelling for my surrender. My daggers lengthen into swords. Smiling, I move.

A shape blurs past me, catches my arm, and spins me. Knowing the feel of him I relax and let him throw me at the group of men. Flipping mid-air I spin my body and the swords become a deadly version of a blender.

Landing on my knees, I lean all the way back in a mock dance pose to see Phobe lift a truck and bring it down on another truck. Effectively smashing everything in between.

'You just made a truck sandwich,' I say to him, rolling backwards to a crouch.

Swinging out with my leg I sweep a man's feet out from under him. As he falls Phobe appears above him and slams him several inches into the pavement. His eyes meet mine for a second and, then he's gone again.

Dancing to the side, I avoid a spray of bullets, and snatch the weapon out of the man's hands and hit him with it. Shooting someone who has their back turned is just rude. Then I shoot his gawking companion and hit the first man with his gun again.

I finish him off by kicking him across the clearing. Seeing him broken and bloody hits me in the gut with guilt.

'This is going to cause a war and these guys? They're innocent. What the fuck am I doing?' I say to Phobe, staring at the damage around me.

'These humans are not innocent soldiers. They are not soldiers at all. Stop feeling fucking guilty.'

I ponder him a moment. He is many things but, he won't lie to me. With a mock salute, I say, 'Aye, aye, captain dick.'

Another truck pulls up and, as the driver begins to open the door, I run at it, jump, and hit it with both feet—effectively trapping the legs of the driver. A sword through the window finishes him off.

A quick breath and I move again. Over and over, blood and more blood. They just keep coming and, Phobe and I keep killing them. He's quite good at it.

A lot better at it than I am because at some point I can't move anymore so, I stop and simply watch him. Phobe doesn't seem tired at all and, I'm pretty sure the bastard is having fun.

A walkie-talkie squawks on the ground at my feet. Weary, I ignore it. It's taking my precious last drops of energy to watch Phobe.

And what a thing he is to watch. The runes on him are lit up slithering around on his skin like glowing snakes. It's rather awesome actually. How do I get some of those?

Looking up at his face I find myself blushing because he caught me staring so, I give him a cheesy smile. With fiery eyes focused on me he smirks as he starts walking towards me.

Uh-oh.

Eyes searching, he cups my cheek with a bloody hand.

"What the fuck are you things?" someone screams in my ear as an arm snakes around my throat. The cold metal of a gun presses against the side of my head right at my temple. A bullet shouldn't kill me unless it's to my head. That just might.

I sigh. I'm not nearly as worried about it as I should be. If he shoots me I'll get a nap. Might be a permanent one but still.

Phobe doesn't break our staring contest.

'Do you ever take anything seriously, Iza?'

'Sometimes, but mostly no,' I answer honestly.

Phobe grunts at my answer and punches the man holding the gun to my head. I look over my shoulder to see him several feet away his face a bloody mess of pulp and bone.

Well, I can never accuse Phobe of hitting like a girl.

Speaking of hitting like a girl I look over to where I left Jarvis and he's gone. He's alive then but, I think the problem of him is temporarily solved. There will be other more dangerous problems to deal with in the immediate future.

Mentally shaking myself I call out to the fiends to check that the truck made it to the Sidhe. My poor fiends are faint they're so tired. I'll have to find a way to make it up to them. A present of some kind.

"Iza, are you ready to go?"

"Home?" He nods at my question.

Frowning, I look around me. Walking home will take too long. I eye a Humvee. I've been meaning to teach myself how to drive. Crossing to the truck I drag the dead driver out of the seat and climb up in it.

"You are serious?" Phobe asks from outside the door.

Smiling, I turn the key. It makes an awful grinding sound.

"Iza, it is already running."

Oh. "Get the hell in. We gotta go."

Rolling his eyes, he walks around the truck to climb inside.

Did Phobe just roll his eyes at me? My smile broadens. I'm rubbing off on him. All right, now, time to get this sucker going.

"Put your foot on the brake and move the gear shift to the D," Phobe explains patiently.

With a small jerk, I manage to do this. Aha.

"Gas pedal time?"

"Yes, you lightly—"

I floor it. The crunching of metal brings us to a jarring halt.

"Lightly, Iza."

"I did!" I defend. Even though I didn't.

This time when I put the gear shift on the R, I lightly tap the gas. We crash into another truck. Perhaps my version of lightly and his version of lightly aren't the same?

"Now you—Iza, do you need me to drive?"

Frowning at him I put the gear shift back to D. "No, I'm driving and, you're going to deal with it."

"I am very glad I cannot die from a car accident."

"Why do you think there will be an—oops." The tree came out of nowhere, I swear.

"Iza."

"The car still moves so I'm driving, Phobe."

CHAPTER THIRTY-FOUR

 hobe

IZA DRIVING IS MORE disastrous than any other experience I have ever had in a vehicle. She is managing to drive worse than I suspected she would. It is the closest thing to fear that I have felt ever. The handle above the window is the first casualty of this adventure with her.

The second is more than likely going to be the law enforcement vehicle currently following us. Something Iza is aware of but she refuses to pull over until the truck dies. If the noises coming from it now are any indication it is in the process of doing so.

Considering she has struck at least five cars and a couple of trees since this started I am surprised it is moving at all.

"Why haven't they gone away yet?" she mutters under her breath.

"They will pursue you until you stop."

She sighs dramatically and says, "Fine, I'll pull over."

With a shudder and a mechanical cough the truck dies the minute she puts it into park. With an annoyed smack of the steering wheel she climbs out of the truck.

'I recommend using your glamour. You are covered in—never mind.'

There is already a gun in her face and an officer yelling at her to get down on the ground. Iza is staring at him in confusion. This is not going to end well.

Frowning at the officer, Iza grabs his gun and crushes it then hands it back to the shocked man. In reaction he sprays something noxious at her. Mace, they call it mace. She staggers and leans against the truck rubbing at her eyes.

I suppose I should help her. Otherwise we are going to be here for hours.

"Get out of the car with your hands up!" someone yells through the window.

"Don't hurt them Phobe no matter how much I kinda want to. They are just doing their jobs,' Iza says, still rubbing at her eyes with the hem of her shirt.

She knows me well enough to know I was about to eat him.

Fine.

Opening the door with just enough force to knock him down I climb out of the truck. Grabbing a bottle of water off the floor I walk around the front to Iza. Her face is beet-red and her eyes are now bloodshot.

Opening the bottle I turn it up and dump the entire bottle on her face. That should help.

"On the ground or I will open fire," yells the officer who maced her.

"Okay, that's enough of this shit. Let's go," Iza says blinking to clear her vision some more.

I grab her around the waist and run.

CHAPTER THIRTY-FIVE

Iza

GOD, my eyes are still burning. What in the world kind of torture device is this mace? Do I need to get some for the assholes who keep coming here trying to kill me?

"Iza, you can stop whining now. I've healed the actual injuries," Nika chastises.

Apparently, I was complaining out loud. Again.

"It still stings."

"It will for a few hours. There is no way to get it off your skin completely. Not even with Magiks," she answers, smacking me on the arm as I walk off.

"Did you get the new Feyrie fed? I need to ask them questions and, I'd rather they have some comfort first," I ask Jameson as he catches up to me.

I'm already heading towards the wing the Sidhe made for them. I ask for Auryn to be summoned.

"Yes, and the healers have already been to see them as well. Arista is asking for you," he answers, sliding his finger across the screen of the brand new iPad he's carrying.

I kind of miss the sound of the pages flipping.

The Sidhe makes my walk a fast one taking me straight to their wing by forming passages for me to walk the most direct route. I find several of the healing Feyrie there, hovering—especially over the small ones.

Most especially Minos.

Goblins are flashing in and out of existence bringing supplies and tending to the ones who need tending. I look around at all of them, but, my eyes are drawn again to Minos.

He's sitting up in a baby seat his red eyes following me.

I feel the smile form on my face while bending down to pick him up. "Well hello there, handsome. I have someone I want you to meet."

"My lady, I was told you—god, is that a Nightmare child?" Right on time.

"Yes, Auryn. I have a feeling he's connected to you. All things considering."

Eyes wide, she puts a shaking hand out for Minos to wrap his own tiny one around her finger. Clearing her throat, she says, "One of my daughters disappeared. This… this is her child."

"His name is Minos. I think that he wants to be with Grandma." I hand him over to her and look for Arista. Minos will be taken care of incredibly well. He needs to be with his family.

Arista isn't a wingless so, it's strange that Kael gave her up to the humans. There's a story there and, I want to hear it. In clean clothes, she steps out of a room off to the side and smiles at me hesitantly.

I smile back and hope it's kindly. I'm still working on it.

"I need you to tell me how—" I indicate the room full of people. "—this happened."

"The king came to me a year ago…" Arista looks around and hesitates. The room blurs around us as the Sidhe sensing my need for privacy obliges. Well, that's neat.

"Continue," I urge.

"He came to me a year ago and said I needed to go into town and meet a man who was going to provide some much needed supplies for our colony. I was surprised by the request. I'd never been asked to leave before, but I went because the King ordered me to." For a moment her eyes burn amber with anger.

Then she continues, "They knew exactly what was. They were prepared for a fight and, I didn't even shift before I was knocked out cold. I woke up in that place surrounded by other Feyrie." She clenches her jaw a few times and continues.

"There were other dragons there in the beginning—special ones. The wingless. They are supposed to be revered by dragonkin but, our king insisted that none survived birth since his father's reign. He lied to all of us. Wingless cannot shift but, they wield potent Magiks. Some of them are children, my lady."

"How many?" I ask.

"Eleven. They moved them somewhere else a few days ago. Our king he betrayed them. He betrayed us all."

He's the one who told them about me but, he isn't the spy still here. That sonofabitch bartered people—I'll get them back and, then I'll deal with Kael. Or perhaps it isn't me that will deal with him.

"You're safe here. Kael can't hurt you. I'll find the wingless."

And I will.

"My lady, in the time I've been there—there have been hundreds of Feyrie brought there."

This brings me up short. Hundreds?

"Where are they?" I demand.

"They've sent them to other facilities spread throughout the world. I heard the humans talking."

"Do you know of any specifically?"

She wrings her hands in anxiety as she answers. "I know some of the towns."

"That's a start. Can you please give them all to Jameson?" She nods and, because I have no idea how to help her feel better, I stand there awkwardly.

"Come, Arista, let's get you some hot food." Nika to the rescue. The adrenaline that's been sustaining me for the last month is

185

gone I think. And the mental momentum I manage to keep up falls around me in broken shards. I'm shaky and there were dead Feyrie in some of those cells. They were dead. A car's ride away from me and they were dead.

Minos's mother is dead.

My mother is dead.

At damn near a run I head outside.

The crunch of snow under my feet is strange and sort of soothing. It's the first time I've seen snow in... ever. I slow my pace and watch the fat snowflakes fall dancing like fairies on the wind.

They fill the air everywhere and a slight breeze makes them swirl around me in a little snow tornado. As I walk the long-buried memories of my mother carrying me on her scaly back in the snow-choked winds of the sky bursts in vivid detail in my brain.

The heat of a tear sliding down my cheek is quickly followed by another. I shove my hands in my pockets and keep walking. And the tears keep falling. Just like the snow.

For the first time since I escaped I can let go and truly grieve. For my mother, for the childhood ripped away from me and for the pure injustice of it all. Not because I have to but this time because I can.

Something I haven't let myself do. This will be my choice!

I walk until the toes of my boots touch the edge of the lake. Looking down at the calm waters my rage boils up. Letting the tears pour I scream into the night. Then I start kicking the ground. Over and over I kick it and, with each strike a little more pain comes out.

The pain for the people I didn't save. For the people I can't save. For the mother who died because of me. For everything I've lost and will lose. The wind and snow rip it away from me and pull into the cold waters of the lake.

"Why them?" I scream, into the night sky. "Why me?" I scream again, sobbing.

Tired of it all I collapse onto my knees in the snow. Ignoring the cold wetness seeping into my pants, I say, "To whatever god is out there, I beg you. Help me. They can't fight. If the Light Fey come they will be slaughtered and, I can't live with that. Please—" I sob, "—help me save them."

"Have you ever heard the story of creation?" The voice startles me. I look up to see the homeless man from the park. He's still wearing the orange filthy coat and no hat.

I hiccup, wipe my face to hide my shame and climb to my feet.

"No, can't say I have." I answer, pulling the hat off my head and putting it on his.

The Sidhe has no idea he's here. A human who can sneak past the Sidhe is an interesting human. Or not a human at all? He doesn't smell —well he smells a lot but, he doesn't smell non-human. Isn't this interesting? He smiles at me exposing the gap where his front teeth should be.

Hiccupping a sob—damn things don't go away—I try to smile back.

"I have a shack just over the hill there with a fire. I hope you don't mind it's there. I don't bother anyone." He turns and starts shuffling along.

Not really feeling like going back to the Sidhe—and incredibly curious about him—I follow.

"I heard all the yelling and came to make sure no one was fiddling about. When I saw you kneeling there I figured you might need someone to pull you from the place you were heading to. Not a good road to travel, grief." He pauses to catch his breath then continues, "Besides I kinda wanted some company."

He does indeed have a little shack. It even has a small window in the front that has the glowing flicker of a fire inside. He opens the door and ushers me in. Closing it behind him he dusts off one of the milk crates around the small fire and waves towards it.

Sitting on it I watch him move around to hang up his coat and the hat I gave him. He dusts off his own crate and smiles that gap-toothed smile again at me before sitting down.

This home is small but surprisingly clean.

"That's a fine hat. I appreciate you sharing it," he says, rubbing his hands together beside the fire.

I simply watch him. The feeling of calm I'm getting from being near him is nice and, I'm not going to question it. Not this time.

"Like I was saying—the story of creation. Strange that one like you has never heard of it. But then again not many care about it anymore. Shame that, it's a good story." He runs a wrinkled hand down his scruffy, bearded face then continues.

"When this world was born there were three: Light, Life and Darkness. And two of those three together created the first five. The sun, water, air, earth, and of course spirit. These first five were all given specific things to do and, because they were so happy doing it they became the things they were born to be." He pauses and blows his nose loudly into a worn handkerchief.

Then he resumes his story, "Life and Light, having made the first five, felt satisfied in their creations. But Darkness was the first to touch the world and didn't know what to create. So, Darkness made nothing." He pauses and opens up a can of sardines that he dug out of one of his pockets.

"One day, Life and Light go off to create in other places, other worlds. Darkness was left alone." He takes a long drink out of a dirty cup and offers it to me. I take it, sip then hand it back. It's the best water I've tasted in my life.

"Years later, Life stops in to check on Darkness and sees how empty the world is. Life shows him how to create and Darkness makes the Eldest, the second born." Slurping up a sardine, he smiles his gappy smile with fish on his teeth and says, "Life was concerned about the strength of these creations so, he gave each of them a specific task much like the first." He offers me a sardine, and of course I take it—it's food.

"When Light saw what Darkness created, Light became angry with Life for showing Darkness how to create. You see, worshiped by all the Light creations, Light considered themselves to be superior to Life and Darkness. So, when Darkness created the Feyrie, Light made ones opposite them. It became a competition to Light you see? So were born the races of the Light Fey. Oddly enough, the schoth were the first race of the Light Fey to be created. Humans call them elves here,

ya believe that?" He smiles at me again and eats the rest of his
sardines.

"Life, seeing how Light was so jealous, decided to make other
creations in other places. Including this world. Humans and every
animal and insect that graces this planet." He sighs. "Life ran and hid
like a coward."

He stares into the fire his blue eyes seeing something I can't. I wait.
I can sense the story isn't over.

"It's then that everything went wrong. The Light creatures began
to fight the Dark ones. And in that war a foolish vain creature tried to
capture and enslave his creator, the Darkness. So the Darkness ate
him. And in eating him, Darkness became aware like a man and in
that he began to hate and, as he hated he destroyed." A single crystal
tear runs down his cheek.

"For the first time since he became aware of existence Life touched
his feet to the world. Saddened by the bloodshed that existed even
before his brother took on the thoughts of the mortals he came to try
and stop it. And on his walk through the world he found a Feyrie
child dying on the road. A beautiful child with red eyes and wings.
She was given a mortal wound from a schoth arrow. She was days
away from her sixth birthday." Another tear falls down his cheek and,
my chest gets tight.

"With a heavy heart he sat and pulled the child onto his lap and
discovered just how special the child really was. "It was not the Darkness that caused this, she said to him.""

A shiver races up my spin. I know who this story is about.

"As she lay dying in his arms she whispered words to him in a
voice not her own speaking the very first Prophecy. This senseless
death made Life angry but, being the creature that he is, he cannot
take a life. He can only give it. So he did the only thing he could do.
He told another of the first Prophecy. And they told another. And so
forth and so on. Until it's taught to every Feyrie child born."

He lights a cigarette and offers me one. I decline.

"The rules always the rules, right? Stonewalled by his own rules,
Life could not change what was to come but he could nudge it. So he

did. So he does." He smiles a sad smile and, blows his nose on a stained tissue.

"Nice story," I comment.

A story told by a man who isn't a man. I just have no idea what he is. Still smells human and, I can't detect any glamour or Magiks.

So I ask, "How did a human come to know it?"

"I'm an old man who likes to gather stories. I have a good memory and, I've lived a long life." He smiles his gap-toothed smile and I smile back.

And I'm a rocket scientist.

"I heard you asking for help and, I bet you're not someone who asks for it often. So I'll put my two cents in this... I wouldn't be too surprised if the answer you're looking for is waiting right outside the door," he says with a rather smug smile on his face.

Standing I start to cross the small room to the window to see what's outside the door.

"Just a little longer if you don't mind. It's been a long time since I had such pleasant company."

Laughing a little I sit back down. Silly of me to think he meant literally.

"What kind of person do you think you are?"

I sigh. That's a good question. "I kill things." Oh, such eloquence I have.

"You know the girl at the prison? You gave her freedom from more suffering. She begged you for death and, you gave her the mercy of it. The others? They deserved what they got. Be what you were created to be."

Shocked, I lift my eyes to meet his and find they are no longer just blue. They are the prettiest, brightest blue I have ever seen. And I know them. They were the eyes of the girl I killed in the cafeteria.

And I thought of the few others that I tried to help over the years all with identical blue eyes. How did I not notice the sameness?

"It wasn't fair for you to suffer alone. So I tried to make sure that sometimes you had a little company or a way to show that heart you hide so deep. You gave everything you could to help others. Your food, your water and occasionally your laughter. That was the greatest gift of all. That despite all the shit you went through you still laugh. And you shared those laughs with me."

He reaches across the fire that moves away from him and wipes a tear off my face.

"The creature you are is what they need. Your Darkness is your army, Iza. He is the First, infinite. And he will fight them all for you. Let him be your wrath, your justice. Let your pain feed his rage. But still give him your hope, your faith and your love. And that laughter, Iza. Give him the laughter." He wipes away another tear.

And in a voice so gentle that it makes me fight to keep from crying harder, he says, "Does Phobe know you named your son after him before you even knew him? That the child they ripped from your body and murdered is the reason you will never bear another? Do he and your father know that the blood locks who did it haven't been brought to justice?" The words suck the oxygen right out of my lungs. "They do now." He leans forward and pats my cheek. "Your son is with your father. He has been for many years but, now your father knows it."

Frowning at me he says, "You need to stop hiding from that pain, girl. Use it."

He stands and he's no longer an old dirty man. Light and warmth radiate from where he stands. Pulling me by my numb hands to my feet he embraces me. With that embrace something inside of me that has long been broken heals a little.

As I pull away, and look into his blue eyes, I see things I will never see again.

"Destiny is what you make it. And you, my girl, will make yours count. I grant you what you asked me for from the deepest part of your heart—from that place that many forget. And even as you take life you give it. A rare balance that few can find but you have managed to find accidentally. Never lose that thing that makes you who you are." He kisses my cheek and then he's gone.

I plop back down on the crate. Holy shit, my mind has been completely melted. And to top it off, now I'm afraid to look outside.

CHAPTER THIRTY-SIX

hobe

IZA SNUCK out of the Sidhe without telling anyone again. The last time she did this she was taken by the humans. An endeavor, that although annoying in the beginning, ended up being a bit of fun towards the end.

It was a good learning experience for Iza as well. She needs to be pushed. Not babied like these creatures keep trying to do. I only stepped in with the humans because of the light Magiks. They caused her too much pain for me to it allow to continue.

Those are a weakness for her, light Magiks. There is no way to protect her from them unless I am there… which I cannot always be if she sneaks out.

Walking outside I find her footprints. The snow is falling, and I can see as I follow her trail where she stopped to look at it. Her tracks are deeper there.

I suspected she would like the snow.

Her tracks lead to the lake to a spot where the ground is torn up.

The smell of her anger is strong here the smell of… sadness even stronger. And something else a whisper of scent then it is gone with the breeze.

Frowning, I follow her tracks away from the lake to where they end at the top of a small hill. I can feel her ahead of me but, I cannot see her. Something is blocking me.

No, not something. Someone. A very familiar someone who should not be here but cannot seem to stop meddling. Instead of breaking through the barrier in front of me I wait. No one will harm her in there. Not this time.

Using my Magiks to poke a hole in the shield protecting her and the creator of it I peek in. A small shack with a light glowing merrily in the window greets me.

I can see her looking out the window then, she is gone. I can feel echoes of her turmoil through our bond. And there is something inside of me that is pulled to her because of it.

Fighting that pull is irritating but necessary. This time I will not interfere. This time.

But I can listen and what I hear… death will not be enough.

CHAPTER THIRTY-SEVEN

Iza

WALKING into the Sidhe after the disturbing but enlightening encounter with the All-Father—because only an idiot wouldn't know it was him—I head straight for the kitchen.

I'm starving.

"I've looked for you everywhere, Iza." Jameson says, coming up behind me at the counter where I decided to make myself a sandwich.

I chased a house goblin off with a relatively good-natured growl. I want to do this my damn self.

"Yes, my lady. Alagard informed us that you were having him train the children." Nika says, before Jameson can speak up.

I pause mid-mayo and look up at Nika. Understanding her concerns is fine but she needs to understand mine as well.

I say, "I don't want them defenseless. They aren't going to be on the front lines of anything but, they have every right to know how to protect themselves. Those children *need* that." I start to make my sandwich.

Going back to the fridge I rummage around for things to put on it besides mayo and lunchmeat. A can of sardines snags my attention making me smile a little. I grab pickles and hot peppers too. And spray cheese, spray cheese is good on everything.

I'm going to make a supreme sandwich. Throwing it all together with a grunt of satisfaction I take the first bite. Oh my god, it's so good.

"That's disgusting, Iza. I have no idea how you're eating that right now," Jameson comments, covering his mouth.

Taking another bite I smile and very maturely open my mouth and show him my half-chewed food. When he gags I laugh and immediately choke. Coughing and laughing at the same time I'm able to breathe again and continue eating my masterpiece.

Nika and Jameson are watching me with mirrored looks of horror. You'd think I just killed someone with the way they're looking at me.

"Back to the children. Iza you cannot let them be taught weapons at such a young—"

I cut her off. "Those children have already suffered because, they couldn't fight back. I will *not* have it happen again. They will train the same as everyone else. They will learn how to use their own abilities. They will learn weapons and, they will learn hand-to-hand. None here will be defenseless ever again, understand?" Speech done I eat the last bite of my sandwich and start looking for chocolate. I know there's some hiding in here somewhere.

"Iza, I don't think—"

Turning to Nika I frown at her. "The shit done to them... you really have no idea. You saw the wounds on the outside not the ones on their souls. They want to stop being victims and, I'm going to make sure that they can."

She looks at me and I can see the urge to argue in her eyes but, she clamps her mouth shut. I have a point and, she knows it. The old ways of doing things are over.

"But with guns, my lady?" Oh, there's the real pickle with Nika. Guns.

"I love knives and swords. They work against a lot of things... but not everything believes in a fair fight. This world here is full of creatures that don't believe in honorable combat. They only believe in putting a gun to your head and pulling the trigger," I explain.

"I feel like they are blasphemous to our ways," she grumbles.

"Nika, they will be using them so, we need to be using them. It's not the 1800s anymore. And you're forgetting one very important detail."

"What's that, my lady."

"I don't believe in your ways." I grab a bag of cookies and leave the kitchen.

The patter of feet trying to catch up makes me sigh. Jameson was strangely quiet during our little chat in the kitchen. I'm betting that he's—

"Iza... my lady, I don't disagree with Nika."

—just dying to say something.

"That's nice." I keep walking.

"Children are helpless. They should be cherished and protected."

At his words I stop walking and, he walks right into my back.

"Those children, our children... have had things done to them that would turn your hair white. They had their innocence, their freedom, their pride stripped away from them. Do not argue with me about allowing them to have their dignity." My tone is firm. I'm not going to change my mind.

The kids asked me, all of them. Even little Cadey. So yeah they can learn to fight and, no one will stop them. Not unless they want to deal with me... in a bad mood.

"Are you sure this is the right thing to do?"

I turn around at his question. He's a breath from me so stepping up into his personal space is easy.

"You had a pretty good childhood didn't you?" He nods at my question. "I didn't. Those kids didn't. Ruthie's mother was murdered and, she was bartered to the pack alpha for a debt of two hundred dollars. Michael's parents were murdered in front of him and, he lived on the street as the errand boy for a bunch of blood suckers." I have no choice but to tell them—otherwise they'll fight me tooth and nail.

So I keep going. "Lissa was raped when she was seven and, even though she fought back it wasn't enough. Cadey and Louise were beaten and starved right along with their sister. And Knox—" I swallow the lump in my throat. "—he was used for years as a sex slave by a pack of perverts that I pulled apart like bread for what they did to him. This is the kind of world we live in, Jameson, not the one you both imagine exists. Now, if you question my judgement on it one more time, I will rip your goddamn heads off." By the end of my tirade, because it's absolutely a tirade, I'm yelling.

Both are staring at me in shock.

Laughing humorlessly, I continue, "You two thought they were just poor and maybe slapped around a little?" After a moment they both nod. "God, open your fucking eyes."

With that said I turn around and head towards my room. That shit gave me a headache. Stress-ache. How can those two call themselves Feyrie? To roll over and show their bellies. No wonder the Feyrie lost.

CHAPTER THIRTY-EIGHT

hobe

IZA'S ANGER calls me to her. I find her sitting at the end of the dock at the lake her feet hovering inches above the freezing water. She is wrapped in a fluffy coat of some kind with a neon pink hat on her head.

The cold does not really bother her, so I imagine it was one of the many mother hens. I go to work once again on her shields. Her thoughts are hidden from me. Thoughts she is putting effort into hiding.

This is becoming a bad habit for her. But now it is only ever a temporary one.

"When will you stop keeping me out?" I ask softly, coming up to stand beside her.

She tosses a stick into the water. "We've had this talk before, Phobe."

Yes, we have. That does not mean I have changed my stance on it. "We can try that thing again."

She laughs a little as she says, "You mean talking?"

"Yes, that thing."

"Nika and Jameson are pissed off I'm letting the children train."

Foolish Feyrie. Iza is doing what is best for her people now. "You are doing the right thing," I say in agreement with her.

"Oh, I know. What bothers me is they think it's okay for the kids to be completely defenseless. That really fucking bothers me."

Then it is not their judgement concerning her. It is their naivety.

"When they see that the atrocities actually exist they will change their minds," I say.

She looks up at me and her eyes flash black.

"I don't care if they change their minds. My gut tells me it's the right thing to do. My Magiks tell me it's the right thing to do. They can take their opinions and shove—" Her words cut off suddenly and, she frowns at me right before she is yanked off the dock into the water.

Something she is kicking at under the water is dragging her towards the middle of the lake. Water nymphs.

Fuck, she distracts me too much!

Feeling my Magiks flare angrily to life I watch and I wait. I cannot and will not coddle her. Iza needs to be strong. She can do this. She meets my eyes and gives me a smile of pure mischief. The tightness in my chest eases.

You'd think since they live in water they'd use soap once in a while.' She would comment on something so unimportant to the situation.

'They snuck in during the barbecue, I imagine, and have lurked here waiting. There is a bounty on our heads.' It is the only way they could have gotten past the Sidhe.

My shadows lash out and come into contact with one of them. They pulled her away from me because they were warned about me. In this case it is not me they should fear. Watching the churning surface, I find it hard not to jump in and help her but, I know she can do this herself. And she wants to.

Iza has some scheme in her head I am sure. Plus the chit is having fun with it. The sound of running feet comes from behind me. I am not the only one who watches her.

"Where is the lady?" Adriem asks as he stops at the edge of the water.

Nightmares are not keen on swimming. The fact that he is considering it will impress Iza.

"Water nymphs," I answer.

I start counting down in my head. One hundred and twenty seconds is how long she has before I go in after her, whether she wants me to or not. I feel her irritation waft across our bond.

'One hundred seconds,' I say to tweak her tail.

"Iza doesn't know how to swim." Michael's soft voice sends a wave of irritation straight through me.

That sneaky fucking—

Water explodes upwards in a funnel, and Iza rises out of the water, her Magiks a dark shadow around her. She is laughing at the spout of water that rises to reach for her missing by mere inches.

Darkness crawls down her arms covering them in her Fiend armor.

Clever.

With a smile directed at all of us she turns and dives back into the water chasing the nymph who failed to recapture her.

'Enough fun, Iza. Telling me you cannot swim is an important thing to share before you play with water nymphs.'

I feel her exasperation, but it does not stop me from diving into the water. Cutting through its cold, murky depths I spot the first nymph. Grabbing her foot when she tries to flee my touch turns her solid. Her blue eyes turn to me and fill with fear.

Someone definitely told her about me.

With ease I toss her out of the water onto the shore. I know, with her being locked in solid form, the water is no longer her salvation. I also know that the others are waiting on shore and will take care of her.

Iza holds one by the throat studying her. The third nymph is trying to sneak up behind her, and I get a surprise. Iza turns her body slightly, her gaze not leaving that of the one she holds, and the bone sword appears running right through the neck of the nymph behind her.

The nymph dissolves in death, and the sword vanishes as quickly as it appeared.

Her eyes meet mine.

'I did survive a long time on my own, ya know.' She smirks and floats toward the surface the nymph in tow.

I follow more slowly double-checking that there are not any more. When I find nothing I surface and jump onto shore.

Adriem is holding the first nymph I tossed out close enough to the water to give her hope of escape but far enough away to make sure she does not. It is cruel, comical and well-deserved.

Focusing my gaze on Iza yields yet another surprise. She is walking across the water as if it were solid ground dragging the nymph along behind her by her hair. That is innovative.

"Cool, eh?" she says, smiling at her newfound ability.

Everyone standing at the shore watches her approach curious as I am. I try to look into her thoughts and find yet another shield in place. I can feel intent churning behind the block which means one thing for sure.

She is going to do something I will not like.

'Iza.'

She unashamedly ignores me. "Auryn, come here please," she calls.

Auryn steps easily through the crowd an inquisitive look on her face.

"You wish me to kill her?"

Iza shakes her head at the question and grabs Auryn's hand.

The nymph freezes, her mouth open in a silent scream. Iza's face takes on a look of total concentration as her mouth tightens in pain. Before my eyes, the nymph starts to shrink in on herself as Iza pulls her very life energy from her.

Which I know causes her pain. Iza cannot tolerate Light Magiks without pain.

Auryn's eyes widen as her face becomes more youthful and healthy. Iza tosses the dead nymph aside, releasing Auryn.

"Give me the other one," she says through a tightly clenched jaw.

Adriem does readily. There is no disobeying that command.

The nymph screams and fights to no avail. Iza has her. Once again Iza pulls forth the life force, except this time she is using it differently.

Slinging her arm out the sword appears. With eyes shining darkly, her aura flares to life. A purple and black mass of tentacled Magiks surrounds her. I do not like what she is doing, because I now know what it is. But I cannot stop her without it causing her even more pain.

The sword begins to glow and Iza groans. Clenching her teeth so hard that muscles in her jaw stand out she pours more Magiks into the sword. Swaying on her feet, she pushes even more in.

The power she is using is incredible but also draining.

Sweat beads on her forehead and upper lip, but what she is doing is working. The sword is starting to morph into the shape of a man. As she releases it the form solidifies and there stands the naked, shivering form of Licar.

Who is staring at Iza with absolute marvel.

She tries to step forward and stumbles. Catching her I lift her into my arms.

What she did she should not have been able to do. The miracle because it is a miracle she wrought... cost her. Dearly.

Auryn sobs loudly as she embraces her lost husband. She also looks at Iza with worship. Without a word, tears streaking down her face she drops to her knees her head bowed. Like dominoes every single creature there does the exact same thing.

"What did I tell you about the kneeling thing, Auryn?" Iza mumbles from my arms.

The others are talking to Iza, but I block them out. I am too busy looking at the white streak in her hair.

Do not ever do that again, Iza.' The cost is too much—she gave of her own life force. Risked it for someone she barely knows. I am not pleased at all. And if she ever tries it again I will stop it.

'She was dying. I couldn't let one of my strongest die, Phobe. I could feel his soul in that sword.'

"I would have never asked such a thing, my lady." Auryn's voice is breathless with emotion, as she stands, hands clasped with her lost mate.

"I really want a milkshake." Iza's voice is barely above a whisper but everyone hears.

This creature in my arms sacrificed something of herself with no expectation of anything in return. And she wants a milkshake. That is all, a fucking milkshake.

"Go get her a milkshake!" Auryn orders one of her children.

Licar steps close to me his eyes on Iza's face.

"We shall guard her with our lives, to the last one," he proclaims.

I nod my head accepting on her behalf. Iza is sound asleep in my arms. In a roundabout way I am proud of her, but I am not happy about her hurting herself. I do not care who it is she is helping.

Turning away from all the well-wishers, I head back into the Sidhe.

Stupid, soft-hearted woman.

CHAPTER THIRTY-NINE

hobe

Harvest Moon came and went with no Romiel. His absence slightly surprises me. Something has happened to change his mind or send him running.

Either way he is not here.

Iza is watching the lake again. She likes the water. She is thinking hard about her shifter child again. Knox. There are no shields currently between us.

'He has done nothing strange or suspicious,' I reassure her. I have been watching him and had others watch him too.

He spends much of his time with the boy Peter. Who, other than being oddly quiet, has done nothing out of character either. At least this time she is not sitting on the dock. I think she is a little wary after the nymph incident.

Stopping beside her I stare at her face and brace myself for the coming conversation.

"It was you outside of the shack wasn't it?"

"Yes." I see no reason to deny it.

"How much did you hear?"

"Enough."

Although she is bringing it up she is not comfortable talking about it. In her eyes this discussion is another task on her list that needs completed. A task she dreads.

Later that night, I saw the child in her memories—the child that carried my name. The name no living creature has spoken before... and survived. How Iza knew it is a mystery.

She was fourteen years old when it happened. A child herself.

One God, a stupid name that gives him more credit than he deserves, shared the names with me. They sung out on the shadows to my mind. The names I will never forget—and one day will meet the owners of.

"He was beautiful, perfect in every way," she says quietly after several minutes of silence.

I say nothing. Instead I wrap my finger around her finger.

"Well, looks like the lizard is a chicken. Can we still kill him?" she asks, changing the subject as her finger tightens on mine.

"Yes." That will happen when he does show up if for no other reason than I am annoyed he did not show up today for me to kill him.

Just like I am going to kill the locks who hurt her so deeply. Slowly and painfully. As I study her pale face, see the frown between her eyes, I decide that I am going to stretch it out for days.

Also in the process of hunting those locks I will kill every other one I cross paths with. Anyone who hurts her will die.

CHAPTER FORTY

*J*za

STANDING in my massive closet I flip through the clothing hanging up. Most of it still has tags on it, because I'm extremely protective of it. And haven't worn it. Which I know is borderline obsessive, but I can't help myself. Dad says it's the dragon in me, hoarding and all that.

There's no denying he's right; I just don't like admitting that to him.

This instinct inside of me convinces me to buy everything that catches my eye, lock it in this closet and then guard it like a... well, shit. Like a dragon.

Laughing, I pull out a pair of faded blue jeans and a long-sleeved shirt. Not the fanciest outfit but I'm tired of standing here looking. Nika actually started to comment on my clothing choices this evening. Well, she was commenting. I think the Fiends chasing her around the room might stop the nagging.

She needs to understand that I don't wear dresses—they'll get ruined with all the blood and, then I'd be pissed off for ruining them.

Jameson gave me a two hour crash course on the information he dug up on the shifters. They really like their pissing contests. Hopefully it doesn't come down to my balls being bigger than theirs, because they are,and I don't even have any.

Phobe does though. Which makes me laugh as I pull a shirt over my head. Pulling on jeans, I dig around for my boots. With a dismissive glance at the vanity with all the unopened face paint on it I grab my jacket and head out the door.

I have no idea how to put makeup on and tonight is not the night I want to experiment. I have a feeling things won't turn out well with me and makeup.

I keep seeing horrible images of clowns.

When I see Phobe I stop a minute and simply appreciate him. Good god, he really is too pretty. He even fixed his hair and it's perfect too. How the hell does he do that shit?

Wearing his normal black t-shirt and faded jeans—no shoes or socks, of course—he looks like he just walked off a runway model show. It's something that's purely him. No frills. The only thing technically fashionable is the black metal bracelet on his wrist.

I like it. I'll have to ask him where I can get one.

Unlike my other two self-appointed bodyguards he doesn't carry any weapons. He doesn't need one: he's the weapon.

"Everyone ready?" At my question Auryn opens the door and walks through ahead of me her eyes sharp.

She looks really nice too. She's wearing a sleek black pantsuit that looks as if it were made for her. If not for the big sword hidden in the back of her jacket and the gun bulge I could see under her armpit she'd look like any professional woman.

Licar is dressed suavely as well. Smiling at me like I'm Santa, ha. He's wearing black slacks that are complimented by a white button up shirt with two guns strapped on and a sword slung over his shoulder as well.

A peek of bright blue makes me look further down. Laughing out loud, I point at his flip flops. Smiling, he winks at me and follows his wife out the door.

Adriem, he's all grunge including the sunglasses he's sporting. Torn blue jeans and a band t-shirt. I also know he has knives strapped all over his body. He prefers them and, he's fast enough to get away with it.

He then motions for me to precede him out the door so, rolling my eyes, I do. Phobe is a shadow beside me. I'm not even positive that anyone besides me can see him.

Somehow I end up in the middle of the group being bounced around between them like ping-pong ball. I mutter a few complaints under my breath, but they have no heat in them. I already argued the arrangement and lost. Repeatedly.

I will say I almost feel sorry for the first idiot who tries to get to me through them. Almost.

When I received the stupid invitation for the club—called Bled of all things—I knew right off the bat it was from the shifters. So just to be a dick I made them wait a full day before answering them, and I had Jameson do it versus myself.

Bet that pissed them off.

In retaliation we were informed I could bring four guests, because I am considered a 'minor' power only and do not require a large guard. The Nightmares didn't give me a choice about it and Phobe… well, he's a given.

I climb into the limousine Jameson ordered for us—he said for appearances sake, I think it's because they don't want me driving. What's the big deal? It's not like I can seriously hurt any of them. They have Magikal airbags.

Besides, driving would've made this night more bearable. I'm not looking forward to this outing. It's almost Halloween time here and, I still need to go pick out costumes for the kids. I promised to take them trick or treating.

One way or another I am too.

Parking myself in the seat next to the door I stare out the window. Snow comes early here in North Dakota. I kind of like it. The snow swirls around us as we drive making a pretty, white smoky trail. I'd rather be out there walking in it, enjoying the night, than dealing with this mess. Maybe making a snowman, or better yet having a snowball fight. I've seen those on TV.

Unfortunately the drive is relatively short and when the door opens any thought of getting back in the car and leaving flees. I'm committed now.

Looking up I get my first look at the club. It's very… fancy. The walls are made from faded red brick that are faintly illuminated by the lit-up entrance boasting velvet ropes and suit-clad bouncers. There are two lines of people that stretch all the way around the building's corner and disappear.

There are at least six men guarding the door, big boys too.

Eyeing them a moment, I can tell they aren't human either.

When they spot us they move the rope that crosses the doorway. Why use a rope to dissuade entrance? It can't stop anyone who wants to get in.

'It is merely a symbol not an actual deterrent.' Phobe supplies the answer.

Still seems like a waste of pretty rope.

My first look in the club and I love it on sight. Gives me a great idea too one that I need to talk to Jameson about. This place is packed full which means money. Not that I personally need it, but others had been asking about jobs. A club of our own will provide those.

'What do you think?' I ask Phobe as we make our way through the crowd of people.

'It is loud.'

I hide my smile. He would say that. *'It's supposed to be loud.'*

I swear I feel him roll his eyes in response. *'There are a lot of diluted half-breeds— what do you call them? Blood suckers?'* he says calmly.

Sometimes I have a hard time sensing them. They are more wrapped up in humanity than most Feyrie half-breeds. 'vampires' interbred more with humans than even the shifters did.

'What are you planning on saying to the alpha?'

I smile, unable to help it. I have no idea what I'm going to say. Probably something rude. I feel Phobe peek in my brain. He tugs on a lock of my hair when he snoops.

I laugh out loud.

The dance floor is massive with colored lights all over the place. The DJ is on a raised platform in the middle that's spinning in place. I have to admit he's pretty good. The crowd loves him too.

"Let's go find where they stuck us," I say to my group.

At least I think they'll stick us somewhere. They did invite us. Plus, I imagine they have better manners than I do.

As soon as my foot touches the table area a man appears before us quietly. Focusing my attention on him I bite my tongue to keep my mouth shut. He's wearing a leather jacket with a pink tie. Either he has a great sense of humor, or he's making a statement. Maybe both.

"Good evening," he greets, turning towards Auryn who frowns at him.

I catch on to the situation quicker than she does. He thinks Auryn is me. It's an easy mistake to make—she's all regal and I'm... well, whatever I am.

Of course, she's totally irritated about it, and her thoughts are written all over her face.

"I'm here to welcome you to the club. If you will follow me, please?" He turns and heads up the stairs.

I raise a brow and motion Auryn to lead us. She gives me a dirty look and then does as bid. I'll catch hell for this later but it's totally worth it.

Pink tie casts one look backward and keeps walking.

"I do not see the humor, Iza," Auryn scolds.

"It's going to be a constant thing with these people. I don't have the look." Or the fashion sense but I keep that part to myself.

"You let them think it on purpose but one day you'll be too strong to do that, and they will know you whether you look the part or not."

I make a face at her and then say, "I'll deal with that when it happens."

She smiles at her small victory. I usually don't give in with so little argument. In this case there is no point in arguing a lost point. It will happen one day.

Pink tie shows us to a large, enclosed VIP area. So says the sign on the door.

'There are a lot of eyes on us. Including some hidden Feyrie.'

At Phobe's observation I put my sunglasses on and use the cover to look around without turning my head. I don't want to draw on the Web and alert them that I'm aware of them.

But I can distantly feel them there now.

'How many?' I ask, knowing he knows already.

'Twelve inside. Twenty outside. There are powerful ones among them, old ones.'

I mull over his words as I cross to the booth we're directed to. A bunch of shifters are standing around it. Hostility bleeds off them.

'They're going to be pains in my ass aren't they?'

His silence is the answer to my question. Of course they are. We had some debates about this visit. Phobe thinks I should force their dormant marks active. It's something I really want to avoid.

Doesn't mean I won't do it.

I take in all the occupants of the booth both in and around it using all my senses to get the information I need. The large blonde man sitting at the center of the booth, although I'm pretty sure he is being presented as the Alpha... isn't. The ego is there—he wears it like a piece of armor—but the power isn't.

My money is on the slimmer gentleman hiding just in the shadows to the side of the booth. Letting my eyes rest on him I feel him raise his gaze to meet my own.

Pink Tie comes to stand beside us and says, "May I introduce—"
He looks at Auryn expectantly. She smiles that beautiful smile of hers that can melt a man at fifty feet. It's also the same smile she uses before cutting a head off with that big sword of hers.

"I am Auryn, Guardian of the Shepherd," she says, stepping back to leave me standing in the front.

"I'm sorry. Did you say the shepherd?" Pink Tie stammers out.

So the mention of a Shepherd makes him nervous? That's interesting. I file it away for later.

'This shifter is on the submissive side. His thoughts are a mess, but he has

no shields against me. Right now he is thinking of the prophecy his people have about the shepherd.'

'I'll have Jameson do some more digging when we get home.'

"Introduce me to the real Alpha," I say pointing at the real one to make sure he understands I already know who is who.

A chuckle wafts out of the shadows. He steps forward.

"It's okay, Malcolm, have a seat." Pink tie, I mean Malcolm, skitters away.

So now that alpha boy isn't playing peekaboo anymore I study him. His hair is white blonde and pulled back into a tidy ponytail that looks strangely ridiculous on him. He's tall, over six foot I'd wager, but he isn't a large man.

He's not solid like Phobe either. He's half- Feyrie with a dark mark. Meeting his amber eyes evenly I blatantly smell the air around him. Some type of big cat. Tiger or lion, I bet. He's also got a good poker face. That means I'll be playing the guessing game.

I hate the guessing game.

My Magiks brush against him the web tinkling with the knowledge it can give me. Which other than some basics, isn't a lot. Shifters are weird like that even half-blood ones.

"I'm Iza. Who are you, kitty cat?" I'm not one for pretty words and stupid formalities. He'll learn that quick. Time is short and valuable.

"I am Adrian, Alpha of the Dakota pack," he answers. "You are not what I expected."

He is mostly what I expected. Arrogant, powerful for a shifter, and if I'm not mistaken, a bit of a know-it-all.

"I get that a lot." I say after a few moments of silence.

The shifter who came to meet me the first time steps forward with a look of surprise on his face.

"That was you in the ugly coveralls?"

I shrug at his question. I don't think they were ugly. "You expected me to say, 'Yeah, I'm her. Lemme bust out the five thousand thread count sheets for your boss?'"

He lets a smile slip at my words.

Adrian takes his rightful seat at the booth. The big blonde one vacates in a hurry.

"Please, sit," he offers, waving towards the spot across from him.

Remaining silent I slide into the booth. It's better than snapping out something impolite, which I really want to do.

A waitress comes to stand beside us waiting patiently. I order a diet soda from her. I motion for the others with me to sit but am ignored. Oh, the whole guard duty thing they took upon themselves.

"Not a drinker?" Adrian asks, his amber eyes intense on me.

He's trying to figure out what I am or at least trying to gauge what kind of threat I am. Something I'm familiar with—I'm giving him a similar look.

"Nope. Can't say I am." My metabolism burns through any human alcohol, and the last time I drank Fey Ale I had a hangover to top hangovers.

"Smart woman. I don't drink much myself. A shifter's body burns through the alcohol too fast for it to be enjoyable." He leans back and displays himself just for me.

He's wearing a white button up shirt with the sleeves rolled up his elbows. Black baggy jeans with some kind of chain hanging from the pockets. For a wallet maybe? I can still smell leather on him, so he had a leather jacket on recently.

He's a good enough looking man I guess. Has the broody look that probably makes women throw themselves at him until they break. Because there's no doubt in my mind he breaks them.

He's not Phobe, though, not even a smidge. So I give him a quick once over and deliberately look elsewhere. He isn't selling anything I want to buy.

"How did you call to us and, why are you here?"

Good, he isn't going to drag it out for hours.

"I called you through the web and, I'm here because you invited me here."

He looks clearly disappointed at my answers. "No one has ever been able to give a call more powerful than an Alpha before. None of us understand it, but there are many who cannot resist it."

I stir the straw around in my drink while I think about his words. There's no nice way for me to comment.

"Most of the shifters want me to request you leave our territory." His words drag my eyebrow up.

Their territory? The Sidhe has been here before human or Feyrie stepped foot on this world.

'Your inner dragon is not happy. She is very territorial.' I can't ignore the humor laced in Phobe's words.

I kind of want to turn around and kick his shin. I fight the urge to look at him. Part of me thinks he wants to feed my irritation. Phobe likes it when I bite.

"We won't be going anywhere. Asking us to leave is just a waste of your time," I finally answer.

It's nothing but the truth. I'm not about to have a territory pissing contest with kitty here—he'll lose. This is our home; we aren't leaving.

His amber eyes brighten, and he says, "You realize this club is full of shifters?"

Oh, here goes the 'my balls are bigger' contest.

I shrug. "Why should I care?" I say it so matter-of-factly he leans forward in surprise.

Shifters have a form of group telepathy, the lucky bastards, which is demonstrated when the area starts to fill with more of them.

I sigh. "Look, I'm trying to go about this in a nice way. Giving me shit isn't going to help you."

I will not be pushed around by testosterone-filled men who think they rule the world. Doesn't matter if they can turn into animals or not.

"You're elves, nothing more. Shifters can tear you apart in seconds," Blondie speaks up from beside the booth.

When Adrian doesn't correct him I realize he let him say it on purpose. Perhaps he even agrees with him. Briefly, when I first met this putz, I thought things might be different and our groups could be friends. I hoped to find a reasonable way to work things out.

Fine I'll give it one more shot.

"Okay, kitty, let's try this a more diplomatic way. I suck at it, but why not?" I force serenity into my voice.

I take a drink of the cold soda in front of me to give me some patience. It's not something I really have in abundance, and this is stretching the limit.

I continue, "We aren't leaving, but considering you're all sort of Feyrie—it shouldn't be that hard for us to get along." This is as nice as I can get. Will get. I didn't threaten to awaken their marks and be done with it… yet.

"I'm supposed to let your authority overrule my own in my territory?" he says haughtily.

Well, there goes the nice.

"My authority does overrule yours." I feel the shifters around me stir at my words.

The Web flickers with the emotions building up in the room. I do have some sympathy for them—it's why I'm trying to give them a chance versus just pulling on their marks. I know what it's like to be forced into something you don't want to do.

"We're at the top of the food chain here. No elves can displace us from that spot." Food chain? He's really looking at it that way?

Apparently, anyone who hikes their legs to pee can't think with anything but their egos. If he looked closer at my group, he'd see the power packed into the four of them. Only an idiot—well, there's the answer to my next question.

'Stop trying to be fair to a creature who will not appreciate you for it,' Phobe scolds.

"She's not even a magical elf. I've seen them before and, they have a glow around them. They must've sent a fraud." Auryn growls at the blonde shifter's words.

He looks over at her and keeps running his mouth, "Now her, I can believe she's some kinda lady. She's even dressed like one. But you, you're dressed like a bag lady."

Not that I care about him thinking she is more of a lady than I, since it's true, but being called names—that's just not nice. My friends think so as well. I can feel the hostility leaking off them.

'They are protective of you, Iza. Insults to you are insults to all of them,' Phobe says.

Well, that's going to take a while to get used to. I send some reassurance through the web and the level of anger drops but doesn't vanish completely.

"What the hell was that?" the blonde asks.

"What is your name, so I can stop calling you blondie in my head?" I shoot back at him just as rudely.

"Lawrence."

"Okay, Larry, much better. I was convincing Auryn not to rip your face off."

"How can you do that? Elves don't share group telepathy." Larry snots back at me.

Funny how ignorant they are about Feyrie.

"You know nothing about Feyrie. Keep that in mind." I stir my soda again. One more time, I can do this one more time. "In this case, we should take the opportunity to get to know one another's customs and races—"

"Races? There is only one race on your side we have several."

Adriem coughs into his hand at Larry's very rude interruption and the blatant ignorance coming out of his mouth.

"Your stupidity is going to be costly." Auryn's words are spoken softly, but there's no mistaking the threat underlying them.

"None of you are welcome here. We don't want your call or your presence. We are the top pack in the state, and it will make us weak if we allow a bunch of elves to come in and think they control everything," Larry continues.

Modest, isn't he? I watch him with a look of boredom on my face and let my eyes drift to Adrian. He's watching the exchange with interest. He's letting the idiot run his mouth to see what type of reaction his words will get. Might have even put him up to it.

It's rude, yes, but in a clever kind of way. I might have done something similar myself in this situation.

'Do you have anything to add?' I ask the ever-quiet Phobe.

216

'You are their Lady this is your decision to make.' A very neutral answer coming from him.

'And if I ask you to kill them?'

'Then they will all die.'

I catch myself almost looking over my shoulder at him. He's usually a voice of reason at a time like this. He agreed to that way too easily.

"What do you have to say about any of this, Adrian?" I lean back in my seat and cross my arms, studying his face.

"He doesn't have the most eloquent way of saying it, but what he's saying is similar to my own opinion," he answers in that same snotty voice.

"Basically, you don't believe we have a right to be here and, you want us gone?"

After a moment, he nods.

I continue, "What will you do if I refuse?"

"We will consider it an act of war," Larry chirps up.

I won't allow Feyrie to fight amongst themselves. I can't. They need time to grow and heal. War is coming soon enough as it is. War that will affect these morons the same as us.

I climb to my feet letting my glamour fall a little. Adrian's eyes widen. He slides out of the booth and climbs to his own feet. His nostrils flare at what little bit of scent he can get from me.

A kitty who uses his nose? Interesting.

The big mouth Larry takes a step back, and his blue eyes widen in disbelief. They aren't connected to me solidly on the Web yet, but any idiot can feel the power I'm letting leak out.

"You couldn't just let this be easy could you?" My voice echoes. Adrian stares, completely unsure what to do. "You know for a minute I thought you were reasonable, then you started trying to pee on things." I turn the fullness of my gaze on him.

"Clear this area." My orders leave no room to be disobeyed. With shock on their faces several of the shifters step back away from us.

'Control it,' Phobe cautions.

Now he's being the voice of reason which is strange. Especially since he said he'd kill them all if I wanted him to—and because I can feel his simmering anger. Anger that is totally unrelated to my own.

Irritation at a manageable degree, I walk over the window that looks down at the dance floor. This time I managed to not hurt people. I deserve a damn medal for it.

"You're not the plain elf I saw moments ago," Adrian accuses.

"No shit, Sherlock. I never said I was an elf. That was you making assumptions."

"Your deception doesn't change anything, Iza," he states, using my name.

"It's worse than you hiding in the corner while letting an idiot pretend to be you? You were fooled by your own arrogance not my glamour." I know the point hits home when he looks at me in his silence.

"So what will you do now?" he asks softly.

"Well, we aren't going anywhere. You can get that out of your head." Tapping my finger against my lip I study him. "Do you even know what a Feyrie is?"

He frowns at me. I bite my tongue to keep from yelling at him.

"I'm not talking about the ones you think you've met. I'm talking about the Feyrie people. Feyrie is made up of several species and races." I lean on the railing. "You lot are descendants of Feyrie and humans bumping uglies. And you have no idea where you come from, none of you, which is a shame."

"Shifters and this Fairy crap aren't related. The first shifters—" Larry begins.

I cut him off. "Go back to whatever type of life sucking, shape shifting Feyrie bred with humans to make the first vampire or shifter. You're all half-breeds of half-breeds. How's that for lineage?"

Larry gasps in anger at my words.

All this shit about bloodlines and pure lineage is crap. A person is who they are. Doesn't matter where or what they came from.

"You see, I'm a half-breed myself, so I can understand the stigma you feel."

"You're part human?" Adrian is way too amused by this prospect.

"No." I watch the amusement drain right out of him. "Neither side of my heritage is human." I walk back to the table and sip the now flat soda. "You should thank the folks with me for saving your ass. This would've probably gone much worse, otherwise," I say to Adrian, giving him a toothy grin.

"Your teeth."

I can clearly tell it's a thought he didn't mean to voice.

"Yeah, they're hard on a toothbrush, lemme tell ya." My smile broadens, exposing just how many sharp teeth I have. I hope this works for the 'my balls are bigger' requirement.

"You assumed—wrongly, I might add—that we're all harmless elves with little pointy ears. Assumptions are dangerous things in our world," I explain, bending the straw from the drink. It's better to take my frustrations out on it than him.

I continue, "I'm not patient, not even reasonable most of the time. Yet I made a genuine attempt with you."

"Are you saying you want to war, elf?" Larry pipes up.

My eyes flash. I've had enough of him.

"See there's something you didn't seem to pick up in my explanation: you're all watered-down descendants of Feyrie. There will be no war."

"I'll cut your throat myself, you bitch." His face reddens when Adrian's eyes flare. He steps back, but unfortunately it doesn't shut him up. "If you don't leave our territory you will all die."

"I'd shut him up if you want him to keep breathing, kitty cat."

I'm not the nicest person in the world but, I wanted them to have a chance. All this bullshit is making me regret that decision.

"All right, let's clarify a few things. I didn't want this job, but I got stuck with it—so, let me explain some of the perks." I walk slowly towards him letting my Magiks awaken a little more. Knowing my eyes are now black and bright.

"I'm *the* Shepherd, which means I'm at the center of the Magikal web that connects all Feyrie together. Every Feyrie and every descendant of a one is born with a mark. In this case yours is a dark mark." I smile a little at that.

"I am the Alpha. My pack is only connected to me and the higher alphas," Adrian insists.

"Yeah, blah, blah, blah. My steward Jameson has all kinds of books on this shit you should read. Might help you look like less of a tool right now." I stop a foot from him and look up into his amber eyes.

"Like I said there won't be a war. However, I'll give you one last chance to make the right choices. Either you gradually come to the dark side and try to rub along with your Feyrie kin, or I call all of your marks right now."

He laughs at my threat. "Magiks aren't effective against this pack. It is what gives us the edge against vampires. Perhaps you should've done your homework."

My Magiks are effective against any Feyrie.

'Take them,' Phobe urges.

'I genuinely loathe the idea of forcing them no matter how much the prick is annoying me right now. We are outsiders to them.' I feel his disapproval, but he says nothing.

I decide to switch tactics.

"If I understand your laws correctly to become alpha someone has to beat the current one in combat, right?" Adrian's eyes swirl with suspicion but he nods. "Death or just defeat?"

"Either."

I smile, unable to help myself.

Adrian frowns at that smile. "I sense no shifters in your people, I should be able to feel them as alpha here."

They aren't shifters you big ninny head. "Does the competitor have to be a shifter?"

"No," he replies.

"But didn't you say that shifters are descendants of Feyrie so logi-cally wouldn't that make them a shifter?" Adrian asks slyly.

He's not very logical for saying logically.

"Feyrie are not shifters. Shifters are mostly human, half-breeds of Feyrie, that take on the traits of an animal. Your true form is a human." I glance over my shoulder at Auryn, Licar and Adriem.

"The difference between you and a Feyrie is that they are creatures

that change to look humanoid. Their creature form is their true form."
There are a lot more differences than that, but we'll be here all night
debating what he doesn't know.

"So, you have a choice. You can fight any one of us." I sweep my
hand around to indicate the five of us. Auryn chuckles.

Adrian's eyes weigh me and then move on.

'You will kill him, if he challenges you, Iza. No argument,' Phobe says,
his irritation clear in his voice.

I ignore his bossy ass.

Instead I watch Adrian closely. He dismisses Auryn and his gaze
moves on. He'll ignore me because in his eyes I'm the weakest of the
group and to fight the weakest makes him look weak. She is a woman,
and I'm pretty sure Adrian is a bit of a sexist. Licar is big and bulky.
Adriem is just a bit smaller.

Phobe is closer to him height-wise but smaller weight-wise. It's
not because Adrian has abs for days either because he doesn't. Adrian's little belly tells me he has a sweet tooth.

As I thought Adrian's eyes stop on Phobe. Honestly, he might have
survived one of the others. He won't survive Phobe.

"Him, the blond-haired elf." At Adrian's words, Phobe steps
forward, his bare feet soundless.

Auryn cackles in glee, her mandibles clacking together as she pulls
Licar and Adriem closer to me.

"What the fuck was that?" Adrian questions, his face half-changed.
His features melt back into those of a human. Auryn's cackle can
creep out even the stoutest heart and makes me want to laugh along
with her.

"Okay, the rules. You lose, and you willingly ally with us and
remain as alpha whatever bullshit title you have. You win... well, you
won't win but carry on." Smiling as I talk I turn to Phobe and blow a
kiss at him. The smile he surprisingly directs at me shows the glinting
of his sharp teeth.

"That is not an elf," Larry the king of the peanut gallery says in
shock, as Phobe with eyes flaming, looks dead at him.

Ha, he let his glamour drop a little. That's hilarious.

ZOE PARKER

'My, what big teeth you have, Mr. Wolf.' I smile at my own silly words. *'The better to eat you with, my dear,'* he responds.

I laugh out loud, I can't help myself. It earns me a bunch of strange looks, but I don't care.

"This is Phobe," I introduce, laughter still in my voice.

"His name changes nothing. He will still lose." Adrian says in a cool, dismissive voice.

He peels off his shirt and starts his arduous change again. He changes into more of an animal than most of the other shifters that I've seen. Explains why he's top kitty, among the shifters anyhow. A Feyrie would tease him for his kitty face and little claws.

I sit down at the booth to watch wishing I had some nachos or something. I don't know what it is but every time I'm watching something interesting I want to snack.

The shifter I met days before comes to sit across from me.

"You look very pleased," he says after a moment of staring at me.

"Phobe's kinda hot, can't help myself."

"I never thought to see the day I met a woman turned on by monsters," he says.

Shifters don't think much of themselves, do they? I lean closer to him. He isn't insulting me, not in the way he thinks.

"Monsters do it better," I whisper, then turn back to Adrian warily circling Phobe who is standing still as a statue watching him.

There are more here watching now. I let my glamour fall back around me, snoopy bastards. Jameson comes strolling up the stairs like he owns the place. He's not supposed to be here, but I smile at him and wave him over anyhow. He slides in the booth beside me and takes a drink of my soda. The face he makes is priceless.

"How do you drink this shit?" he questions, looking inquiringly at the shifter across from me. "Why is that idiot fighting Phobe?"

"They don't believe anything I'm telling them, so we challenged them to a dual or whatever it's called."

"What the hell made him pick Phobe? He had a better chance with the big guy."

"He went for the medium one."

"That was a mistake," he says, signaling the waitress like there weren't two men getting ready to fight two feet away.

"He could've challenged me," I say.

Jameson snorts. "Phobe would've killed him had you accepted."

I can't argue with him. I'm suspicious he's right.

"You really think that skinny guy can beat my Alpha?"

I nod at the shifter's question.

Phobe is just toying with Adrian right now. For some reason he's pissy with the shifter which means he's enjoying the idiot's pain.

"What's your name?" I ask the man across from me.

"David."

"Nice to meet you, David." I hold my hand out and wait for him to shake it which he does. "You seem to be smarter than most of them."

He shrugs. "Adrian is the smarter one, but he's got an ego the size of Texas. We were the first pack to break the vampires hold on us. So he has a right to be a little cocky."

I still think David is the smarter one; he feels smarter. Why isn't he the Alpha? So, I ask him.

"Adrian is my older brother," he answers.

Oh, that's it. Brotherly love and all that business. At least Adrian has someone with brains close to him—wait.

"Were you the one who cooked up the word game?"

"Yeah, that was me. Sorry about that." His eyes are full of worry when he watches Phobe. "Why do I get the feeling that fellow is just playing with my brother?"

Because he is.

"Don't worry I'm pretty sure he isn't going to kill him," I attempt to reassure him.

I go to pat David's hand and Larry yells, "Why don't we kill the bitch and end it now?" Then I hear a very distinct pop.

Something with the impact of a small truck hits me in the chest knocking me sideways into the booth. Pain fills me as my body fights to heal the wound, but something is stopping it.

Distantly I hear a roar that raises the hair on the back of my neck.

Jameson is leaning over me yelling something, but I can't hear him through the ringing in my ears.

What the fuck hit me so hard?

'Iza!' Phobe yells into my head.

Taking a deep breath I cough choking on blood. Well, that didn't work. Ignoring the yelling and scrambling around me I go inside myself to the object causing me so much pain. I find the offensive piece of metal quickly, just outside of my heart. A Fey-Iron bullet.

'That motherfucker shot me with Fey-Iron.' I say to Phobe, I figure me answering him will calm him down.

Which is very important considering the circumstances.

His face appears above my own. Peeling my shirt up, he looks at the small bleeding hole right above my bra. Letting the claws on his first finger and thumb lengthen into precise points he begins to steadily dig the bullet out. Gritting my teeth I curse vehemently.

It hurts like a sonofabitch.

He drops it in the table with a 'tink' noise, and with fiery globes of fury he watches the hole close. Putting his face directly in mine, he says out loud, "If you want to save them call their marks, Iza." He adds in my head, *'Or I will kill them all.'*

He means it, too.

He kisses me. His lips are hard and bruising and angry. Then he straightens and vanishes.

Sitting up I look around me. The Nightmares encircle me protectively, backs to me, eyes forward, along with a few unknown Feyrie. The shifters circle them uneasily. Poor David is sitting there white-faced. Looking at the blood spattered over my neck and chest my own temper burns in my belly.

Sticking my hand out for Jameson to pull me to my feet I pull off my shirt and toss it to the Fiend that appears out of thin air and disappears with it.

I liked that shirt.

Surveying the damage around me I see that the table is broken—glass strewn everywhere. The fabric of the seats is stained with my blood. I imagine that the glass is what my body is pushing out of my back. The seat smolders and I smell Jameson's Magiks.

He's smart, I'll give him that.

Focusing on my anger I dig my claws into my palms to bring my temper to a manageable level. I offered them peace, offered them a choice that I and many others didn't have. I was diplomatic and flipping *nice*.

My nostrils flare.

"Is she okay?" a bloody Adrian asks from outside my ring of protectors.

"Jameson why are you here?" I ask, my eyes on Adrian.

"I figured I'd come help out." He pulls off his shirt and hands it to me. Eyeing the pink alligator on it I slip it on.

Turning my full attention to Adrian I walk towards him. My Feyrie part for me to walk through them.

"Did your homework on Feyrie, eh, Adrian?" I ask.

"My sources say we outnumber them five to one, Adrian," Larry yells from across the room. It's followed by his yelp of pain.

Phobe has a hold of him now.

"My sources say that's not enough not nearly enough. The Feyrie in this room can kill every... single... one... of... you." I smile calmly.

I'm anything but.

Phobe's fury is feeding my own, feeding that darkness inside of me.

"Wow, you really pissed him off. I'm going to go get a drink. These are new shoes, and I don't want to get blood on them," Jameson says, pausing long enough to kiss me on the cheek. "Have fun, Iza."

"The elf bitch told me you were nothing more than a whore!" Larry hisses from under Phobe's foot on the floor.

I feel Phobe's fury reach its peak. Grabbing Larry's arm he dangles him in the air and crosses, the room with Larry in tow. He stops in front of Adrian.

I step back.

Without any visible effort, he calmly rips the writhing man in half tossing both halves at Adrian. Eyes on fire, he looks at Adrian's gore covered face and smiles a predator's smile.

Yeah, that's the last time I'm nice. I tried to respect their freedom, their beliefs, and the motherfuckers shot me for it.

"Was that planned by you, Adrian?" I ask, stepping around what's left of Larry. The Fiends are snacking a bit.

Adrian shakes his head looking nervous for the very first time since I got here. "Lawrence brought a woman here, a witch—and she said that the bullets will kill an elf. I ordered them to be left at the den house. He apparently didn't listen to me."

I nod along as he speaks but my decision has been made.

"I called you here... to our home. Yes, OUR home. We all worked hard to get here to have some freedom for the first time in our lives. Yet you never once considered that." I poke a black claw into his bare, gore- covered chest. "You claim you're top of the food chain? I'll show you top of the food chain, fuck head."

My eyes take in all the shifters with dormant marks. "I did it your way; now you're going to do it mine." With those words I let my Magiks loose.

With my inner eyes I seek out the dormant mark connecting me to Adrian and, through him, every shifter he is connected to.

"Now, kitty cat, you're all mine."

Pulling on the Magiks inside of me I awaken his mark. I watch him open his mouth in shock while hearing the gasps from him and all of those present that are connected to him. Their marks flare to life solidly tying them to the dark and to me. In seconds, I touch them all, every single shifter now connected to me.

Adrian is now staring at me with a dumbfounded look.

"Now I need a shirt that doesn't have a pink alligator on it."

It appears out of thin air compliments of the goblins who decided to join the party.

Thanking them I promptly pull off the one I'm wearing and throw it over the railing towards Jameson. It smacks him in the head and, he looks around a little lost.

Feeling the gazes of many on me I pan my gaze around the room. I know it's not because of the nudity. There isn't a creature here weird about it except Jameson.

"What?"

"Your scars." Adrian supplies.

Frowning, I look down. What's the big deal? "Did you think I'm some pampered princess sneaking out of the castle for the first time? That maybe I came to play fetch?"

These idiots have no idea what I've gone through. I pull the clean shirt on. They can suck it, too.

"Things could've turned out better for you." I look at him expecting to see anger or accusation. Instead I see a combination of awe and confusion, then resolve and acceptance cross his face.

"We respect strength—we honor it. This bond with you gives us something we've never had before... complete immunity from vampire control."

Well, that's nice. And something I need to look into. I had no idea that vampires could control them.

"So, you're not going to rant shit about me being a dictator?"

He shakes his head. "We can feel you inside of us." He looks around him sensing the Fiends for the first time. "We never outnumbered you here, did we?"

I shake my head. The fiends were here the entire time. So were the forlorn although I can't sense them. Phobe's and my hidden weapons are a force to be reckoned with all on their own.

Not to mention the Nightmares and Phobe. Hell, I think Phobe could take on everyone here... probably even the Nightmares.

Speak of the devil. Phobe grabs me and hauls me to a darkened corner away from everyone. I shiver as his glamour falls around us. Shoving me against the wall he kisses me until I'm breathless.

'What's that for?'

His answer is to kiss me slowly, languidly.

Pulling away, he rests his forehead against mine.

'I was going to kill them all.'

I sigh.

'I know.'

CHAPTER FORTY-ONE

 hobe

THAT EASILY SHE acts as if she was not shot mere minutes ago by metal fatal to Feyrie. It is just another day to her.

That is something I find charming about her. Her ability to move forward. But she did get shot and bleed all over, and it hurt her more than she admits. This is why I am keeping my mouth shut about her drink.

Jameson is watching her drink it with deviousness in his gaze. My payback for her letting it drag on until they hurt her is my silence. He slipped some Fey Li'quer into her soda. The overly sweet taste covers up the Li'quer taste. This is her second one. Sneaky bastard. Normally I might do or say something about it, but not this time.

The stuff is so potent it is already affecting her. Her speech is slightly slurred, her laughter coming easier, as she listens to Adriem's stories.

Adrian, the former Alpha, is silently watching her. I let my eyes rest on him a moment. He is thinking things that make me want to smash his face into the floor. Which I might still do before the end of the night.

He has wanted her since she said the first cocky words to him. Shifters are attracted to power and, she is the epitome of it. I do not dislike him for his attraction; it is for his willingness to hurt her even though he wanted her. All for his ego.

Right now he is plotting how to have her. He does not care if she has a mate or even no interest in him. I wonder how long before I remind him he is not in the shifter world anymore.

Iza is not capable of sharing herself so carelessly.

She staggers to her feet and grabs my hand. "We're so dancing," she slurs.

Everyone at the table stands. She wobbles her way to the dance floor with all of us in tow. Slipping through the throng of people she stops next to the DJ who in turn notices her presence and turns the music up. With a smile directed at her he eyes the crowd for a threat. That is interesting.

There are still threats here. She pulled the dormant marks of the shifters, but there are other half-breeds and even Feyrie hiding. Those Feyrie are unknown and not all will be loyal.

"I've never danced with a person before," she whispers drunkenly.

Then she proceeds to grind her pelvis against my leg. Stunned, I stand there and watch her. Watch her move her hips back and forth and then find her rhythm. It is so bloody sexy I can only watch with pure male appreciation.

The song comes to an end and she stops moving while I find myself slightly disappointed.

"Oh my god, that was fun. Can we dance more?"

The DJ, hearing her, starts another song. This one is peppier and less hip swaying, but it is still interesting to watch her dance.

I simply stand there and stare at her. She is moving her head side to side and hopping around in circles. I like the effect this music has on her.

A chill runs down my spine. Tense and alert, I find Licar's eyes on me. I move closer to her signaling him with a jerk of my head.

There are more vampires in the club now. Vampires are predominantly Light Fey. I will not allow her to be hurt again tonight. To distract her I pull her into my embrace while also blocking her from the view of others.

A slower song comes on. The drunken Iza who would never slow dance sober wants to now. If you call her snuggling up to me and giggling slow dancing. There was a time when this kind of moment with her would make me uncomfortable, and in some ways, it still does.

But not enough for me to stop it.

Allowing myself a look at her I see the frown on her face. She is a suspicious little thing. The smile she is wearing lets me know she is aware of the threat here. My chest tightens.

How did I exist without her? She gives my world color and life. Iza is all over the place and, I like chasing her there.

Suddenly she stops moving. Every single Feyrie connected to her stops as well. Even the shifters. Half the club now stands stock-still watching her, waiting. She is watching something over my shoulder with so much focus she is not paying attention to anything else.

Turning to look I spot a vampire feeding in the corner, on one of the younger human women in the club. He is doing it carelessly unfazed by the innocence shining from her.

My shadows feel around carefully.

There are at least fifteen vampires in the club now. Some of them are old, powerful. The one feeding is neither. A small group of them slink nearer to us. Their leader is one of the old ones—most likely three or four centuries old. A rarity here in this realm. Most do not live to see one hundred. Vampires have a habit of killing their own.

Without saying a word, Iza starts walking towards the feeding vampire. Licar and I step in behind her, Auryn and Adriem at our sides.

The older vampire pauses and watches Iza. He is surprisingly dark. The other I can feel, but not see are as well. But they are protected from my intrusion. Vampires this old can protect themselves from mind reading for a time.

Iza approaches the object of her interest, calmly grabs a handful of his hair, and rips his face from the woman's neck. Motioning to Licar she indicates the human and focuses on the vampire she has ahold of.

He is not very pleased by her hold. He is thrashing against her grip, but it is unbreakable. His head is twisted at an odd angle, so he cannot reach her with his hands. It is not for lack of trying.

She pulls his head back, so she can look into his face.

"That was a young, innocent girl," she says quietly.

I know the vampire can hear, even over the music. Iza is using her special voice.

"She's food," he insists with a lisp through his two pointed teeth.

Normally Iza laughs at such a thing, but she is not entertained by him at the moment. "No more innocents die here." She puts her hand on his shoulder.

"How are you stronger than I am?" he demands belligerently.

Instead of answering him she twists his shoulder holding on to his head. There is a crack as his neck breaks, but she does not stop there. Levering her foot on his shoulder she pulls and twists until his head comes right off.

"Snack time," she says quietly, tossing the head to the ground.

The body slides into an unnatural shadow and is gone. Then she turns to the group of vampires approaching including one of the old ones. Her glamour is still up hiding her from their green eyes.

"Okay, Count Chocula, what's your agenda? Are you going to threaten me too then challenge me to some type of wrestling match? Because right now I just want to go home, and you're in my way."

Iza's patience is gone. Her mood has turned sour. It makes me want to kill the vampire she killed again.

"Does she make up names for everyone?" Adrian says from beside Licar. "Is she always so impatient, too?"

"This is patient for her. The mess with you was a world record," he answers.

"You are the Shepherd?" This gets Iza's attention—someone recognizing her. It also rouses her suspicions. He continues, "Some of us, including me, received a call to come here."

She reached vampires as well. Interesting.

"What do you eat?" she asks instead of answering the question.

"Humans, of course, my lady. We are blood drinkers after all."

"What kind of humans?" She taps her foot impatiently as she asks.

"We do not take innocent life, my lady."

She shakes her head and argues, "I just killed one of yours for it."

"He wasn't one of mine. He came with—"

He is interrupted when someone shoves him out of the way. "We do not owe this woman any type of explanation. The Duke will not take kindly to them being in our area."

Iza turns immediately to the speaker. "And you are?"

"I am a representative of the Blood Duke's court. I have come to see if this clan is being run correctly. We heard rumors that Darius here is not keeping blood houses for nobility."

Iza makes a face. A blood house is self-explanatory, and she does not like it... or nobility either.

"Can't they just order takeout?" At her joke multiple people snicker.

I catch the hand that he lashes out at her an inch from her face. Iza does not even flinch.

"I am a noble from an old, respected family and no person of your status will treat me in such a way—" His words choke into silence.

I had enough. He tried to slap her. The smell of his fear fills me.

It is oozing off them all now.

"This is my friend, mister representative. It looks like he's happy to meet you."

I hesitate, unsure if I should kill him or not. I can feel her anger but not her bloodlust. She wants me to wait.

Funny her being the sensible one.

"So what's this about a duke. I thought your people were ruled by a prince?" she inquires. It is a good question.

"Our Blood Prince has disappeared. The Duke is leading our people in his absence," Darius answers, not sounding happy about the situation.

"He is part vampire?" someone asks from in front of us.

Reluctantly I drop the man turning to see the speaker. I ignore the anger in the green eyes of the man looking up at me from the floor.

"Ha, ha. No. He's something scarier than the lot of you," she says, amusement in her tone.

'I can kill them all, Iza. Then we can go home,' I offer.

'Not yet. But it's starting to sound like a good idea.'

'Are you going to try diplomacy again?' I ask her, hoping she will not.

It will be much simpler to just awaken the dormant marks, kill the ones that are light marked and be done with it. My preference is for them to die sooner rather than later.

The coldness of a blade sliding through my chest surprises me a lot more than it hurts. Iza's shock filled gaze looks at the blade sticking out of my chest then up to my face. But before I can turn to deal with the man on the other side of it Iza's eyes bleed straight to black and her skin turns blue.

"Oh, fuck," Jameson whispers.

I smile. Finally, she is pissed.

CHAPTER FORTY-TWO

 hobe

WITH HER POWER FULLY AWAKE, her hair a mass of thrashing anger around her head, Iza literally walks through me. Her Magiks melting the blade sticking out of me and healing me completely. Her reasonable side knows I will heal in seconds, but her temper does not recognize reason.

Her arms crawl with darkness as her armor materializes. The shadows begin to come alive and move in the club—the fiends and forlorn making themselves known. Roars of anger sound in the club; her fury is contagious.

We all feel her rage.

She stops an inch from the man's face and then, in a blindingly quick move, grabs his ears with her armored hands bringing his face down to the level of hers. He fights her hold, hard, but there will be no getting out of that grip.

"I'm sick of assholes like you." Iza is using that special voice again.

They can see her now, these mortal creatures. See her Magiks alive, powerful, and displaying some of the true monster she really is.

"Blood Prince, can you hear me?" she speaks out loud but also through the connection this vampire has to the prince. Her Magiks are making this vampire a form of telephone. It is something she should not be able to do at all.

But Iza likes to do the impossible.

"I suggest you get your ass back here and fix this Duke person. Darius is mine now as you will be when you get here. I suggest you do it NOW."

Then she smashes his head between her hands like a fruit. His headless corpse falls limply to the ground.

She looks at his companions with a completely evil smirk on her face. "Anyone else?" she asks, so coldly the temperature of the room drops. Ice begins to form on glasses causing some to shatter from the cold.

"The duke will send assassins now," Darius states.

Iza cocks her head to study him. He grows uncomfortable under her gaze.

"The Blood Prince will come and take care of him." Her voice echoes in the small area. "Between the shifter's shit and this crap I'm not in a good mood anymore." She wills it and the dormant marks of the vampires burn to life.

"All of the dark are mine now." Her Magiks glow like purple fire around her. There are several noises of surprise.

She turns to her right. "Those three." She points at three vampires clumped together. I do not question her meaning; the intent is there in her eyes. Moving, I kill all three of them with one swipe of my dagger.

If there were not others present I would have eaten them.

"Oh, tsk, tsk Darius. You have a spy close to you." She points at a female off to his left side who is trying to disappear back into the crowd.

"But she's my—"

"Girlfriend. Yes, I know. She's a spy for someone who's trying to kill your Blood Prince." She studies Darius a moment. "She's dark too, but she isn't loyal. You see when I claimed all the marks I got the goods on everyone that has one. She isn't very loyal to you either." She leans close to him and says, "She was sleeping with tomato head."

Iza steps forward and calmly guts the woman with her sword.

"All right, I'm done for tonight." She starts walking towards the door as her sword disappears in black smoke. "Adrian, I want the name of the person who gave you those bullets. The timing is too coincidental. Jameson, get the Sidhe folks ready, I have a feeling we're about to get a big influx of people." She kicks the door open and steps out into the cold night air.

"I didn't get all of the vampires or shifters but I got the quality. The Blood Prince and Alpha Lord are mine." She stops and Adrian almost runs into her.

"Actually I don't want to talk to you right now. It's because of you this bullshit started. Get me the name and give it to one of them to give to me." She indicates the Nightmares and Jameson.

Who still does not have a shirt on. The vain creature.

Adrian opens his mouth to argue, but Licar pats him hard on the back and says, "Our Lady has given a command. It is in your best interest to obey."

After a moment of regarding the big Nightmare Adrian nods and retraces his steps.

"The shifters have children. Guard them." She is whispering to her Fiends.

I take advantage of her distraction to piggy back her thoughts. She is already planning for a conflict with the shifters and vampires. She is strong enough to trace the strands she shares with them to the strands they share with others.

"The vampires will need help transporting their families too. The others won't take kindly to the ones now connected to us. Their hierarchy is a lot like shifters, small pack-like families all connected to a local leader, who is then connected to a Prince. Rather complicated but it works for them." She stops walking halfway to the limousine and turns to us.

"This is going to be a goddamn mess." After that statement, she climbs into the car and is silent the entire drive home.

CHAPTER FORTY-THREE

*I*za

THIS WHOLE SHEPHERD thing is a pain in the ass. The one time I try to be fair and all that garbage it blows up in my face. Then I go and lose my temper.

A knife can't kill Phobe. Much worse has been done to him. Why did I react like that? I search inside myself as I walk towards my room. The answer comes to me with a quickness that damn near takes my breath away.

Because I can. I did it simply because I can. Before, I couldn't fight back, I couldn't stand up for myself or him. Now... now I can.

Wow. How is this realization just now hitting me?

Hallways and doors appear in my path, taking me where I want to go, where others can only go if I wish it. There is only one thing I want right now: solitude. I don't even want Phobe around. I need to think. I need to digest everything. I can't think when there are other people around.

Especially tall, dark, and distracting ones.

"Iza, are you hurt?" The little voice stops me in my tracks. Knox. The Sidhe let him find me.

I turn to him and force a smile on my face. "Nah, I'm good. What's up, little man?"

He stands there with his little hands tucked behind his back, staring at me. Something is different with Knox. He's been avoiding me a bit, so it's great that he finally searched me out.

My solitude can wait for a little while.

"Who is Phobe to you?"

I frown but make the smile stay on my face. That's a weird question for him to ask me. "He's my friend. You know this." I cross to him and kneel in front of him. "You wanna go watch a movie?"

Knox loves movie time. He shares my family movie addiction.

"No." With that, he turns around and walks off.

There's a sour note in the voice of the Sidhe. It brought him to me reluctantly. That was incredibly weird but kids go through phases, or so says the Google God. And Knox has a lot of shit to work through. I'm probably being paranoid.

Fuck that.

I pursue him and easily catch up. "Knox, what's up with you?" I ask, grabbing his shoulder to turn him around.

Green eyes study me with hurt in them. "Peter says that you don't love me anymore because of Phobe," he says quietly.

Hitting my knees in front of him, I pull him to me, hugging him tightly against me and say, "Oh, babe I will always love you. No one will ever replace you in my life."

For a moment he stands there unmoving, then his skinny arms wrap around my shoulders and he begins to cry.

"Peter said when his Mom met a guy she started being mean to him," he sobs out.

God, how do I fix tears? Wait, I'll buy him a bike. He mentioned one of those before. Presents fix things.

And with these kids so do hugs. I keep hugging him.

"Well, I'm sorry that happened to Peter, but it won't happen to you," I reassure him as I pull back and wipe the tears from his cheeks.

With a sudden smile he kisses my cheek and turns and runs off. Kids are so freaking weird.

Walking back to my room I shake off the weird encounter and file it away to think about later. Maybe I really do need some quiet time to myself.

Flopping on the bed I turn on the TV. TV makes your brain numb. This will work for now.

First to think on the shifter situation...

The door to my room flies open and, Ruthie staggers in giggling. Her arms are full of snacks and DVDs. Behind her walks Michael, carrying Cadey, with Lissa and Louise bringing up the rear.

I sit up and sigh, but it's a happy sigh. I wait for Knox to come in the door, but after a full minute I realize he isn't coming.

Isn't he the one who told them?

"Where's Knox?"

"No idea. He made a new little friend and has been hanging out with him," Michael answers, handing Cadey off to me.

He immediately buries his hands in my hair. It's not a big deal. My hair loves him.

He must be with that kid Peter right now. That part of me that was worrying about him is more relaxed after our little talk mostly.

Juggling the baby and some chocolate—*that* I'm quite happy to see —I laugh at the kids settling in for the movies. They brought four, so they plan on staying awhile.

I guess solitude is overrated, ha.

"Iza, there's a woman who wants to be our new mommy," Louise says.

All the noise ceases at once.

She crawls up on the bed and onto my lap. Brushing her hair out of her face, I smile at her. "Now what's this about a new mommy?" I ask her.

"An imp wants to adopt us." Lissa ever the kid/adult, answers.

Well is this a good or bad thing to them? "And what do you think about it?"

"She makes good cookies," Louise says.

"She's really nice," Lissa chirps up.

"Hugs," Cadey adds, flopping onto my shoulder.

"I suppose the most important question is do you want her to be your mommy?"

All three of them frown in concentration.

"Yes." Lissa says after a moment and Louise nods. Cadey just hugs me again and drools a little on my shirt.

"Good, then. We'll have to throw you a party!"

A big party where I can go cry afterwards. I'll be glad to see them happy but sad because right now they are kind of my kids. And soon they won't be.

"Movie is starting!" Ruthie says crawling up beside us. Michael flops at our feet.

Let the movie marathon begin.

CHAPTER FORTY-FOUR

Iza

SINCE THERE ARE SO many children getting adopted, which is spectacular, we decided to have an actual party to commemorate it. By the end of the evening several of the shifters and vampires showed up with their families.

There are a lot of awkward silences, but for the most part people are rubbing along together. The vampires are a snooty lot though. The shifters too in their own way. It's a work in progress.

The best reaction so far is from Florenta. She is out-snobbing the snobs. It's entertaining to say the least. The indulgent smile she sends my way on occasion makes me laugh as well. I think she's messing with them on purpose.

Florenta is a bit of a snob, but she's not stupid.

Sighing in satisfaction I survey the occupants of the room. This is a big step for our people. Auryn waves at me from a few tables over; she has little Minos in her arms.

For this little pocket of time, the people look damn near… happy.

Tomorrow is also Halloween so another party but with candy. Excited for the holiday I stand up and clear my throat. The silence is immediate.

"Attention guys and gals. Tonight is special for two reasons. One: all the kids finding loving families. Everyone deserves to be loved, right? And two: tomorrow is Halloween!" The room breaks into cheers, mostly from the kids.

"Now, first—I want to thank all of the folks who stepped forward to take these wonderful kiddos in. Thank you for realizing they are special and need to be treated that way!" That about sums up my speech abilities. I move on.

"Second, did you know that you can dress up as monsters and go door to door and get free candy?" I ask the room in general.

Some laugh, some seem really surprised.

"So, for us that means one thing… well, two, if you count free candy. We get to wear costumes, or in some cases take them off!"

The kids cheer again. Someone even howls.

"The party will start after trick-or-treat time. And yeah." Awkwardly, I sit down.

That was not fun. How the hell do people do that all the time?

'What costume are you wearing?' Phobe's questions surprises me so much I turn in my chair to look at him before catching myself.

'Little Red Riding Hood.' I'm joking, but the teeth comment made days before comes to mind.

'Then I shall be the Big Bad Wolf.'

Giggling, I turn back to a bunch of folks staring at me. "What?" I ask them.

Immediately they shake their heads and turn back to their own conversations. Is it that strange for me to giggle to myself? I know I do it at least once an hour. Or more. Probably more.

Rubbing my hands together I start calculating how many kids will be trick and treating. And how much candy I'm going to get out of it —a candy tax sounds super fair to me. One piece of chocolate and one piece of hard candy. Or gum, but I always end up swallowing mine and Ruthie said it'll get stuck in my... well, that area I'm currently sitting on.

I'm not sure I believe her, but I should be careful just in case. I tried to ask the Google God but got a lot of nude butts and no real answers. It's Ruthie; why would she lie about such a thing?

"Iza." The sound of Jameson calling my name breaks into my candy daydream.

"What?" I ask blinking to center my attention on his face.

"Let's go get the costume shopping done. We still have the limo and the bus, so we can get all of the kids to the store," Jameson says.

Great idea. That makes perfect sense and I love shopping.

Jumping up, I grab my coat and head out the door. Two seconds later the slushy, cold feeling of the snow squeezing between my toes makes me turn around and run back inside to put shoes on.

"You're not driving," Nika insists, stopping to put her own shoes on. The laughter and excited chatter of the kids fills the hallway next.

For once I agree with her, mostly.

The kids can get a lot more injured, and I'd feel bad if they got hurt. But right this second there's a point of principle that I need to address. Standing, I cross the hallway and stop beside her. She's taller than I am, so I look up into her face and lean so close my breath moves her hair.

I whisper, "You're welcome to ask me to do something or give your opinion. But this needs to be the last time you try to tell me what to do, okay?"

Childish it may be, but I'm done being controlled and ordered around by people. If she says to me that she thinks something is a bad idea I'm alright with that. Anything along those lines really. But this bossy thing she has going on has got to go.

Her face blanches and her mouth opens and closes.

"I'm so sorry my lady. I remember you as a child, and perhaps that is something I need to stop picturing you as." Her apology surprises me.

244

I pat her arm and say, "Yeah, that ship sailed. I haven't been a kid since the day I was taken." Then I head back outside. This time with shoes on.

CHAPTER FORTY-FIVE

*J*za

WATCHING the reactions of the cashiers at Wally-World is almost as entertaining as the shopping part itself. There are seventeen kids between the ages of six month old Minos and eighteen-year-old Michael. At the looks of wonder on some of their faces I realize that they've never been to a store.

"All right heathens you get a costume, a toy and a food. Go!" I wave them forward with my arms as I say go.

For a moment they all pause, then in a stampede of little feet, they're off.

Laughing, I follow behind Knox and his little group. He's walking slower than the rest of them with his arms behind his back. His face has such an adult like look on it not like the Knox I know. He stops and looks at me and the familiar smile creases his face.

Thank god. I was seriously starting to worry again. With a wave at me he takes off running to catch up with the other kids.

An hour later I start tracking them all down. I'm pretty sure the manager is threatening to call the police, and I can't be banned from this store too.

Seventeen kids leave a lot bigger mess than I usually do. There are costumes and bags of candy everywhere. That's not counting the toy aisles. When I get to the bicycles aisles I laugh out loud.

A bunch of them are hanging upside down on the rack like those hairy apes on the zoo show.

"Kids, time to get down and get going, clean up your mess! Five minutes!" I yell over my shoulder as I walk towards the next aisle full of giggles.

Finally we get them all rounded up—costumes, toys, and food in tow—and get them herded outside. I can feel their happiness through my links with them.

A sign at the door way catches my attention. It says Happy Thanksgiving and there is a big roasted bird of some type on the table. I know this; it's the next holiday.

Oh, oh. I'm totally cooking a big bird. When I get home, I'm going to get on the interwebs and find the biggest bird in this world. Maybe get a few of them.

The family looks so happy in the pictures. I want to make my family look that happy. Decision made I catch up and climb into the car. These human holidays are fantastic. A candy day, a bird day and then a fat man will climb down our chimney to eat our cookies and leave us presents.

This is going to be a great few months.

Wait, where the hell is Phobe?

CHAPTER FORTY-SIX

hobe

THE SUDDEN SHOT of happiness that bleeds through our bond catches me off guard. I am not sure what made this miracle happen, but I will need to find out what and find a way to replicate it.

This feeling... feels good.

"Hey there kid, what are you doing?" a voice demands from behind me.

Letting the glamour of yet another new face fall around me I turn and pretend that I am completely surprised by his appearance.

"I'm sorry, dude. I was just looking for my dog. She got out of the house." As I talk I walk closer to him.

This human has information I need. Information I am going to get. One way or another.

Snatching him from his post is easy. Pulling him along behind me, unconscious, is even easier. Leaning him against the wall of the park bridge I slap his face to wake him up and start asking him questions.

Human minds are incredibly frail, so I am careful to extract what I need. This man provided some; I need more. Other than information, the humans provide no real sustenance, but I eat him anyhow.

Now I can really dig into his memories.

Heading back towards the nondescript building I pull the hood of the jacket up over my head.

"Here, boy." Whistle. "Come here, buddy," I say, working my way back towards the other set of guards. Time is limited; they will eventually catch on to their missing companions.

Realistically I could walk into the building and take what I need. But there is more going on here—I can sense it. Precision is required. I will whittle away at it until I find out the cause of the unease.

One man at a time if I have to.

"What are you doing here?"

Number two. There are forty more guards spread throughout this hidden compound. This is going to be a long night.

CHAPTER FORTY-SEVEN

*J*za

HALLOWEEN ARRIVED RIGHT on the tail end of another light dusting of snow. The previous snow melted super-fast which disappointed me a little bit. The muddy mess it left behind I can do without.

Thankfully getting dirty is kind of fun.

We put the costumes on the kids and let them 'do' their own makeup, sort of. Basically they get to be what they already are without any glamour—no hiding tonight. Which is spectacular.

The town is a mass of talking, laughing kids wearing a wide variety of what they consider 'monster' costumes. The younger ones are followed by a mix of harrowed looking parents and humored ones.

After telling one of the kids to pay attention for the fifteenth time I kind of understand the look. I keep bouncing back and forth between the two. But I don't trust the humans who kidnapped me to not try and take one of the kids.

That's why everyone from the Sidhe is out here helping me watch them.

And the candy tax is being fully enforced. So far I've managed to swipe a candy bar per kid. I was keeping them in my pocket, but all the walking around made me hungry.

Now I have seventeen wrappers in my pocket.

Phobe is nowhere to be found. I feel him out there, but I haven't laid eyes on him for more than a few minutes at a time. And he's not on Sidhe land. He hasn't told me what he's doing either. Not that it's really any of my business. When I get curious enough I'll go hunt him down.

That will probably be soon.

It boils down to the fact that I don't think he needs to be at my side 24/7. We are our own people who do our own things. God knows I like my time alone. Look at how I was kidnapped... okay, that's not the best example.

"Lady, what kinda monster are you?" The adorable little voice talking pulls my gaze down. A little human boy, wearing the fake armor of a video game, looks up at me with big brown eyes.

I kneel going down to his level. "A nice one... for you anyhow. I like cute little human kids."

He smiles and he's missing one of his front teeth.

"Kenneth, get your worthless ass over here. If you keep wandering off I'm going to beat—" The intent, the hate in that voice makes me react before I think about it.

The older rather squat human man is now up against the wall, his face turning a pretty purple, because I'm choking the life out of him.

"Kid, who is this guy?" I ask.

"My step-dad." Kenneth, because that's what this ass called him, says, coming to stand beside me.

Calmly he looks up at his step-dad and not one look of worry sparks in those brown eyes. Step-dad here did something horrible for this child to be this way.

Pushing my face right into the man's, I smile, showing him my real teeth, and say, "I'm going to borrow Kenneth for the night. He needs to be someplace safe to have fun. When I bring him home you will be nice to him. Because if I find out you hurt him in any way, I will flay you alive and feed you one piece at a time to my Fiends. Understand?"

A Fiend appears at my shoulder and gnashes her teeth at him. Warm, wet liquid comes into contact with my shoe, and the smell of ammonia burns my nose.

Did he just pee on me?

Disgusted, I drop him.

"Come on, Kenneth, I'm going to show you what a real dinosaur looks like," I call over my shoulder while sneakily peeking to make sure he follows. "And get new shoes," I add.

With a look at the pussy coughing on the ground, one that finally holds a bit of fear, he runs after me.

Kids shouldn't be afraid of their parents. Not in those ways. A little afraid of getting in trouble sure. But not violence to the magnitude I bet this little guy has experienced.

Kenny, because Kenneth is way too formal, slips his hand into mine and starts swinging our joined hands as we walk. He's talking a mile-a- minute about all the costumes around us. It makes me smile.

Maybe I should feed the step-dad to the Fiends anyhow?

We get to the rest of the kids and everyone is welcoming and bring him right into the group. Everyone except one.

Knox.

"Why did you bring a... human?" he asks his tone incredibly snide for someone so little.

Is he jealous?

"Knox, that's not nice to say. You want me to have someone take you home since you're being a jerk?" I ask.

The transformation from the super serious, snotty Knox is immediate. He smiles and pats my hand before running off to be with the other kids.

Can jealousy make people act that way?

"He's going through a lot, Iza. Kids do weird things sometimes. He's jealous you're showing someone attention other than him," Jameson says, stopping beside me.

Rolling my eyes I start walking to catch up to the kids.

Jameson might be right, but I don't need to tell him that. It'll go straight to his ego and his ego is plenty big enough all by itself. He's dressed like a model for Halloween. A freaking model.

Who does that?

His costume consists of fake leather pants, a too-tight white shirt made of straps, makeup—lots of eye makeup—and enough stuff in his hair to stick it straight up.

He looks ridiculous. But it is a night for wearing costumes or taking them off.

"Where's Phobe?" he asks.

I shrug at his question. Changing the subject, I say, "I'm going to buy the biggest bird I can find for the day of thanks. So make sure we let everyone know."

He clears his throat and says, "Iza, are you going to cook? I mean the goblins do—"

"Is there something wrong with my cooking, Jameson?" I ask in mock-seriousness biting my lip to keep the smile off my face.

"Uh, well…no. I mean—" He straightens his shoulders. "—the last time you tried to cook you melted the spoon into the soup and ate it."

"I have the tube to watch. They have all these how-to videos on them. We'll be fine," I reassure him.

The truth is I'm a terrible cook. Mostly because I have no idea how to cook. More than likely I will let the goblins cook most of the meal —but I'm cooking the damn bird.

"Oh, okay. I'll be on hand with a fire extinguisher," he says, saluting me.

Shoving at his shoulder I laugh when he topples over. "The Sidhe puts the fires out, silly."

Climbing to his feet and dusting the snow off he catches up to me his eye makeup now smeared.

"Exactly how many fires have you started, Iza?"

Quite a few really. I like the idea of cooking. I just lack the follow through. "Once or twice." I fib.

"Why don't I believe that?" he counters.

"Because you're smarter than you look," I answer and run to catch up with the group of kids.

We are going to the graveyard to see if there are really zombies and ghosts. The Fiends can eat the zombies and Phobe can… Well, shit he isn't here.

"Can anyone eat ghosts?" I call into the crowd. When the laughter dies down I shove my hands in my pockets. "I'm serious, guys."

"Ghosts aren't real, Iza. Why in the world would you think that?" Nika says from across the small clearing in front of the graveyard.

"TV," I grumble.

"Not everything you see on TV is real," Nika replies.

"The Addams family could be our cousins!" I insist. "They might be real. Definitely more real than those soap opera shows you sneak and watch, Nika."

"Their stories are legitimate romantic stories, Iza. It is perfectly plausible that she was pregnant with her sister's dead husband's baby. We had no idea that her mother was sleeping with him and killed him in a jealous rage then called her alien family. No one saw the aliens coming either or their amnesia!" she defends heatedly.

"Nika, everyone knows that aliens with amnesia aren't real," I tease.

"Amnesia is a serious ailment that needs more people to be aware of it. Especially amnesiac aliens," she mutters.

"The next time you say my shows are weird remember this conversation," I say, ending her little tirade about aliens with as serious of a look as I can make.

She pauses with her mouth open, and then does something completely surprising—she sticks her tongue out at me and walks off.

CHAPTER FORTY-EIGHT

hobe

IZA SURPRISES ME AT TIMES, especially in moments like these. After doing the nightly routine of sniffing out the human authorities interested in Iza and removing them from the equation I find her in what they call the 'living room.'

Sitting in the middle of the room's floor she has candy scattered all around her while she divides it up equally among the children. While doing this task she is entertaining them with stories about Halloween that she read off the internet.

They are so enthralled with her they are uncaring of the occasional piece of candy she sticks in her mouth.

Her candy taxes.

Also surprising is that she has not asked me about where I am going when I leave. Her curiosity is so strong sometimes I can feel it, but still she does not ask. Then again I am not so sure I will tell her if she does.

This particular endeavor needs subtlety. Iza does not possess any.

Dismantling them a few men at a time is effective. As of right now the commanders of this human organization are not aware that one building—formerly full of them—now sits empty. They will notice soon enough, but their cameras will not be telling any tales.

Humans are not my preferred meal, but their memories serve a good purpose. In this last week I have learned much from them.

For example they have been experimenting on the half-breeds for decades. Their blood tests outed the creatures. As well as using the dragons as subjects, that Kael has provided over the years, they have breeding programs where they are attempting to make better soldiers for war.

It is failing.

The half-breeds are not strong enough. The dragons are but they do not breed well with humans. And they only produce once.

The other Feyrie at the Sidhe… are more than strong enough. The child Minos provided them valuable intel. I erased as much of that as I could. But I have not been able to locate their main facility where they house the information.

That is something I will discuss with Iza.

Withholding the information is only temporary. Iza needs to be a part of the bigger, noisier moves on the board. Leaving her out of that would be a mistake, and I am sure would piss her off.

Her being pissed off at me is not appealing.

Coming out of my thoughts I look towards her and grit my teeth. She is gone. How is it that this woman distracts me so? Even from her! Crossing the room I head outside using the door that appears with the Sidhe's assistance. Apparently Iza is outside. Following that thread that attaches us to one another forever I locate her quickly.

Another surprise from her today.

She is in the practice area, barefoot in the snow, her Fiend weapons glowing in the night. Her stance is somewhat tidy, her foot-work precise. The blades flash out in blurring speeds moving in the identical motions I practice with her.

Propping my hip against the fence, I let my shadows fall and I watch her. She knows I am here now; I saw the flashing of her eyes over her shoulder.

Watching the steam rise from her moving body and the way she moves… I decide I am not longer content to be a bystander.

Walking across the clearing to her, I let my own sword materialize and, I take a stance in front of her. Teeth flashing she smiles and lunges right at me. The dance begins between us. But this time it is not me teaching her. It is her showing me what she has been taught.

I am a good teacher.

There are things she throws in there that I did not teach her. That makes me have to work a little to stay out of the reach of those blades. I smile. I am proud of her.

Flipping backwards to avoid a swipe of my sword she laughs as she rolls around in the snow. Studying her, my feet subconsciously bring me closer to her.

I blame the soft feelings she evokes in me when I kneel in the snow next to her. I blame the way she makes my heart beat faster when I do not move out of the path of the snowball she hurls at my face. I blame this bubbly feeling she raises in me for grabbing snow and packing it into a hard ball and lobbing it back at her.

Like children we begin this thing they call a snowball fight. And it is… fun.

"So when you gonna tell me where you've been going?"

And there it is.

"Patrolling," I answer.

The look on her face speaks plainly of her disbelief, but she does not push it. Knowing her she will follow me next time.

That does not surprise me.

"The humans are being quieter than I expected them to be. Any idea why?" she asks flopping down in the snow beside of me.

"Perhaps. What is this about a big bird that has Jameson in such turmoil?"

She rolls her eyes at me. "It's rude to answer a question with a question. And as far as the bird is concerned I'm going to cook it for the Thanksgiving."

Iza's cooking is dangerous to everyone.

"I used the Google God and found out that the biggest bird in this world is called an ostrich. It's not as big as a dunlick from Juras, but the birds here are dumber. There are a lot of jokes about them burying their heads in the sand."

As she talks I check over her body. She is covered in mud, snow and spots of red here and there from where I nicked her. With a growl of frustration I grab her and sling her over my shoulder.

Giggling, she beats on my back but there is no real strength behind it.

Moving through the Sidhe I take her to her room and dump her on the bed. She kicks out at me and I dodge to the side.

"Take care of yourself. You are bleeding and—"

The impact of her hitting my chest automatically brings my arms up to cup her hips. Her legs are around my waist, her arms locked around my neck.

"Iza." That is all I say, her name. But there is a wealth of meaning in it.

The smell of her, all wet from snow and mud, fills my senses.

"Phobe, go shower, you stink." Then she slides down my body and goes into her own bathroom.

Leaving before I do something I want to do—but know I should not do—I head towards the room the Sidhe made for me. I only use it to shower and think, but otherwise I spend my time doing other things.

I remove my clothes as I walk through the large bathroom I need the shower. The water will come on automatically and is always the perfect temperature. Climbing under the hot streams of water I rest my forearms on the wall and relax.

Only to immediately tense when I feel Iza coming. What is she up to? I hear the bedroom door shut with footsteps leading to the bathroom door. I frown as the other noises coming from her register in my mind.

Was that a zipper? Clothing rustles as it hits the floor.

The shower door opens, and Iza steps inside magnificent in her nudity. She smiles and says, "You want me to wash your back?"

I straighten, absolutely stunned.

Her face turns a very pretty shade of pink. "I mean, you were covered in mud and stuff. I thought maybe you'd want help getting clean." She is offering much more than a shower.

I close the small space between us and stare at her unable to form one coherent thought in my head. All I can think, see, feel is Iza standing there offering me something I have waited on for so very long.

Every single inch of her body is forever in my memory, but this time is different. I study her face closely. Is she ready for this?

Then she takes the choice completely from me. She steps forward and softly kisses my chin then my bottom lip. Watching my eyes closely, she licks that same lip.

Her eyes flash and she bites me, hard. My body instantly responds. I stand stock-still letting her experiment. Her little bite made me hard as a rock in two seconds.

She licks my lip again. *'Touch me everywhere, Phobe.'*

At her words I tense even more. If she needs gentleness right now I cannot give it to her not with sex. Maybe not really with anything. I have wanted to be inside of her so badly, for so long, my own nature will work against me.

'Iza, I-I cannot be gentle.' Hell, I am stuttering like a school boy. In my long life I have never felt as unmanned as I feel right now.

She smiles again showing me all those sexy sharp teeth. She opens her mind completely to me. I rush in eager to know why she chose to do this. Her thoughts quickly fill my mind.

That is all the answer I need.

Her eyes bleed to black shining in the semi-darkness of the shower. I can clearly see my own reflecting in hers. I can also see the heat and want in her dark eyes matching my own staring back at me.

I pin her against the shower wall. My nostrils widen filling with the scent of her arousal. God, she smells so good. My body slides down her water-slicked one as I drop to my knees.

I want to taste her. *Need* to.

She is so short I push her up, so I can see the core of her. The view is hot enough to almost make me fuck her right then. With my tongue I trace a path from her thigh to the inside of her leg nudging her thighs apart. I let my tongue slide against the heat of her, the very center of my Iza. She moans as one of her hands buries itself in my hair. And she pulls, hard.

Iza tastes like darkness, sweet seductive darkness. My long tongue slips up inside of her trailing over her little nub as I withdraw it. She whispers my name.

The sound of it, thick with passion, sends a shiver through me.

I want to pleasure her this way, but I want to be inside of her when she climaxes. The undeniable need had to have her around me is a desire I will no longer deny.

Standing, I lift her roughly by her ass and guide her legs to encircle my waist. I bury my tongue in her mouth the moment I bury my dick as deep inside of her as I can go. She is wet and so fucking tight. I moan in her mouth.

Tearing my lips from hers I take deep breaths against the wet skin of her neck, biting and kissing it, as I fuck her as hard as I can.

Iza is the only creature I can fuck this way. Love this way.

Every thrust takes me all the way to her core, to her womb. Her claws dig deep into my shoulders and back adding to my excitement. She is panting my name her cries getting louder and louder as she gets closer and closer. I watch her face, watch how her mouth hangs slightly open her lips still bloody from my kisses. I cannot look away from how her eyes are half closed as she moans my name over and over and over.

Vaguely, I am aware of the Magikal storm our passion is forming, but damned if I care at the moment. We are surrounded by a bubble of black power. This moment will change something, seal something, lock in that last little bit that needed to cement our bond.

"Oh god, Phobe—don't stop—please, don't stop."

Her body tenses in my arms as I feel her warm liquid heat surround me as she comes. Feel her muscles squeeze me so tight it sends me over the edge of my own orgasm. I roar as I lose myself deep inside of her and swell, locking us together as wave after wave of pleasure ripples through me.

Resting my head on her shoulder, breathing heavily, I fight for control. That is the most pleasurable experience I have ever had in my life. I rest my chin on her hair.

Time is no longer trackable as I stand there listening to the rhythm of her heartbeat slow to normal. My eyes are closed, every nerve-ending in my body hyper-sensitive.

Slowly, I soften enough to pull myself out of her and set her gently on her feet. I look down at her, down at the one thing in any world that I cannot be without. Will not be without.

She opens her black eyes and stares at me with a look so fathomless I feel myself sinking into it. A drop of blood weaves its way down her chin only to be carried away in the spray of the shower.

I jerk my eyes away from hers and study the damage I know I did to her body. Her shoulder has healing bite marks, big ones. I know my claws dug into her bottom causing her to bleed there too. I wait for her to get angry for my roughness.

Not to mention how tender she must be inside.

"That was amazing. Can we do it again?"

At her words I feel the smile spreading on my face. Pulling her directly under the spray of hot water I kiss her. Then I make her stand there while I wash every single luscious inch of her.

It is a long time before we get out of the shower.

CHAPTER FORTY-NINE

*I*za

DURING PEACEFUL MOMENTS like this I keep expecting to wake up and find myself still in a prison—starving, angry and waiting for the next beating. Waiting for the pain that comes after the sound of feet in the hallway.

I often wonder why they hadn't killed me sooner.

Somehow I know it's connected to this prophecy I'm... well—living. This prophecy that puts me in a place that, honestly, I don't really know what to do with. Yes the dark and my own instincts guide me often, but they're not what ultimately makes the decision.

These instincts help shape them, but the dark itself brings out the more—bossy part of me. The controlling part. It's the deeper part of me that feels like the Feyrie are mine and somehow I'll restore them, my people, to their rightful places.

My life shaped me into who I am. Between that and what I am now will ultimately shape into whatever type of person I'm supposed to become.

Who I will be for *him*.

It seems since I woke up that first night in the cell next to him it's been one crazy moment after another. One more person doing something horrible or trying to kill me or someone I care about. Yet each of these moments led me to this man beside me. Led me to the man I don't know how to live without. Can't live without.

I sigh and relax against him. Every single moment that was painful, scarring… is worth what I have right now. Worth these arms of his wrapped around me like they are now. I wouldn't change a bit of it. It's worth the time I've spent with this scary, quiet, beautiful man.

Before him I never knew an honest touch, never knew there could be something soft between two people. Before him I didn't know what it's like to—love. No, more than love.

Something that there isn't even a word for.

It's he that awakened this emotion in me. He that gave me the ability to freely love my father and all the rest of them tied closely to me. If not for him I would still be dead.

A dull ache takes up residence in my head as the music that the Sidhe speaks to me with sends a sour note. The next notes are of confusion.

I sit up in bed concerned. Somehow something just hurt the Sidhe. "Iza?"

"We're under attack," I answer.

Then Phobe is gone moving so fast I can't follow him.

Dragging on clothes as I run towards the front of the Sidhe I'm hit with another sour note. The Sidhe is fighting to protect itself. So I lend all that I have to give.

How dare they!

It's someone outside. Someone who can hide from me and the Sidhe. How fucking powerful are they to be able to do that? The answer comes swiftly and makes my stomach turn.

As strong as Phobe.

Running to the front room and out the door I'm surprised to find absolutely nothing but snow and trees. What the hell? There is no one out here.

Then, just as suddenly as it began, it stops.

The entire building sighs with relief. The attack has stopped.

"Iza? What the hell was that? My bedroom disappeared," Jameson says from inside the doorway.

"Someone was attacking us. But they're not now."

"Who?"

"Someone outside," I answer, looking at the thread of each being in the Web that's on Sidhe land.

For the life of me I can't see who did it. Everyone is loyal.

'Phobe, it doesn't make any sense.' There is no way they could disappear that quickly.

'What? Did you find someone?' he asks appearing at my side.

'That's just it—I didn't. But the Sidhe told me they were just outside of the door.' I start pacing and thinking.

'I cannot find any intruders nor can the fiends or forlorn.'

'That's so strange. How does someone get away so quickly?'

'A portal, Iza,' he responds.

Shit. I didn't even think of a portal.

'Go. Rest. I will stand guard tonight.'

I make a face at him, prepared to argue. The yawn catches me off guard so big that it cracks my jaw. Well, there's that. Apparently I gave more to the Sidhe than I realized.

'Wake me up in four hours.'

Of course he says nothing. He doesn't say anything when I turn, unsurprised at finding him so close, and I stand on my tiptoes and kiss him either. A quick kiss that no one sees. Now is not the time.

But he does smile.

CHAPTER FIFTY

Iza

THANKSGIVING IS tomorrow which is why I'm standing outside this stinky ostrich farm waiting on the man to bring me my big bird I bought. Watching them peck at him while he goes after the biggest one in the field is mildly entertaining.

Having them peck at me because I got too close to the fence is not.

My pocket starts vibrating. It takes me a moment to figure out why. The thing rings so rarely that I forget about it unless I'm on the interwebs.

"Hello?"

"Iza, you need to get home. There's some humans here claiming that they can take the kids." Jameson's voice wavers; he's in damn near a panic.

Are you fucking serious?

Impatient, annoyed and heading towards angry I hop the fence and go after the same bird the farmer is having no luck catching.

Three quick steps and I have the stupid bird by the neck. One twist and it's twitching in death.

I'm not leaving here without the freaking bird. Dragging it to Nika's car I toss it in the trunk.

"Nika, either you drive faster than a grandma or I'm driving. You pick."

She nods at my words and drives faster than I've ever seen her drive before.

The Sidhe is in an uproar when we get there. Outside the door are a few law enforcement officers and a couple men and women in cheap suits waving around papers. Alagard is blocking the doorway, and he doesn't look like he's moving any time soon.

Shit.

Hopping out of the car I jog to the front door.

"How can I help you?"

"Are you the owner of this property?" a rather round gal questions, stepping forward to stand even with me.

"You could say that. Why?"

"Are you aware that children are required by law to be in sch—"

Forcing my voice to be as pleasant as possible I interrupt her, "They are homeschooled. Jameson, can you please get these nice folks the paperwork we have? Do you need copies?"

That shut her up.

Jameson returns quickly, his face red from exertion and pokes his head out the door, papers in hand.

Thank god I have money. Money can buy you lots of things here. She rifles through the papers, and her lips take on a more puckered look with each piece.

"Are they in order?"

"Yes, surprisingly they are," she answers, not happy about it either.

Jameson snatches the papers out of her hands and goes back inside. Good boy.

"Now, any more questions?" I ask.

The law enforcement officers, seeing they aren't needed, are already heading back to their cars. The other two people accompanying this woman are also walking off.

She is the last one standing here.

I lean close to her and whisper, "I know they sent you. If you aren't gone in fifteen seconds, I'll let them eat you."

Her face pales and then goes beet-red. Without a word she turns and stomps off. Yeah, my gut's right. The humans who captured me sent her.

Dirty bastards.

Waiting until all of them are gone I go drag the big dead bird out of Nika's trunk and into the Sidhe headed right for the kitchen. This visit of theirs was just a poke at me saying "Hey, I can get to you."

Do they realize that I can also get to them?

'Have you been killing the humans?' I ask Phobe.

'Yes.'

'Where do we need to go to kill the rest of them?' I ask as I start to pluck the feathers out of the bird.

Some of the goblins are hovering, but they won't step in unless I ask them to. Following the instructions on a tube video, I gut the bird —which I think I was supposed to do first—and then I dress it for the pan.

One of the goblins is crunching on one of the feet behind me. I toss the other one to him. He shares it with his comrades giving me a happy, bloody smile. I smile back and keep trying to figure out how to fit the bird into the pan on the counter. I bought a large roasting pan. The biggest one they had.

It's definitely not big enough. It's barely big enough for the bird's leg. Slowly it starts to morph and change before finally turning into a pan that is large enough to fit the big bird. I blow a kiss in the air for the Sidhe. The goblins giggle while chewing on the feet. Sounds like they're eating popcorn.

Three hours later I'm covered in feathers, frustrated beyond belief and after what feels like an eternity almost ready to put the damn big bird in to cook. Dressing a bird is apparently a lot more in depth than they say.

Now I need to make a sauce to pour over it. Playing the video on my phone again I plug in the blender. The video says I'm supposed to stew the giblets in a soup pot for an hour or so but since I forgot I need to hurry it along.

So I figure by using the blender to liquidate the giblets I can just dump them on the bird. Isn't that basically what the broth is?

Plugging the blender in I cram a couple organs into it and quickly run out of space. Okay, fine, I'll do a couple at a time. Forcing the lid closed I hit the 'smoothie' setting. I want them smooth, right?

When it starts smoking I'm only a little concerned. When it starts shaking all over the place and making super weird noises I have a flashback to the microwave horror.

Oh, shit.

It dies and I yank the cord out of the wall. It's smoking like a bonfire and the giblets are not smooth!

Fuck.

The goblins step in and the blender and the mess accompanying it quickly disappear.

I turn and focus on the bird.

Sliding it onto the rack I shut the door of the oven with a sigh of relief. Leaning on the counter I watch the oven start cooking it. Feeling satisfied that it didn't immediately catch on fire I head to my room to shower.

Leaning against the doorjamb is this tall, solid wall of muscle that smiles that dimpled smile that makes me want to poke his cheeks. He goes to kiss me and I dodge under his arm.

Bird. Stink. Wash. Off. Then we can make out.

When I hear his laughter, I know he heard my thoughts. Climbing in the shower, I almost hope he climbs in. He pokes his head in the door, kisses me hard on the mouth, and then he's gone.

Oh. He was still in my head.

So, like I normally do in the shower, I think.

Think, Iza, think.

Someone attacked the Sidhe. The humans sent people to try and take my kids. I add it to the growing mental list of things I need to research.

Phobe was also sneaking off and eating humans, but that doesn't really bother me that much. I mean, I get it. He's sneaky, I'm... not.

And if I have to guess he was after something specific.

'Yes, locations. Information about your missing dragons. And how much they know about you,' Phobe supplies.

Gone but not gone, I see.

He still scares the hell out of me in some ways. Especially now. We had hours of the best sex imaginable. Something inside of me knew it was time to take that step. But now I feel awkward—no—that's not the right word.

Shy? Am I really being shy? Chuckling at myself, I wash my face.

'Does this mean you still want to... make out?' he asks smugly.

Throwing my head back I laugh. The shower door flies open and he drags me out of the shower to the bed.

I forget all about the big bird cooking.

CHAPTER FIFTY-ONE

 hobe

WATCHING her sleep is strangely enjoyable. And if the memories in my brain serve probably somewhat disturbing.

Before me lay the salvation of the Feyrie whether they realize it or not. Their ideas and beliefs are skewed. They think all she will do is awaken the dark king who will save everyone. She is the only reason an attempt to save them will be made at all. That makes her much more important than the dark king in the scheme of things.

Honestly, I will only fight for her. I do not give two shits about the prophecy or the Feyrie, but I care for her. I will do anything that needs to be done to make sure she survives even if it means destroying every single creature in existence.

Whatever threat exists I will find.

For her I will go to war—not for vengeance, not for freedom but for her and only her. I will make sure she gets where she needs to be, and may the so-called gods have pity on anyone who gets in my way.

I will not.

Moving her hair out of her face I stroke her cheek with my thumb. It concerns me that the Sidhe was attacked. That it came from someone unknown. Something is fishy with some of the people here. Iza should be able to feel a traitor but if they are not always the traitor —what if someone is borrowing their bodies?

There are two ways that a body can be borrowed. One that is parasitic and burrows into the brain of its host, and one that can take them over spiritually. I think this is a case of the latter.

I am not sure who it is.

I have my suspicions, but those are not enough. Not this time. I know that Life is sticking his nose in especially with Iza. The prophecy has always been his baby.

"You know, when you think super hard, you get little lines right here," Iza says, poking the space between my eyes.

"I did not know this."

"So what ya thinking about?"

"Who could be doing the attack here without you knowing."

"I dunno. I checked all the strands and, I found nothing."

I tell her about my theory.

"So you think someone is borrowing someone's body?" she asks me.

"Yes. It would explain their ability to get through the wards and avoid detection by either one of us." I watch her face closely.

"We aren't going to be able to find them are we?"

Kissing her slowly I enjoy that still-sleepy look she is wearing. Then I give her the bad news. "More than likely no. Unless you see them try to use Magiks while borrowing the form they are undetectable."

"That's how they evaded the slaughter of the Feyrie?"

I nod to answer her question.

Chewing on her lip she climbs out of the bed to slip a robe on, all the while thinking through the information I gave her. "I have to check the bird."

Following her through the house I watch her face when she looks in the oven.

"There's a spoon in there on it. Well, what's left of a spoon," she mutters, thumping her head against the wall once. She straightens and says, "How can we draw them out?"

There is only one thing that might draw this creature out.

"Use me," I offer.

She makes a face at me. I know why Iza has been protecting my identity like she has. I have killed many Feyrie—millions. Some of the Feyrie here will remember the face I wore then.

"Iza, I can change my face."

"Do they know the face I see?"

Thinking about it I am not completely sure. But I do not remember ever using that form. Ever.

"How does using you help though?"

"The dark king, Iza. His presence will draw them out."

"Oh, that's a little different." Cocking her head to the side she comes over and surprises me by wrapping her arms around my waist. Then she says, "Are you ready for that?"

Here she is, her life in danger, and she is worried if I am ready to admit who I really am?

Hell.

"The Feyrie are not ready for that, not yet. Let's focus on the humans for now. At least they are a threat we know," she says, and she is not wrong. There is a good chance they will rebel completely.

Lifting her and wrapping her legs around my waist I head back towards the bedroom. While Iza is preoccupied with the humans I will work on figuring out who our mole is here—who is being controlled—and do what needs to be done.

When I find them I am going to kill them.

CHAPTER FIFTY-TWO

Iza

HE HAS that frown on his face again. It's really his only tell that something is on his mind. He's lying across from me on the bed staring at the ceiling. Unlike me he doesn't need sleep. Ever. I wonder if that allows him to get more done or get bored more often?

He rolls to his side and kisses my cheek before climbing out of the bed. Guessing, I'd say he's going to try and see if he can find out who the traitor is while I'm fiddling with the humans.

Or *not* traitor. If they've been body-snatched it's beyond their control now. From what Phobe said, they lose a piece of their soul every single time they are occupied. Until eventually there is nothing left.

For all intents and purposes they're dead.

Sunlight creeps in through the window. I had no idea it was that early. Groaning, I crawl out of bed and drag some clothes on. As I near the kitchen I can smell the bird cooking. It had to cook all night

273

in order to be cooked enough for Thanksgiving. It weighs something like 200 pounds.

The house goblins are taking care of the side dishes. I'm hoping no one notices the melted blue plastic spoon stuck to the right leg. Why did I even have the spoon near the big bird?

Oh, I remember now. I was feeding the not-giblets to the goblins.

Putting on my gloves, because no one likes getting burned, I open the massive oven door and peek in. The big bird is a golden-brown color and, the skin looks crispy and yummy.

Sliding the rack out I lift the bird out and put it on the counter. God this thing is huge. Carefully I tug on the stuck spoon. I don't want the bird to fall apart, because I was a dumbass and left a spoon on it. It takes part of the meat, but otherwise there is no noticeable damage. Good, the bird is still pretty.

Smiling, I stab it with my daggers, lift it out of the pan and put it on the huge decorated plate the goblins made for me. Grabbing the plate by its fancy gold handles I carry it to the dining room. The huge table is covered in all kinds of fantastic foods both human and Feyrie. Some are even still moving.

The goblins went all out today.

Grinning, I place the bird at the center of the table and stand back feeling a little tiny bit proud of myself. I cooked a bird for our day of thanks.

"My lady that actually looks edible," Nika comments, taking a seat across from me.

Casting a dirty look at her I fight the urge to throw potatoes in her face. She seems so surprised I made something edible. Sarcastic dragon.

Phobe startles me when he pulls my chair out for me.

'The humans do this for their females,' he assures me.

Shrugging, I sit down and giggle a little when he lifts the chair and I both up to scoot us to the table. Looking around the room I discreetly touch each individual with my Magiks. Noting each face, whether they are smiling or sad, and what I see… makes me smile so hard my face hurts from it.

People are serving themselves, talking, smiling. Some of them simply look happy.

Thanksgiving is a great day to have with my family.

Christmas will be even better. We can give presents on that day. And have lights everywhere that twinkle to music. And cookies, and hot chocolate and the kids and I can try to catch the fat man. Maybe we can bake lots of cookies to lure him down our chimney. Not that we have one yet, but we will for the holidays.

Jameson and I need to do more research... Wait, not everyone is here. I climb to my feet and search the room and inside on the Web for him. Only one thing is loud and clear.

Jameson is afraid.

Climbing up on the table I shout, "Where the hell is my nerd?"

ACKNOWLEDGMENTS

Thank you, the reader of this book, for all the support you have given me to write it. Without you this world wouldn't exist to anyone but me.

Jason, you are my rock. And yes, while there are days I might want to punch you right in your pretty face I still love you to distraction. Thank you for feeding me when I zone out all day. For making sure I have enough sense to sleep, for being the one person who tells me it'll be okay, no matter what. Love you tinkertits. (Every book will have a diff nickname for you)

Vicki Ward Duran, Kelly Stephens, Amy "The Biscuit" Naylor, Heather Endsley. Thank you, ladies, for your laughter, support and for keeping me on task. Love you!

Thank you, Squad!

As always, my kids. You were the only beautiful things that came out of my existence.

ABOUT ZOE PARKER

Writing has always been a dream and a curse of mine. It seems I've spent more time living in my head than skydiving or climbing mountains. But really, why stop at skydiving when I can explore other worlds? Writing is as important to me as breathing. I think I'd rather lose a limb then stop writing. The places I've visited, the things I've seen in my imagination were better than climbing mountains any day. In here I can fight for the poor dragon, I can cheer for the black knight. I can make the little guy strong enough to toss cars. And if you allow it, I'll drag you right along with me.

AUTHOR MEDIA

Facebook group:
https://www.facebook.com/groups/ZoesSavagesquad
Website:
www.zoeparkerbooks.com
Facebook Page:
https://www.facebook.com/ZoeParkerAuthor
Twitter:
http://www.twitter.com/zoeparkerauthor

74533280R00175